Producer & International Distributor
eBookPro Publishing
www.ebook-pro.com

THE CODE GIRL FROM LONDON
Deb Stratas
Copyright © 2024 Deb Stratas

All rights reserved; no parts of this book may be reproduced or transmitted in any form or by any means, electronic or mechanical, including photocopying, recording, taping, or by any information retrieval system, without the permission, in writing, of the author.

Website: debstratas.com

ISBN 9798326059833

The Code Girl From London

A WWII Historical Fiction Novel

DEB STRATAS

DISCOVERING THE NEXT BESTSELLER

Sign up for Readmore Press' monthly newsletter and get a **FREE audiobook!**

For instant access, scan the QR code

Where you will be able to register and receive your sign-up gift, a free audiobook of

Beneath the Winds of War
by **Pola Wawer,**
which you can listen to right away

Our newsletter will let you know about new releases of our World War II historical fiction books, as well as discount deals and exclusive freebies for subscribed members.

Dedication

The Code Girl From London is dedicated to my dear friend, Debbie. You are always my bestie, through good times and bad. I couldn't manage without you in my life. I love you, sweetie.

xo

CHAPTER ONE

May 1944

"I don't know what to whinge most about – burning eyes, crick in my back, or aching fingers. That was an interminable watch." Ruby plunked down and threw a weary smile at her mate.

"Definitely my fingers," Katie replied, as she removed her navy-blue hat and tossed it on the worn wooden table. "I can hardly feel them after taking down so many messages today." She fluffed her dark curls to give them a little life and flexed her fingers.

Ruby nodded and stood.

"Can you fetch me a cuppa, Katie? I'm off to the head. My bladder is fit to bursting."

Katie laughed and nodded.

"Of course, luv. I'll be waiting here, trying to stay awake."

After collecting two lukewarm cups of tea and a couple of stale biscuits, Katie sat down. She was so tired that her mind was numb.

"Is that tea for me, sweetheart? Looks like I'm just in time to join you." A tall American soldier with a short, dark brush cut loomed over her table.

"No, thanks just the same. This is for me and my chum." Katie smiled politely.

"The name is Alan Bailey. U.S. Army. What is a pretty little thing like you doing sitting all alone? I guess it's my lucky day." He scraped back a chair and sat. A silly grin spread across his face.

"I said this was for my friend. I'm sorry, I've just finished a long watch duty and I'm washed out," Katie said through gritted teeth.

"Washed out? You Brits sure have a funny way of talking." The soldier hooted.

"The lady said she doesn't want your company. Are you having trouble understanding her and all?" A lilting Irish voice floated somewhere above Katie's head.

She looked up, and locked eyes with a green-eyed, auburn-haired Irishman. He took her breath away. He was that gorgeous.

The American stood.

"I was here first, Paddy. Take off."

"The lady doesn't want your company," repeated the tall Irishman. He took a step towards Alan.

"Boys, please. I'm not worth fighting over, really." Katie stood to her full five feet, two inches and inserted herself between the men.

"Hey, I can tell where I'm not wanted." The American backed off with his hands in the air. "There are plenty more gals on the base. Alan Bailey doesn't have to beg for female attention." With a backwards smirk, he left the mess.

Katie sank down.

"Thanks ever so much, er…Lieutenant?" She motioned her khaki-suited hero to sit.

"Lieutenant Ciaran McElroy, Wren." He removed his cap and gave her a small bow. "Happy to be of service. Sorry that Yank was troubling your fine self."

"Normally, I can put them in their place in no time flat. It's just been a long day. Or should I say, a long night? And I'm Katie Kingston, Petty Officer." She nodded at him. He was so handsome that she felt wide awake.

"And I'm Ruby Rhodes, also a Petty Officer," Katie's mate appeared at the table.

Ciaran immediately jumped up to give her his seat.

"Sorry, Petty Officer." He smiled, showing even, white teeth. "Sure, and I'm in the presence of two of England's finest female sailors."

"Please stay, Lieutenant. I can fetch you a cuppa. It's the least I can do to thank you for ridding me of that brute."

"No need. I'm too whacked to even drink. I'll leave you to it. Nice to meet you. Katie, I'll see you for supper at half-past. I'm going to take a turn 'round the castle to keep my eyes open." Ruby was gone in a flash.

"Tactful Ruby, that's what I always call her," Katie said with a wry grin. She motioned again for Ciaran to sit. "Sorry about that, but no point letting the tea get any colder than it is."

He grinned and sat, removing his cap.

"Sorry that eejit troubled you. May I call you Katie?"

You can call me anything you like. Just keep talking in that gorgeous Irish accent.

"Yes, of course." Her words tumbled out, too fast, as always. "But don't bother about him. It happens all the time. Comes with working alongside men, I suppose." Katie shrugged and smiled. "We don't see too many Irish sailors here in Dover. You're one of the rare ones." She took a sip of tea to stop herself from chattering too much. She shuddered at the cold, watery taste.

"True enough, Katie. But me da fought in the Great War, and I wanted to carry on. And you can call me Ciaran." He sat back and picked up the teacup. "Or Mac. That's what the blokes call me."

Although Ireland had fought alongside the English in World War I, they had declared themselves neutral in this war. Regardless, thousands of Irish had signed on to support the Allies. This pleased Katie to no end.

"Alright, Ciaran. And we're chuffed to have you on board with us. We need every pair of hands to win this war against Hitler and his dreadful Nazis." Katie found herself beaming at him. "What do you do for the Army?"

He wiggled his eyebrows.

"Special forces, Katie. I can't say too much, but it involves a parachute."

"My, that sounds dangerous." Katie's hand flew to her mouth.

"It can be," Ciaran replied shortly. "Many of the lads didn't pass, but somehow I've made it through."

Katie leaned forward and whispered, "You'll be involved in the big push, then?" she asked, brown eyes wide.

For months, soldiers, airman, and sailors from all the Allied forces had been amassing across the south of England. Whether it was

English, Scottish, American, Australian, New Zealand, or Canadian troops – everyone knew that a big European invasion was coming. Tons of equipment, planes, over-water tanks, and more were collecting in ports strategically along the coast, positioned to attack points along the French shoreline.

"It certainly seems like it. This base is teeming with swarms of servicemen. There's hardly room to swing a cat in our barracks."

Dover Castle housed nine centuries of Kentish history – dating from Roman times. It was one of the first English Norman castles, built by Duke William of Normandy in 1066. High and imposing atop the famous white cliffs, anyone sailing could see it across the Straits of Dover.

Playing a critical role in defending the country for centuries, the fortress had been at the center of the extraordinary Dunkirk evacuation. It had also been bombed continually during the war, albeit this was not widely known. Because of its strategic location at the southern-most point of England, the Kentish coast became a restricted zone, bringing with it stringent rules about secrecy. Locals were prohibited from using binoculars and cameras in the area. Like many other coastal locations, the beaches had been closed and fenced off since the beginning of the war.

Known as Hellfire Corner, the area around Dover had been heavily bombed from far-too-close occupied France. Batteries had sprung up in defence, but with attacks coming almost daily, the destruction of life and landmarks truly defined the Kentish coast as a war zone. To date, something like 10,000 buildings in and around the town were damaged by shellfire. Hundreds of civilians had lost their lives or were injured. The entire area was under relentless assault.

Dover was now poised to play its part in the largest Allied coordinated attack to date on mainland Europe – or so it seemed.

"Ours too," sympathized Katie, picturing her billet, rooms bulging with Wrens.

"I suppose yourself is rather occupied as a busy Wren, then?"

Katie tossed her dark curls.

"It depends on the day. Sometimes we're rushed beyond belief. Others, we sit idle for hours. Like everyone else, I suppose." This was the way of war – hours of dead boredom, followed by fear and furious toil.

"How did you get that job, then, Katie?" Ciaran took a bite of stale biscuit, made a face, and ate it anyway.

"After being accepted in the Women's Navy, I was first posted in Liverpool as a postal censor. I felt ghastly, having to black out parts of letters coming from overseas to mums and girlfriends back home, but that was the job. Loose lips and all." She smiled. "I somehow picked up little bits of other languages in the letters. French, German, and so on. The navy decided I would better serve as a clerk, handling correspondence, assisting senior officers, general office dogsbody. So, here I am," she finished briefly.

Katie hated to be so vague, but she couldn't say more. She'd signed the Official Secrets Act, and could never speak of her position to anyone – friends or family – for the rest of her life. She was under strict orders never to reveal the true nature of her work, upon serious retribution.

Ciaran gave a low whistle.

"I'm sure it's trickier than you are making out," he replied with a slow smile.

"You get used to it. I suppose all of us are proving we can get accustomed to anything in this war. Bombs, the Blitz, rationing, endless queues. We've all had to endure so much. But yes, it is tough at times." Katie was getting the distinct impression she wasn't fooling this canny Irishman one bit.

Yet, she was impressed. It wasn't often that a man showed much interest in her work. She'd found most of them were self-absorbed, droning on and on about their training, missions, life back home – wherever that was.

"I'm pleased to do my bit. And it's going to be even more hectic in the coming weeks. When do you think the invasion will be?"

"I dunno, Katie. But it's a matter of weeks, if not days. Then we'll show Jerry what we're made of." He smiled again, making Katie's heart thump.

Get a hold of yourself, girl. He's just an Irish bloke. Nothing special.

Katie was rather shy of men and entanglements these days. She'd had her heart broken earlier in the war, and guarded it carefully now. She would not open it for just anyone, certainly not a parachutist who could die on a dangerous mission.

Mentally shaking her worn-out mind, she glanced at her watch.

"Bollocks," she jumped up. "I'm meant to meet Ruby for supper. She'll be hungry – and cross. It was lovely to meet you, Ciaran. Thank you again for your gallantry with that oaf. I didn't have the energy to shove him off." She held out her hand for a shake.

Ciaran also stood.

"When can I see you again, Katie? You've brightened a proper dismal day."

"I don't know," Katie flustered. "I'm on day watch for the next four days."

"How about a walk tomorrow? Or whenever you're free. We must make the most of every moment. We never know what tomorrow will bring."

Katie had heard this before – usually whilst a soldier or RAF flyer was kissing her and trying to paw at her uniform. It steeled her.

"We're bound to meet up again. The base isn't that large, even with all the servicemen arriving hourly. Goodbye Ciaran." Good, that should put him in his place.

"Goodbye Katie. I'll look for you tomorrow around this same time. And the day after." He smiled again.

Katie ran off, feeling confused. This red-haired Irishman stirred something in her. But she wasn't ready quite yet to open herself to love. And yet, blimey, he was so attractive.

"Sorry I'm late, luv. I got caught up talking to that—"

"That gorgeous Irishman. Yes, I noticed," Ruby teased. "And here I thought you were immune to all men. Anyone that can make you glow like that is welcome in my books."

"Sod off, Ruby. It was just that he told off that cheeky American good and proper. That's all. Being so tired, it was just brilliant to have someone step in for a change."

"Whatever you say, Katie. Ready for whatever passes as the evening meal? I'm half-starved."

"I'm ready. And sorry again, Dusty," Katie apologized.

In both the men's and women's navy, it was common for everyone to pick up a nickname from somewhere or other. Ruby was Dusty as a play on her last name – Dusty Rhodes. And Katie was Queenie – an obvious twist on Kingston. Her first training officer had given it to her.

"Oh, I almost forgot. You received some post." Ruby handed her chum a letter. "One of the girls brought it from Capel le Ferne on the way to watch."

Katie said, "Oh, goody," as she fairly ripped it from Ruby's hands. She loved receiving news from home.

"I suppose we're waiting for you to read it then…" Ruby sighed and picked at a loose fingernail. She knew Katie would be fit to bursting until she'd read it.

"It's from Tillie," Katie said excitedly, as she leaned against a cold wall, skimming through the short letter.

"Dear Katie,

How are you getting on, dear sister? I understand from Trevor that things are heating up in the south, so you're in the thick of it. Please be careful – you can be so reckless. Please don't put yourself in harm's way.

Young Jamie is quite the handful these days. Now that he's walking, he's into everything and we've had to move all Mum's precious bits and bobs higher and higher. At least, he's past the point of falling all the time, so that's something, I suppose. He's babbling constantly, but only he knows what he's saying. I keep practicing with him to say Mama and Dada, but so far, he just gives me a blank look. He's a precious pet, though, and getting totally spoiled by Mum, Aunt Shirley and Trev's mum. Once Trev and I get our own home after the war, it will be a shock to young Jamie having to mind just his parents.

Maggie and Micah's wedding is coming so quickly – it's almost here. You know Maggie – she is determined to keep it a small affair, but Mum and I are equally set on making their day special. Even though it will be a civil ceremony at the registry office, we are still inviting a few friends back to the house for a small wedding breakfast. I don't even think the poor things will have a honeymoon. Maggie will need to get back to the ack-ack command base just a day or two after the wedding. Can you imagine, luv? Even though Trev and I only had a short honeymoon in Scotland, it was heavenly, and I wanted that for my dear twin. This wretched war makes life and love near impossible, doesn't it? We're that heartsick that you won't be able to come to the wedding, but it's understandable given the current situation. Rumor has *it most leave has been cancelled across the board, so I'm hoping this means enormous news for the Allies soon. I still remember how surprised we all were when you turned up at our wedding. It was marvelous to see you, luv. It made our day just perfect. And you looked ever so smart in your Wren uniform. The blue is so flattering.*

Everyone else is carrying on as usual. They all send their love. And speaking of love – any handsome seamen in your life? I should think with all the flyers and soldiers about, there must be someone you fancy? You can tell me, Katie – I promise I won't spill the beans to anyone. Well, except maybe Maggie. And Trevor. Alright, you know I can't keep a secret. I do hope you find someone that means as much to you as Trev means to me. Maggie and I have found our soulmates. Now it's your turn, little sister.

You are rotten at writing, but please scratch us a few lines and let us know you're getting on alright. We miss you desperately and can't wait for your next leave.

Loads of love,
Tillie xx"

Katie shoved the letter into her pocket.

"Righto, Ruby. What do you reckon? Corned beef and cabbage or Woolton Pie?"

CHAPTER TWO

It turned out to be another dreary supper – bangers and mash.
"What is in these sausages, Katie? My bet is sawdust and potato peels." Ruby pushed away her half-eaten plate in disgust.

"It's food, and it's filling. That's all that matters to me, luv," replied Katie with a mouthful of mushy peas and dried potato mash. "What did you expect? Steak and kidney pie?" She grinned and kept shovelling in the plentiful, if plain, food. She never said no to a meal and was perpetually hungry.

Edith groaned.

"Don't start, Katie. We haven't seen the sight of a steak and kidney pie for years now."

Edith Birchall was tall, and what Katie's mum would kindly call big-boned. She had kinky light brown hair that never cooperated, especially on rainy days when it puffed and blew all over the place. This was matched by bushy brown eyebrows that seemed to have a life of their own, wiggling and furrowing with every expression on Edith's face.

"Are you going to eat that, then?" Katie eyed Ruby's dish of barely touched sausages.

Ruby waved airily.

"Have at it, Katie. I'm going to queue up for pudding. Perhaps there will be a Victoria sponge cake on offer," she said hopefully as she stood up. Ruby Rhodes was also tall, with straight black hair almost to her shoulders, and a fringe that she was forever blowing out of her light blue eyes.

Katie and Edi burst out laughing.

"You are a dreamer, Ruby," Katie snorted. "More likely a prune custard."

Ruby shrugged.

"I'll take a stodgy prune custard. Anything with even a whisper of sugar will go down a treat."

"Bring us one back, luv." Katie smiled.

"Righto, girls." Ruby turned to join the long queue of servicemen and women in the busy mess.

"Ruby said you met an Irish lad today. I hear he had a twinkle in his eye," Edi teased Katie, raising a bushy eyebrow.

Katie shook her brown curls.

"Crikey, does everyone in Dover know about me chancing upon an Irish lieutenant whilst having a cuppa?" Katie glared.

"Since you've never even glanced at a man in the eight months you've been here, it seems like news," Edi replied, blinking.

Katie sighed. She'd given her heart to a man early in her naval career, and dearly regretted it. She'd been stationed at Southwold Y Station, near Suffolk, after her two weeks probation as a Wren. Green as grass, she'd fallen for a senior officer who'd swept her off her feet, and then broken her heart into a million pieces. Since then, she'd resolutely shut down her emotions, and put all her effort into her work. She would not let down her guard now, thank you very much.

"It was just a casual encounter, Edi," Katie said softly.

Edi nodded. She wasn't a deep thinker and took Katie's explanation at face value.

"How was last night's watch?" Katie changed the subject.

"Busy. This special assignment at the castle makes little sense to me, but just following orders," Edi replied.

Katie nodded. A small group of telegraphists at the nearby Y station had been selected for a special mission assisting their male counterparts at Dover Castle. For the last six weeks, eight of them had been provided lorry transport morning and night between their digs at Capel le Ferne and the demanding command room underground at Dover.

Operating under the codename Operation Fortitude South, the Allies had been mounting an elaborate deception for the better part of a year.

The German high command assumed that the primary Allied landings would be across the Strait of Dover to Pas-de-Calais – the most direct route. This belief assured that German defences and troop concentrations in that region were the strongest in the whole Atlantic Wall, and weaker where the real invasion would occur – in Normandy.

To bolster this falsehood, the Allied forces created a fictitious army – the First United States Army Group (FUSAG). Giving further weight to this plan, General George Patton was assigned to lead this assault – the most senior U.S. field commander – and one feared by Germans.

Dummy landing craft were made from scaffolding tubes, wood, canvas, and empty 40-gallon barrels. From a distance and in the air, they were quite convincing, and were deployed in harbors around the southeast, particularly Dover. As well, great numbers of replica tanks and vehicles were situated strategically around south-east England to simulate an army organizing a massive movement.

Part of this deception included a barrage of fake radio traffic transmitted by multiple bases across the southeastern coast. Supported by double agents who leaked false information about the FUSAG units, the entire operation was strictly hush-hush, but the worst kept secret in the forces was aiding the enormous effort.

This was where Katie and her mates came in. Posted at nearby Capel le Ferne, near Folkestone, the telegraphists were on loan to the Dover radio transmission unit until the big day – whenever it was going to happen.

"It may not seem like we're doing much, running messages for the men, helping with translations, even making tea – but it's all critical to this operation. It's crucial that everyone plays their part to make the Nazis believe these transmissions are real. We've all got to do our bit, Edi," Katie reminded her mate.

"When you put it that way, it makes me dead patriotic. Don't mind me. You know how grumpy we get on evening watch."

"Too right, girls," Ruby breezed as she plonked three prune custards on the table. "I can barely remember my name and rank after a long night watch, let alone carry on a decent conversation. Let's get this down, Queenie. Our transport leaves at half-past, and even on a warm night like this, I don't fancy a two-hour walk back to our billet."

Katie checked her watch and tucked in with gusto. Within minutes, the trio had finished their puddings, washed down with watery tea, collected their tricorn hats, and scrambled up the hill towards the castle gates.

"How is your family getting on, then?" Ruby asked as they jostled along in the lorry. She stayed away from the touchy topic of Lieutenant McElroy.

"All eager for Maggie's big day. Tillie is always so bright and breezy. It makes me feel wretched about not writing more. I always mean to, but…" her voice trailed off.

"Will she be able to get leave with the big push coming?" Ruby asked into the darkness.

"I doubt she'll get more than a forty-eight-hour pass. Maybe a seventy-two if she sweet talks her CO," Katie sighed.

"How ghastly for her," Ruby harrumphed. "This bloody war."

"She's that chuffed to be married at all, I suppose. She's waited a long time for her love."

Maggie Kingston certainly had not had an easy road to happiness. Her fiancé, Micah Goldbach, had faced unimaginable horrors as a Jew in occupied France. Captured during a roundup in the south, he had suffered in Drancy – an appalling exportation camp just outside of Paris. His parents had been transferred to the concentration camp, Auschwitz, and never heard from again. He'd only just been released early this year. Maggie and Micah had overcome tremendous barriers to their love – and now wanted nothing more than a quiet wedding to truly get on with their lives together – despite the raging war.

"I imagine it will be a quiet affair, then? Will she have a proper wedding gown?" Ruby was eager for details. Who didn't love a wartime romance?

"Probably not as modest as Mags would like. They are tying the knot at the local registry office, and Maggie will be in her ATS uniform – like so many women. But Tillie is determined to give them a proper do at the house, with whatever rations have been saved up, a bit of bunting here and there, and some music to make it all quite festive. I wish I could be there, but with this current twenty-mile travel limit, it's simply not possible." Her voice caught. *You really are a rotten sister, girl. Not even there when your family needs you.*

Ruby couldn't see Katie's face in the dark lorry, but reached out to grab her hand.

"It's all right, luv, I'm sure your sister understands. And Tillie will make it special, won't she?"

"She will, and ta, Rubes. With the big push coming any day now, any chance of leave is out of the question." She shook her head to clear it.

"Chin up, darling. If it all goes according to Winnie's plan, this dreadful war may be over in a matter of months, if not weeks. Then, you can have a proper catchup with all your family – the newlyweds, your nephew, your brother Kenny, and all the assorted Kingstons."

The girls nattered for the rest of the uphill trip as the sun sank in the June sky.

The lorry came to a shuddering stop at the top of the hill – Abbot's Cliff.

"Ta ra, Humphrey," Ruby called to the lorry driver. "See you in the morning."

"Thanks ever so much," echoed Katie as the girls jumped out.

The requisitioned Abbot's Cliff House, or HMS Lynx, as it was known to the navy, bustled with a collection of other Wrens in the communal kitchen.

"There's a fresh brew in the pot, girls," called out Jane, alias Jinks. "We were meant for bed three quarters of an hour ago, but we've just been chatting about our important visitor today. Did you hear?"

"We heard nothing, do tell." Ruby plunked down on a hard, wooden kitchen chair and pulled the brown teapot towards her.

"None other than Winnie himself," breathed Jinks. "He was seen walking around the base and near the cliffs with Field Marshall Bernard Montgomery and his aides. How thrilling."

"Why was he here, I wonder…" Ruby poured tea.

"An Ensign at the castle said that Churchill is meant to be seen around Dover in the run-up to the big push. It's all in aid of the Germans believing we'll be attacking straight across the channel from here," Katie offered, as she gratefully took a cuppa from Ruby, adding a splash of milk. "Do you think it will really work – two Allied leaders parading about to show Hitler we're about to invade at Pas de Calais? That, and all the troops and equipment amassing around here. I sure hope it works."

There was a brief silence as the Wrens considered the importance of the days ahead.

"It's all really happening, isn't it?" one of the other girls asked slowly.

"I don't know what I'd say if I saw Winnie," Jinks said. "I should think I'd be rather tongue-tied and make a mash of it."

Katie laughed.

"I doubt he'd take much notice of you, luv. He has far bigger things on his mind just now."

Jinks turned pink.

"I'm going to make sure my kit is turned out proper at all times, anyway. And I won't be caught out without my tin hat and tricorn. Just the same," she added with a resolute set to her chin.

The girls erupted into friendly laughter.

"As long as I don't bump into him on the way to the head in my pajamas and face cream, I'll be happy," joked Katie, as the girls tidied up the tea things.

They dispersed to their rooms. Abbot's Cliff was packed with Wrens, and Katie was glad to share a room with only Ruby and two other girls. The downstairs bedrooms overflowed with six to seven Wrens each. With five bedrooms and only one bathroom, it was chaotic at the best of times, bedlam at others, with disarray always.

Katie wasn't as neat and tidy as her sister Maggie, so the mess didn't bother her a bit, but the noise sometimes got to her. After a tough watch, she spent hours walking along the cliffs and down the paths to the beach. It helped to clear her head, even with the almost constant mist around Capel le Ferne, nicknaming it Capel le Fog.

She'd shrugged off the report of Churchill's duty call, but if she were honest, it shook her a little. It made the upcoming push seem real, immediately real. For months, every Briton had longed for the Allied invasion of France. The country was holding its collective breath, hoping for the best possible outcome – surrender by the Germans, utter capitulation in fact – and the end of this miserable five-year war that was meant to have been over by Christmas 1939.

Katie managed a cursory wash-up amongst the queue for the bathroom and lay in bed, ignoring the surrounding hubbub.

The girls murmured their goodnights, wearied from long watches and chronic lack of sleep.

Hearing the quiet breathing of her chums, and Ruby's light snoring, Katie had trouble clearing her head.

Suddenly, she felt homesick. Desperately homesick. Images crowded her mind – Pops and Mum at the Longridge Road dining room with the whole family gathered for Sunday dinner. She could almost smell Faye's delicious roast beef, Yorkshire pudding, mashed potatoes with gravy smothered atop both, and Brussel sprouts – the table groaning under the bounty. She could see her beautiful older sisters – Tillie and Maggie – Tillie talking nineteen to the dozen, and Maggie observing and making sure everyone was included in the conversation. Kenny joking with everyone, and Mum glowing with pride seeing all her children gathered together. Aunt Shirley fussing with the tea and pudding, whilst Uncle Thomas sat back, waiting for the moment for the men to retire to the library for brandy and cigars.

Katie ached for the busy Kingston townhouse in London – so familiar and so far away. The household had grown since the war – Micah's younger sister Hannah, quiet and old beyond her years after her parents' death and a harrowing escape from France. Trevor's mother Isla, who had her own flat, but was at the Longridge townhouse much of the time, fending off loneliness and delighting in her new grandson. And the light of the house – young Jamie, Tillie and Trevor's son, who daily proved there was life amongst the ruins of war. And Katie barely knew him.

A sob escaped her throat. Katie pulled up her blanket to muffle the sound.

Get a hold of yourself, girl. You've had it luckier than most. Kenny had been reported Missing in Action earlier in the war, and then found and now slowly recovering. Both Micah and Hannah had been spared. Trevor was unharmed in the RAF Fire Service. And dear, brave Maggie, who had stunned them by signing on as an Ack-Ack girl in the ATS, was safe and about to be married.

Katie turned on her side and punched her pillow.

"You alright, luv?" came a sleepy, concerned voice from the other side of the room.

"Sorry, Rubes. I'll be okay. Goodnight."

To the sound of Ruby's gentle snores, Katie resolutely put her homesickness to the back of her mind, and conjured up the image of a handsome Irish Lieutenant. It helped, but she still ached for her family.

CHAPTER THREE

In the event, it was another four days before Katie chanced upon Ciaran again. Her daytime watches ran long, with two Wrens sick with the flu, an air raid, and another night watch.

"Breakfast in the mess, or tea and toast back at the Wrennery?" Jinks yawned as she removed her headset and turned to Katie in the early hours of the morning, when it seemed they were the only people awake.

Katie checked her watch, laid down her own headphones, and gave her hair its customary fluff to revive it.

"It's too soon for transport, so we may as well eat here, unless you fancy a long walk?"

Jinks nodded, and the pair navigated the castle's chilly hallways, which were just coming to life with servicemen and women starting their day duties in Dover's underground tunnels.

Originally built during the Napoleonic wars, Vice-Admiral Ramsey had led the conversion of the abandoned underground barracks into a labyrinth of naval chambers, housing an operations room, offices, and living quarters. Also here were the coastal artillery center of operations, an anti-aircraft nerve center and his own headquarters.

After the fall of France in 1940, two further levels extended the original tunnels of Casemate, including the Annexe – a secure underground hospital, a home of dormitories, kitchens, and mess halls. Dumpy was below that – a Combined Operations Headquarters for the Royal Navy, Royal Air Force and the Army. The tunnels and interior rooms buzzed twenty-four hours a day with servicepeople in all branches of the military doing their part to prepare for the big event.

Walking side by side in the narrow tunnels, the girls went in drowsy silence to the bustling mess, where they queued for powdered eggs, toast, and tea.

"Not a rasher of bacon to be seen, more's the pity." Katie heaped some rather dry looking beans onto her plate.

"Maybe after the big day, we'll be rewarded with a full English brekkie," said Jinks hopefully.

Katie raised an eyebrow.

After munching for a few moments, Katie took a gulp of tea and sat back.

"Who would have thought when we signed on that we'd be working out of a castle just twenty-one miles from France and the German defence?"

"I would have been terrified if I'd been told that," Jinks shuddered. "Basic was horrible enough. I never worked so hard as all that marching, early mornings, and 'scrubbing the deck.' I didn't think I'd last." Jinks had been a London shop girl before the war.

"And all the new terms. Cabin for room, mess for dining hall, deck for floor. I'll never get used to calling a building a ship's name, and having to get shore leave to visit home. Seemed strange then, but now we're proper used to going aloft, turning port or starboard down a hallway, and a duty shift being called a watch," Katie added.

"Why did you pick the Wrens, Queenie?" asked Jinks as she pushed back her empty plate. "Was it the—"

"Uniform," they cried in unison.

The navy-blue double-breasted jacket with two rows of gold buttons, matching skirt, white shirt with stiff collar and black tie, matching navy-blue cap with H.M.S. in gold, and sturdy oxford shoes with black stockings, was considered rather smart, especially in comparison with other women's military uniforms.

"I didn't know which branch of the service to choose," Katie admitted. "Maggie in the ATS, and Tillie drove an ambulance. Neither of those appealed to me. I didn't think I had the head for the WAAF, and neither nursing nor factory work seemed to fit. Once conscription was around the corner, I had to decide fast. The Wrens seemed as good as anything, and I supposed I could put my office skills to good use. What about you?"

"Seriously, it was all about the uniform. I didn't really give it much thought. My father had some connections to the navy, and that helped." Jinks shrugged.

The Wrens were the most popular branch of the women's forces, and not just for the uniform. It was considered an elite service, and was difficult for merely any woman to qualify. In Katie's case, she'd had a chat with her Uncle Thomas, who held a high-level and hush-hush position with the government. He'd put in a quiet word for her, and in no time, she'd been sent for her medical, aptitude training, and ultimately received her call-up papers.

"You're too much, Jinks," laughed Katie. "Too honest by half."

Jinks fluttered her eyelashes. She was flighty and paid more attention to her makeup, hair, and the local dances than anything else. She had pale blonde hair, green eyes, and a mischievous smile. When it came to work, she was all business, though, and Katie enjoyed their watches together. She'd only been stationed at Cape Le Ferne for a few weeks and had slid into the routine effortlessly.

"Where was your first post?" she asked, reluctant to move her tired body from the table.

"I was at Gilnahirk, Belfast, and it was bloody cold, I can tell you. But I learned the basic skills fast – naval terminology in English and German, setting a high-frequency radio receiver, turning the knobs repeatedly to find German transmissions, and then taking down the messages and passing them along," Jinks said in a rush.

"How did you learn German?" Katie asked as a gang of sailors burst into the mess, looking for hot tea.

"Our housekeeper was German, so I picked it up at home. Originally, I was meant to be a despatch rider, but I'm hopeless at driving. How about you?"

"I expected to be given a clerk position, but they started me off as a postal censor, just shy of my twenty-first birthday in early 1942. Blacking out suspicious material wasn't too exciting, but I couldn't let through any post that disclosed important military locations." She smiled, but it didn't reach her eyes. What a drudge that had been.

"I'd learned Morse Code in Girl Guides, and when I started picking out French and German words in the letters, they thought I might manage as a wireless telegraphist. They sent me for training in wireless procedures and electromagnetism and more dull marching. From Wren, I made Leading Wren, and here I am. A Petty Officer in the Women's Royal Naval Service." She saluted to her chum, who giggled.

Katie conveniently left out her time at Southwold Y Station, where she had met Major Ralph Buckley. She'd been briefly assigned to him as a driver. Best to leave that forgotten.

"And jolly good you are, P.O. Kingston." Jinks saluted in return.

The naval salute differed slightly from the standard military gesture. The hand was curved slightly inward – a throwback to the days when sailors didn't want their senior officers to see the dirt on their hands. It was second nature now.

"Enough of that rot. Our transport should be along anytime now." Katie picked up her tricorn hat and stood.

"Not so fast, Petty Officer," an Irish voice boomed behind her.

Katie's heart lurched as she recognized Ciaran's voice. She turned to see his green eyes flashing as a slow smile spread across his face.

"You're a hard Wren to track down."

"I've been on extra watch, and then an air raid kept us in the shelter, and then I've been on night watch," she stumbled.

"No need to explain, Katie. We are all hard at it these days. Are you finished watch for the day, then? Luck 'o the Irish, I suppose," he replied with a lilt.

"Jinks and I are meant to catch transport back to our digs. We're fair knackered, aren't we, Jinks?" Katie looked to her mate for support.

"Yes, we are. I'm Jane Powell and you are…?" She held out her hand.

"Sorry, Jinks. This is Lieutenant Ciaran McElroy."

"Lovely to meet you P.O. Powell," Ciaran twinkled at her.

"Oh, you can call me Jinks," she replied.

Ciaran turned back to Katie.

"How far are your digs? May I walk you back?"

Katie considered.

"It's a two-hour jaunt, mostly uphill," she spoke haltingly.

"That's nothing. Shall we take in a little fresh air? I'm not due on watch for a few hours."

"Oh, all right, then," Katie replied, a trifle ungraciously.

She felt a bit rotten that she hadn't met him on any of the previous days he'd mentioned. She wondered if he'd waited for her. And it would be good to clear the cobwebs with a refreshing walk before kipping down for a few hours.

"Will you join us, Jinks?" asked Ciaran.

"As much as I'd like to, I'm that bushed – I'll take the lorry. I need to write some letters home before bedding down. Ta ra." And she was gone.

"I suppose it's down to us, then. Shall we?" Ciaran offered his arm, which Katie ignored. She jammed on her hat and led the way out of the mess.

Once into the sunshine, her mood lightened straightaway. She was outdoors. Taking in a deep breath, she inhaled the sea air and ignored the throngs of sailors and soldiers around her.

She gave Ciaran her best smile.

"Sorry to be so churlish. Night watch is the worst. You never really get used to it."

"It's alright, mavourneen. I've found yourself again."

"What does that mean then?" Katie furrowed her brow as they started up the hill.

"In Gaelic, it means my darling. Since I've met you, it seems I can't get you out of my mind. We were destined to meet, I reckon."

"That's daft, Ciaran. You hardly know me," she replied with a scoff. But her pulse raced in response to the endearment.

"We Irish are a romantic lot, don't you know?"

"Rubbish. Let's just enjoy the weather." Katie paused and gazed at the white chalky cliffs of Dover and the swell of the blue sea. From the top of the hill, you could see France on a clear day. A little frightening these days.

"Katie, tell me a little about your childhood. Where are you from, and all?"

She looked quite a way up at him – he was a good five or six inches taller than her.

"We live on a street called Longridge Road in Earl's Court, London. Our family has had a home there since – well, since forever. I grew up there with my twin older sisters, Maggie and Tillie, and my younger brother Kenny. Pops has an accounting firm where I worked before the war. Mum looks after all of us, even though she's never sure who will be at home or away serving. Hannah lives with us now, too. She's Micah's little sister – he's my future brother-in-law." *Slow down, girl. Stop talking so fast.*

"That all sounds lovely, but I want to know more about you. What did you enjoy doing when you were a child?"

She blinked, considering.

"I was always the tomboy," she said. "My two older sisters are beautiful and popular. Twins cause quite a fuss…" Katie raised her hands and shrugged. "I always loved being outside, playing sports, but I am a bit accident-prone. I'm always in a hurry. During the early blackout days, I tripped up on the street, and broke my leg." *Stop talking, you daft cow. He doesn't want to hear all this nonsense.*

Ciaran laughed as they climbed higher on the path.

"It's the three Kingston girls, then?" he asked.

"Well, it was until my younger brother Kenny was born. I suppose I was meant to be a boy, but they were stuck with me, so they tried again," Katie tried to sound cheeky.

Ciaran stopped and spun Katie to face him, his eyes intense.

"Katie, I'm sure that's not true. Your parents wanted you. They love you, right?"

"I suppose," Katie agreed miserably. "But if my parents were so happy with me, why would they need a boy?" *Why are you telling him this? Stop it, girl. What are you blathering about?*

"Ah, Katie. I'm sure that's not the way of it. Couldn't it be that your parents loved yourself and your sisters so much that they wanted more children?"

"Maybe," mumbled Katie as she continued climbing. "I dunno."

"I see a beautiful, smart, funny woman. And it sounds like you come from a loving family. I expect you're being too hard on yourself."

"You hardly know me," Katie burst out.

"I want to change that."

Katie's head whipped back.

"Let's take it slow, Irish. My head is spinning."

"Fair enough. For now, let's enjoy this splendid morning."

They walked in silence for a while, the only sound being the waves crashing into the beach below them, ravens cawing above them, and their own labored breathing.

"What was your childhood in Ireland like?" Katie puffed.

Ciaran hid a small grin.

"Very different from yours, mavourneen. I grew up in Howth, near Dublin, on the coast. Me da and mam have a small farm with grains and a few animals. It wasn't easy." He paused. "I'm an only child. My parents didn't have me until they were older. I must admit they dote on me. Me mam is worried sick about me in the war. But I have to do me part, don't I?"

As he talked, Katie felt increasingly foolish. Here she was being rude to this dashing soldier, who was being naught but kind to her.

"This war really is dreadful for those left behind. All the waiting and wondering. When did you see them last?"

"Three months ago. Even though they don't have much, they put on a good show, with a brilliant supper from saved rations, even a slaughtered chicken from the smallholding. I had a seventy-two-hour pass, so with the travelling, I could only stay one night. Me ma was beside herself when I had to leave."

Katie put an arm on his sleeve.

"The war must be over soon, mustn't it? After the big push, the Germans will have to surrender. There's no chance they can rally with the size of this Allied invasion, is there? Then you'll be home again, safe with your parents."

"I hope so, Katie. But once we've invaded France, for some of us – our work will be just beginning. That's if I land safely, which I will." He gave her an impish grin, and wiggled his eyebrows, belying the seriousness of his upcoming mission.

"How long will you be there?" Katie whispered, as she reluctantly removed her arm. She missed the reassuring warmth of him straightaway.

"I don't know, do I? But we must secure our targets and liberate the French. After that, it's not for me to say."

They had reached the top of the cliff. As one, they turned to the sea, and took in the splendor in silence. It was high tide, and the waves crashed into the beaches below. The white chalky cliffs of Dover stood out against the blue water of the English Channel.

"These cliffs always remind me of the Irish coast. I've walked along them often enough."

"Does it make you homesick?"

"Sometimes," Ciaran replied, gazing at the sea.

"We're fortunate today there's no fog. It's often a smoggy hike from the castle. There – you can see France – just there," she pointed out the slim piece of land barely visible.

Ciaran whistled.

"And here we are, just over twenty miles away – amassing a phoney set of troops, inflatable tanks, and dummy landing craft to fool the Germans into thinking that we're invading Calais. It's a tremendous risk, Katie. And no matter what happens, we will lose a great number of men."

Katie gasped.

"You must keep yourself safe, Ciaran. Promise me you will."

Ciaran chuckled.

"So, already you have fallen for me, and all? 'The man who has luck in the morning has good fortune in the afternoon.'"

"What's that, Irish? From a poem?" Katie neatly ignored his first question.

"We have a saying for every occasion, Katie. Today seems to be my lucky day. I can't help believing that it will hold out."

"You really are a softie, aren't you?" She playfully pushed his arm as they continued walking.

"With eyes brown as liquid chocolate like yours, my romantic spirit is rather inspired."

My word, he was a romantic soul. Either that, or filled with blarney.

They spent the rest of the walk chatting about inconsequential things – life on base, living on no sleep, sharing digs with loads of people, the beastly rations – anything but the upcoming invasion.

Katie found she was disappointed when they reached Abbot's Cliff. The walk that she'd been doing once or twice a week had sped by.

"I'd invite you in for tea, but it's too early. There's bound to be a few girls in nighties and pajamas in the kitchen or lounge. They'd shriek and start throwing crockery at me if I brought in a bloke at this hour," Katie was surprised to hear the regret in her own voice. *I like this man. Be careful, girl.*

"I understand, Katie. Are you on night watch again tonight? Could we do this again tomorrow morning?" He sounded so damn eager. *Does he really fancy me that much?*

"Err, yes I'm on night watch again – the 4:00 a.m. shift, which is the worst. But maybe we could." She felt and sounded uncertain.

"Let's meet in the mess at half-past eight tomorrow, then. We'll have breakfast before I bring you back."

"Alright, Irish, I suppose it's a date," Katie took a leap.

"Brilliant," Ciaran exclaimed.

"Thank you for walking me back," Katie said more formally than she meant. She didn't quite know how to say goodbye.

"Could I have a kiss, Katie? Just on the cheek."

How could she deny such a sweet request?

"Go on, then," she said with a smile, her eyes sparkling.

He leaned over and brushed her cheek with his lips. Katie felt a shiver ripple through her body.

"Sleep well and sweet dreams." He turned and walked away.

Katie opened the door and let herself in, paying no mind to the hustle and bustle of a half-dozen girls chattering over tea and toast.

With a jaunty wave in their general direction, she slipped aloft to her cabin. After a quick wash with her flannel and brushing her teeth, she put on her pajamas and sat heavily on her bed.

Picking up a pen and paper, she scrawled a letter to her sister before trying to snatch a couple of hours' sleep.

"Dearest Tillie,

It was so lovely to receive your letter full of news from home. I miss you and young Jamie more than you can imagine.

I can't say much, but it is proper hectic here at the moment. I'm staying in terrific form, trundling back and forth between the base and the wrennery, and watches are busier than ever. Maybe it will be over soon, dear sister.

Please give Maggie and Micah my love at the wedding. I'll be there in spirit, and thinking of you all on the day. This ghastly war keeps us from the most important of life events, and smirks through it all. It makes me feel wretched to miss it.

I've got to manage a couple of hours' sleep before I'm at it again tonight. I promise to write a proper letter soon.

*Love always,
Katie xx"*

Katie put the letter on her night table, ready for the evening post. Thinking of her poetic new Irish friend, she fell asleep listening to waves crashing outside the open window.

CHAPTER FOUR

"This place is crawling with servicemen, transport, and equipment. I can scarcely move," Ruby startled as she alighted from the lorry for afternoon watch.

Katie whistled.

"Too right, Ruby." Katie jumped down and scanned the busy castle grounds, humming with noise, activity, and men in every uniform imaginable.

"It must be coming in no time." She adjusted her navy hat, fluffed her hair, and linked arms with Ruby. "It's sure to be a busy watch today."

"Do you reckon Hitler will send his boys over again tonight on his way to London? He seems to be letting up of late," Ruby asked as the pair swung their gas masks over their shoulders.

Instinctively, they both looked at the sky. It was a reflexive action for most Britons. Four years of war and bombing triggered fearful glances into the air whenever they went outside. It was a cloudy day, and the sound of the sea was muffled by the engine sounds, barking commands, and the general hum of men and machines.

"Who knows?" Katie shrugged. Although the Baby Blitz was not causing as much havoc as Hitler wanted, the Luftwaffe were still sending Junkers and Dornier 217s to London and Bristol. "They seem to miss more than hit nowadays. And our RAF flyers have been knocking them out of the sky before they drop their bomb loads. Which is brilliant for us." She beamed.

"They are getting weaker, and we are getting stronger. At least I hope so." Ruby smiled back.

The Baby Blitz had begun in January of this year. The Germans, stinging from the terrible pounding that the RAF had been inflicting on their cities, had planned to retaliate with new flying bombs, but because of technical development problems, these attacks had to be postponed.

Codenamed Operation Steinbock, concentrated air attacks on industrial centers and ports began. Something like 500 enemy aircraft had begun strategic bombing, but to minimal effect. Besides the highly efficient RAF squadrons, large numbers of radar controlled anti-aircraft guns, Z-rocket batteries and searchlights took a heavy toll on the attackers. Radar had also advanced in both the RAF and anti-aircraft operations which helped to pinpoint defensive manoeuvres.

"At least the Germans have lost plenty of planes so far. It makes me damn proud. I'm not afraid to say it." Katie was equally chuffed with the Allied response to this latest offensive.

Nonetheless, the Baby Blitz had taken its toll in lives, injuries and damages across the southern coast of England. About 1,500 people were killed and 3,000 seriously injured during the first five months of 1944.

"Still, I don't fancy spending most of my watch in the air raid shelter here in the tunnels. Even though the ops center is not far away underground, it's agony spending hours in the cold with no work to distract me. I get proper fidgety. It's wretched enough working in this rabbit warren of damp, chilly rooms. The airless, crammed, dark and dreary shelter is unbearable." Ruby shuddered in the warm air.

"No. *Really?*" Katie feigned surprise. She'd spent countless hours with an edgy Ruby in shelters during their times together. No one liked the cramped, boring, and often terrifying stints below ground, but her mate suffered more than most.

"Let's not borrow trouble. Look on the bright side. We're on watch together. It doesn't happen that often. We'll look after each other. And maybe there will be no bombing tonight if it stays cloudy. Hitler prefers clear skies."

They'd strode down the hill to the side entrance to the tunnels. After queuing and having their identification checked, they made their way to the main communications room, running through Bat Alley and the chilly tunnels to the busy hub.

"I wouldn't fancy being stationed here in winter, Ruby," Katie whispered as they greeted their watch mates. "It's frigid enough here in summer." She shivered, glad of her woollen overcoat.

"That and no windows. It would be grim in here, indeed," Ruby agreed.

Within minutes, each was absorbed in her duties. The First Officer in charge of the shift called the Wrens together, sharing recent reports of E-boats patrolling the Channel. It seemed unlikely that the Germans had caught wind of the upcoming D-Day plans and were skulking around English waters, but no one was taking any chances. There was far too much at stake.

It surprised the girls to be assigned to Y-intercepting during this watch – the work they'd been trained to do. They slipped on their headphones, and slowly, meticulously turned the dials of their HROs to known Kriegsmarine's frequencies, fixed on finding a signal.

The transmissions came through in Morse code or plain German. Both Katie and Ruby could take down and translate either with ease and speed. Occasionally, they picked up odd receptions from radio stations or even lighthouses. In rare instances, they caught a warming up signal before the Germans started transmitting – a familiar rushing sound as they waited for someone to start talking.

What they were mostly listening for were the German MTBs (motor torpedo boats), also known as E-boats, and destroyers that set sea mines and attacked Allied convoys under cover of darkness.

Two hours into their watch, it had been quiet.

"The most exciting signal I've picked up tonight is a German weather report from Le Havre," sighed Ruby, pushing back her fringe from her forehead. "It's sixteen degrees Celsius, if you're curious."

Katie looked up from her desk.

"Did you say something?" she asked, lifting an eyebrow. She'd been concentrating so hard that all she'd heard was the sound of Ruby's voice buzzing to her left.

Ruby giggled.

"Pay me no mind. I'm just prattling, Queenie." She glanced up at the clock. It was time for her break. "I'm going up for some fresh air. I'll bring us back a cuppa from the mess on my way back."

Katie nodded and put her head back down. They weren't meant to talk during watch. She didn't want a dressing down from her CO.

Thirty seconds later, the familiar, wearisome sound of the air raid warning enveloped the hollow caves.

"Bloody hell. It's Moaning Minnie again," a Wren wailed from across the crowded ops room. "Sir, can't we just keep working? The air raid shelter is no safer than this room."

Already Katie could see staff gathering up half-drunk mugs of tea and gas masks, as they hurried down the tunnel to shelter.

"You know the rules, Blackmuir. No one stays behind. No one. Get a move on."

There was no rebuttal. Everyone moved quickly and resignedly towards the crowded shelter.

Katie looked out for Ruby as she collected her bag, grateful for its half-eaten spam sandwich. Squashing herself on a wooden bench next to chattering Wrens, she kept her eyes glued to the small door opening, holding her breath until her mate breezed through.

Minutes crept by as the German aircraft droned overhead. The men called out the names of the individual planes as they passed over. With the amount of bombing that Dover had experienced, they had all become experts in German aeroplane identification and even competed to see who could correctly name them first.

Once the shelter was bursting with servicemen and women, and Ruby hadn't appeared, Katie felt her anxiety rise. Her palms and forehead started to sweat, and she gulped for air. *Where are you, daft girl? Stop messing about.*

After several nerve-wracking minutes, the lights flickered and went out. Katie didn't think. She scrambled from her bench and ran for the door, hoping no one would miss her in the dark confusion. She had to find her friend.

Ignoring the planes overhead, Katie ran through the tunnels and up the steps out of the castle. She knew Ruby would be nearby – preferring the cover of night and fresh air to the smoke-filled crush in the shelter. Nearing the NAAFI building, she called for her mate in a hushed shout.

"Ruby, where are you? It's me, Katie. Can you hear me? Ruby?"

Katie stayed as low as she could. Hearing more planes overhead, she ducked under a tree, taking deep breaths to calm herself. *Dammit, where are you, Ruby? This is not funny.*

Slowly walking the grounds, keeping cover where she could, she kept calling, hoping that none of the planes would drop their bomb loads here – either on purpose or by mistake. So many had gone astray that it was entirely possible that an orphan incendiary could crash nearby.

Reaching the top of the hill, Katie spied a familiar gathering of trees. She and Ruby had frequently eaten sandwiches here, seeking whatever privacy they could find. It was so dark that she crept towards the trees by instinct, and hoped she'd find Ruby huddled there.

"Ruby, where are you? It's me, Katie. Are you there?"

The planes were still flying overhead, but so far, no bombs had dropped.

She heard a rustle and moved towards it.

"Queenie, is that you?"

Katie was never so relieved to hear her chum's muted voice.

"Yes, I'm here, you daft cow! Where are you?"

"Over here," came the frightened reply from deep under the trees.

Within seconds, the two had found each and embraced tightly. They quickly moved deeper into the clump of trees and sat underneath a large oak.

"Why didn't you come to the shelter when the warning went off? It's not safe out here!" Katie shook her friend by the shoulders.

"I couldn't face that smoky, overcrowded, smelly shelter, Katie. I get so claustrophobic – you know that. I thought it would just be a matter of minutes until the planes would pass and the all-clear would sound. And that no one would have missed me," she finished miserably.

"Well, I missed you. And I'm sure the CO will notice that we're both unaccounted for now. Listen to me. You mustn't do this again. It's not safe. You must hang on just a bit longer. We're nearing the end now. You mustn't take chances with your life. We have so much to live for. Don't you have a date this Saturday night?"

As the panicky feelings subsided, Katie thought a little joke might get them back on even ground.

"You're right, I do. With that Yank. I don't want to let that pass." A tiny spark lit up Ruby's voice.

"That's my girl. Whatever made you think a slip of a Wren like you could best the German Luftwaffe on your own out here?"

The pair sat back, watching the sky.

"I dunno…" Katie felt her mate shrug. "Didn't Herr Hitler give strict orders that Dover Castle never be bombed? I'm sure I heard that somewhere."

Katie laughed. She couldn't help herself.

"Because he wants to claim it for his own after he's come ashore? That's your defence? Jeez, Ruby. I can't believe you thought that excuse would pass muster. You are too much."

"Well, the soldiers say it all the time. So, it must be true," Ruby replied stubbornly.

"I love you, dear heart, but you mustn't believe everything you hear. Especially from cocky soldiers."

"You're right, luv, and I'm so sorry I've caused all this trouble. For you and me."

Katie reached for her hand and patted it.

"That's alright. I'm just relieved to have found you safe."

They sat in silence for a few minutes, realizing that the drone of planes had ceased, nor was there any buzzing, whistling, hissing, cracking, or booming sounds that signalled bombs or incendiaries falling anywhere close by. Thank goodness.

The all-clear sounded, and the girls stood up.

"Well, that's us sorted, then. Do you think we've been missed?" Ruby asked as they started back down the hill.

"We'll be lucky not to be written up on charge," Katie predicted gloomily. "Unless you can sweet talk our CO. They are certain to have done a head count whilst we've been above-ground. I need no more black marks on my record."

"How many do you have?" Ruby asked.

"Just a couple of late infractions. But I don't want to chance being refused a pass home when I need it. Let's rush. Maybe if we bring her a cuppa, she'll go easy on us."

"I'm parched myself. That would go down a treat. Come on."

In the event, the CO let them off with a stern warning. Nerves were frayed with the upcoming push, and in the end, no harm had been done. No bombs had fallen nearby, and everyone got back to work with speed and efficiency. After all, the Baby Blitz had been going on almost nightly for the past few months. Besides, the excitement of the big push coming in a matter of days filled the young people with optimism and the chance to do something active to push back the Germans, reclaim France, and stop this war once and for all.

They weren't to know it for some time, but that Luftwaffe air attack was the last England's shores would ever see.

CHAPTER FIVE

June 6, 1944

"Today's the day," Ruby danced around their cabin. The off-duty Wrens had been up since dawn, as Operation Overlord sprang into action. A few of the girls had been out early on the cliff and witnessed history as a convoy of empty landing craft moved towards Portsmouth. It was overcast and nippy, but marginally better than the previous day when it had been foggy and stormy – the original invasion day. Churchill and Eisenhower had given the order to advance when the needed full moon for glider landing visibility and low tide to real German underwater defenses were at their optimum.

They'd been proper gutted when the Allied offensive had been postponed. On pins and needles, it had cheered them to hear that the invasion was back on.

"I've polished my shoes and buttons till I can see my face in them. I want to look my absolute best on watch today." Katie's face shone. "I'm proud to serve King and country in this noble mission." Her voice choked up a bit; she just couldn't help it.

Everyone gathered around the wireless in the lounge when the first momentous announcement came at ten a.m.:

"*This is the BBC Home Service. And here is a special bulletin, read by John Snagge.*

'*D-Day has come. Early this morning, the Allies began the assault on the north-western face of Hitler's European fortress. The first official news came just after half-past nine when Supreme Headquarters of the Allied Expeditionary Force, usually called SHAEP from its initials, issued Communique Number One. This said, Under the command of General Eisenhower,*

Allied Naval Forces supported by strong Air Forces began landing Allied armies this morning on the northern coast of France.'"

This was greeted by loud shouts of "We're coming for you Hitler." "We've got 'em now," and "Brilliant!"

More cheers accompanied this news, as endless cups of tea and broken biscuits were consumed.

Katie brushed her short, dark curls until they bounced and gleamed. Donning her uniform, she tucked her newly pressed white shirt into her navy skirt, carefully knotted her black tie, and slipped on her jacket. Deftly placing her tricorn hat atop her head, she gave herself one last approving look in the small mirror above the washbasin and nodded. *You'll do nicely, girl.* She skipped down the stairs.

She was on watch from noon to four o'clock and was eager to get into the heart of the action on this important day.

"Any further news?" she asked as she gulped a half-cup of lukewarm tea.

"Nothing yet," Edi replied. "You'll doubtless hear more at the base."

"Ta ra, girls. I'm off down the hill. With any luck, we'll be celebrating at The Valiant Sailor tonight." With a backward wave, Katie waited for transport, chatting with other Wrens bound for the castle.

The last few days had been more than hectic, with troops and equipment arriving in an endless stream. She'd managed to see Ciaran twice more, and the pair had walked the cliffs and spoke of the uncertain days ahead. Despite her best efforts to guard her heart, Katie warmed to his open charm and boundless enthusiasm.

Last night, they'd finished their walk at the Abbot's Cliff Sound Mirror – a large concrete structure that provided early warning of incoming enemy aircraft.

She and Ciaran shared a makeshift picnic of spam sandwiches and warm beer that Ciaran had brought from the base.

"I thought of sneaking us up to the top of the Great Tower for our picnic, but this is much more private."

"Not to mention it's off limits for women working at the castle. Now is not the time to be put on charge. This is much nicer, Irish."

"Let's make a pact, shall we, Katie? When I return safely from this mission, we'll meet back up here again, and talk properly about our future?" He gazed at her hopefully. "Sure, and Dover is our place now."

Like many new lovers in wartime, Ciaran and Katie lived in the moment, not thinking too far ahead of the next shift on duty, upcoming meal, or a chance for an evening's sleep uninterrupted by air raids. Whilst some couples opted for early marriages before wartime service separated them, others resisted rash commitments and were determined to wait it out for the duration, certain of a better future together when fear and uncertainty were well behind them.

"It's a deal, Irish," Katie replied impulsively. How could she send him off to a dangerous mission without something to hope for? She crossed her fingers behind her back, hoping the Navy wouldn't see fit to transfer her before Ciaran returned.

Ciaran beamed.

"Brilliant. And in the meantime, you will write to me, won't you?"

Katie made a face.

"I'm rubbish at writing – I have the best intentions, but time always seems to get the better of me. I promise I'll try, but don't expect Shakespeare. My family is chuffed when I can manage a paragraph or two."

"I'll take whatever yourself can spare, mavourneen. I also can't promise when or how often I can write. I don't know how the next days will go, or what to expect when I get to France, and all."

Katie nodded, chewing her bottom lip. Damn, he was going into the heart of the danger. *Don't die. Be safe.*

Checking his watch, Ciaran cursed and rose.

"Bloody hell, Katie – I must get back. I wasn't meant to be gone this long, but I had to say goodbye." He raked a hand through his auburn hair and pulled her up by the hand. Katie found herself quite close to Ciaran, indeed. He smelled delightful – a woodsy combination of sea air and soap. It was rather dizzying.

"Might I have a proper kiss, Katie?" he asked in a husky but respectful tone.

She couldn't refuse and didn't want to.

She leaned in as he put his arms around her. She reached up to wrap her arms across his back. Closing her eyes, she waited for the feel of his lips on hers. Warm against the windy, chilly night, Katie wasn't disappointed with the heat that immediately filled her. He held her closer as he deepened the kiss. Katie felt a tingle that nearly made her shudder.

Ciaran sighed and reluctantly broke away.

"You are a sweet and extraordinary girl, Katie Kingston. You're sending me off with so much to fight for. But I must go. There's a briefing tonight and my CO will have me guts for garters if I'm late."

He walked her back to her digs and kissed her again briefly. She watched from the door as he took off in a sprint towards Dover. *I hope he cadges a lift. It's a long walk down.*

Musing on last night's events on the brisk walk to the castle, a smile played on her lips.

Shocked at how empty the grounds were, she hurried to the watch room, signed in, and greeted her fellow Wrens and officers.

Slipping on her headset, she took her place at a desk with a green-shaded light, pad of yellow paper and pencil, and her HRO receiver – her conduit to messages from the Kriegsmarine – Germany navy.

It was painstaking and tedious work – turning the knob in micro movements, listening intently for U-boat messages, toggling a switch to determine a proper bearing, then taking down the message word-for-word, and passing it along to the watch officer.

Whether taking down Morse code, or translating German messages on the fly, the work required intense concentration and was mind-numbing. The four-hour on, eight-hour off around the clock schedule was gruelling.

Most of the messages were dull, or the operators didn't know what they meant. Regardless, they were given strict instructions to take down the messages precisely, never to guess, and to pass them along as quickly as possible. On rare occasions, a coded message would be of particular interest to the watch officer, and was sent on to a mysterious "X-station," the location or purpose of which was never known.

Katie got to work straightaway, turning the knob almost imperceptibly, straining to catch a German signal that might expose a U-boat, which would be disastrous for their boys on the water. For the next four hours, she barely lifted her head. Translating, transcribing, and passing along dozens of messages, Katie hoped nothing would come through that would sabotage the Allied efforts, particularly that of one Army parachute jumper, perhaps now landing in occupied territory.

"Did you hear that?" Katie's watch-mate whispered quietly.

Katie flipped her knob until she picked up a most extraordinary signal. She scrambled to take down the lengthy message. She looked over at her mate, brown eyes wide.

"That's Hitler himself," she breathed. "He's ordering everyone to stay and die at their posts."

They both shook their heads in disbelief. What must those men be thinking? Ordered to die – it was unthinkable. It was a message transmitted repeatedly that day.

When her relief Wren stood over her desk, Katie realized her watch had flown by. And nary a U-boat or E-boat on report. One of the most important signals to catch was a short one, called an E-Bar, sent from a U-boat that was about to attack a convoy. The operator receiving it shouted out "E-Bar" and the frequency. The switchboard operator would quickly relay the information to the various Direction-Finding Stations around the country to get the exact position of the submarine for anti-U-Boat measures.

No such messages had been received, and Katie was gleeful. She sat back, ripped off her radio set, and beamed around the smoke-filled room, teeming with operators, decoders, and supervisors.

"Three cheers for the Allies."

No one responded, albeit she saw a few smiles.

After a hasty trip to the head, Katie rushed to the mess for a cup of tea and to catch up on the news.

Early reports were triumphant. The mess was abuzz.

"I heard one-hundred-and-fifty-thousand troops landed on five beaches in Normandy. We fooled the buggers."

"The Canadian troops battled through a rough landing at Juno and drove the Nazis inland."

"The decoys worked a treat. The Germans were sitting ducks at Calais."

"We've unloaded over a million men and hundreds of thousands of tons of supplies – heading towards Germany."

"France is liberated."

* * *

Speeding back from North African waters, Kenny's Royal Navy ship was one of many bombardment warships to shell the German defences on D-Day. Seeing active service, Kenny was witness to the devastation firsthand – to his fellow naval officers aboard, ships blown up, and men stranded or shot in stormy waters. He considered himself lucky to have survived the day, and rejoiced with an extra tot of rum alongside his trusty mates, drowning the horrific images that couldn't be unseen.

He thought longingly of the girl he'd met at the last port, and raked a hand through his mucky hair, grinning to himself. With any luck, he'd find another smashing blonde on his next shore leave.

* * *

At the gun park, the squads were called out time and again. Only a few German planes soared across the channel, dropping bombs and creating defensive havoc. Filton Airfield contributed to the onslaught along the Normandy coast, shooting guns into the sky, pushing the enemy bombers away from England's shores.

Scrounging a lift back to their billet, the ack-ack girls were weary yet jubilant. They did not know the extent of the wounded yet, but word of the Allied capture of the coast had trickled back, and was received with joy and pride. Maggie hoped Kenny and Katie had done their part without injury. She wouldn't hear for weeks, probably. But somehow it cheered her to think they were pulling together for a common good – even if their posts and duties were completely different.

Maggie was immensely thankful that Micah was safely home in England. To have worried for his safety in a France under attack would have been unbearable. She dashed him off a brief letter before stumbling into bed without even washing her face. Her last thought before sinking into a dreamless sleep was that surely it would all be over in next-to-no-time. Then life could truly begin for all the Kingstons and those they loved.

* * *

Tillie picked up Jamie, grabbed Hannah by the hand, and danced gleefully around the kitchen.

"The war is ending, the war is ending," she chanted repeatedly. "And Daddy's coming home. Daddy's coming *home!*" She threw Jamie into the air, and they all fell into giggles.

"Is it really so, Tillie?" Hannah asked with wide eyes. "Is the war over? Will Trevor and Katie and Maggie and well – everyone – be coming home soon?" Her eyes shone with excitement.

"I don't know exactly when, Hannah, but this is a major victory for the Allies. Surely, Hitler and his abominable Luftwaffe and the entire Nazi military will give way. They can't hold fast with so much of the world marshalled against them."

"I believe you, Tillie. It will all be over soon. Then I can have chocolate every day."

"And Jamie too," agreed Tillie. "The poor luv has never had it. He won't know what to do with all the sweets we'll be feeding him."

They laughed again.

* * *

Walter and Alice Kingston sat drinking tea with Isla Drummond, listening to His Majesty, King George VI.

"After nearly five years of toil and suffering, we must renew that crusading impulse on which we entered the war and met its darkest hour. We and our Allies are sure that our fight is against evil and for a world in which goodness and honour may be the foundation of the life of men in every land."

"Quite moving, I must say. And His Majesty sounds more himself with every broadcast." Alice, along with all Britons, had felt the King's discomfort as he stuttered during his speeches.

"He's a fine wartime sovereign," Walter declared with satisfaction.

Alice blinked away a tear as her knitting needles clacked furiously.

She thought of her children risking their lives to win this war – Maggie on the ack-ack guns, Kenny at sea serving with the navy, and young Katie clerking for the Wrens. She couldn't be prouder of them, a feeling partnered with daily fear for their lives.

* * *

Katie and all the off-duty Wrens drank themselves mad at The Valiant Sailor, singing chorus after chorus of The White Cliffs of Dover. It was a grand day for the Allies.

CHAPTER SIX

By dawn on June 6th, 23,000 paratroopers and glider troops were on the ground behind enemy lines, securing French bridges and exit roads, supported by 5,000 Allied ships. The British and Canadians overcame defiant opposition to capture beaches codenamed Gold, Juno and Sword, as did the Americans at Utah Beach.

The worst resistance challenged the American forces at Omaha Beach, resulting in over 2,000 casualties. By day's end, approximately 156,000 Allied troops had successfully stormed Normandy's beaches. Initial estimates reported that over 4,000 Allied troops lost their lives in the D-Day invasion, with thousands more wounded or missing.

By June 11th, the beaches were fully secured and over 326,000 troops, over 50,000 vehicles and some 100,000 tons of equipment had landed at Normandy. By any measure, Operation Overlord was an overwhelming success and a major turning point in the war.

* * *

And then, Germany retaliated by launching V1 rocket bombs towards London.

* * *

July 1944

"Are you sure you can mind him, Hannah? He's a handful." Tillie gazed at her young son, currently chasing Robbie around the muggy kitchen.

"I love this young rascal, and he usually heeds me. Isn't that right, Jamie?" Hannah snatched him for a cuddle seconds before he pulled the cat's tail. Grinning with his two top and bottom teeth, he struggled to get out of her arms and back to his game.

"Besides, I must get back to the air force base on Monday, so I want to squeeze in as much time with this little mite as I can."

Hannah had grown into a lovely young woman of eighteen. Her family had been longtime friends with the Kingstons. Early in the war, Hannah's parents had moved to France to help the aging, ill grandfather with his struggling jewelry business. Hannah and her older brother Micah had joined them, albeit Micah was torn between his loyalty to his family and his growing love for Maggie Kingston.

The family had been trapped in the south when Germany had shockingly conquered and occupied the country. Over time, Uncle Thomas had pulled some strings, and quietly worked within his network to arrange for Hannah's dangerous escape across the Channel. Neither her parents nor brother had been so lucky. Samuel and Ruth Goldbach had been deported to Auschwitz concentration camp, and were now presumed dead. Micah had suffered at Drancy holding camp – a transport prison for locations unknown in Poland and Germany. It was appallingly brutal. Micah had been kept in sub-human conditions for many grueling months, with barely any food and enormously overcrowded dorms. He'd been useful to the gendarmes, and quietly did what he could to remove Jewish inmates' names from the deportation list, claiming illness or desperate family situations. He'd only just been released, and was a shadow of his former self. Undernourished, weak, and in a precarious state of mind, he was touchingly grateful to reunite with his sister and his true love, Maggie.

"We shall miss you, dear sister. I hope it won't be too difficult for you to be parted from Micah?" Tillie asked gently.

"It won't be easy, after we've just been reunited. But I must do my duty, mustn't I?" Hannah thrust out her small chin in defiance.

"Absolutely, you must, darling. How are you getting on in the WAAFs? Weather forecasting is such an important job."

"A bit of alright, I suppose, Tillie," Hannah answered proudly. "Helping our RAF bombers to know as much as possible about cloud cover, visibility and upper air winds along their projected routes may seem dreary, but I want to see every flyer come home safe – every time – after doing his job."

"You're so clever, Hannah. You've always done well in school – I'm sure your precision and careful nature make you a brilliant forecaster." Tillie picked up her basket and placed a straw hat on her blonde curls. "Now, I must be off before I lose my nerve." She grimaced.

Just a few short days after D-Day, Hitler had retaliated by launching a dangerous new type of bomb – the V1, or doodlebug, as Londoners nicknamed it. It was pilotless, albeit resembled a small aeroplane – a bomb with wings. The "V" stood for Vergeltungswaffen, German for weapons of reprisal. The Allies had relentlessly bombed Berlin, and Hitler was intent on revenge.

Thousands were launched against London. Sounding like rushing lorries, they flew until they ran out of fuel. Then the engines stopped, and they simply fell to the ground and exploded. Sometimes it was an immediate drop, at others they would continue to glide, gradually losing height.

These attacks had devastated London. Thousands of people had already been killed or injured. After the euphoria of D-Day, people were fearful, looking up constantly to the sky, and taking to shelters again.

Tillie had experienced the terror of a V1 a couple of weeks ago, and it had been a near thing.

"Oh Tils, it must be wretched for you to relive that day each time you leave the house." Hannah was instantly sympathetic.

"That moment when I heard that buzz bomb engine cut, and I knew I only had fifteen seconds to find cover, was the most terrifying of my life. But I was safe. And I can't cower behind closed doors. That would be letting Hitler win. And we can't ever do that." Tillie brushed away a tear.

Hannah nodded.

"We mustn't ever chuck in the sponge, no matter how difficult it is."

At that moment, Jamie sent up a wail. He'd lost his toy under the table, and couldn't reach it.

Tillie scooped him up and laughed.

"And this is what we are fighting for. Thank you, Master James, for reminding us of the truth of it. I better go. I'm meant to pass by Aunt Shirley's at Number Twelve, and then we're off to the shops."

"Shall we find Robbie, then, luv?" Hannah took Jamie from Tillie, as she turned for the kitchen steps.

"Ta ra. I'm hoping for an onion for our stew tonight." Tillie's voice faded as she reached the front hall, and then the door clicked.

***

"Sorry, Aunt Shirley. Hannah and I got to talking, and the time got away from me." Tillie kissed her aunt on the cheek a few minutes later.

"No bother, Tillie. We'll only be standing in queue for hours, in the event. The time goes that much faster when there's company. We can have a right natter. How is young Jamie getting on? Any more teeth?"

The Kingstons and Fowlers were close. Aunt Shirley was Alice's younger sister and best friend. She and Uncle Thomas had lost their only son, Geoffrey, at Dunkirk, and the couple had never been the same. The Kingstons included them in family dinners and everyday life to fend off their loneliness. It helped a little. During the Blitz, the sisters had often sheltered together.

"He's a proper handful at times, but we love him to bits. And no more teeth, at present."

"He is a little love." Shirley smiled. "How are you getting on with sending Red Cross packages to prisoners of war overseas? The need is surely great," Shirley tutted. She was a younger version of her sister, short with greyish brown curly hair and a big smile.

"Now that Jamie is older, I need to do my bit. Trevor won't let me go back to driving an ambulance – too dangerous, he says. But there are still many things I can do for the war effort. A few afternoons a week packing up boxes of essentials for our men at war is the least I can do. It's a small thing, but sending treats from home – tinned foods, tea, cheese, Marmite, and chocolate when we can get it – may make the difference to help those POWs to survive another day. Or barter for needed items. You understand, Aunt Shirley. You must have knitted a thousand scarves and pairs of mittens by now. You're one of the WVS secret weapons."

"I don't know about that, but as you say – we must all do our part. And it makes the time pass – especially during the long nights in the Anderson," Shirley replied softly.

Tillie nodded and the two women linked arms and set off down Longridge Road.

* * *

"Dear Katie,

It's been a whirlwind since the wedding, so my apologies for not writing sooner.

Albeit the ceremony was private, we missed your sparkling smile and cheerful presence at the small wedding breakfast at the house.

Mum, Aunt Shirley, Tillie, Hannah and Isla did their best to make it special – even with the rationing. The house was decorated with bunting and rummaged ribbons. Everyone clubbed together to create a veritable feast, and Alfie came up trumps with a Lyons wedding cake. Jamie snuck up before we cut it and smashed a huge handful in his mouth. He stole the show, little darling.

Even though I just wore my uniform, Hannah arranged for a small posy, and Tillie made a fuss over my hair and makeup. Mum even loaned me her diamond bow brooch – you remember the one I loved to try on when I was little? So even without a gown, I still felt bridal.

Micah made a small speech, thanking everyone for coming, and raising a glass of wine for those who were no longer with us. He was dignified, but tense. He has never liked crowds, now more than ever. We will need to find a quiet place to live when the war is over. He finds the townhouse a bit much.

Married life is smashing, dear Katie. I only had a 48-hour pass, so no *honeymoon, more's the pity. But it was still heaven to book into a small hotel as Mr and Mrs Goldbach. It was such a wrench to say goodbye to Micah, but needs must, and here I am back on the ack-ack site.*

I've just had orders to relocate to a London ATS site. The V1 attacks are so widespread that we're needed for local defence. We'll have to train on how to shoot the guns against pilotless bombs. I'll be close to home and Micah when I can get time away from the guns, which is wonderful.

How are you getting on as a Wren? Your letters are scanty and lacking detail. No surprise, dear Katie. But we long to hear you are keeping safe. Surely, you will be as occupied as the rest in the services. I'm sure Churchill is putting your clerking skills to good use. I hope your time working with Pops in his firm over the summers is standing you in good stead.

Do you think this will all be over soon? After the Allied successes last month, surely this war can't go on much longer. We are buoyed but now demoralized as we determine how to fight this new battle in the air.

Please write soon, Katie. It seems so long since all of us Kingston girls were together, laughing and sharing makeup. Those days will come soon, but perhaps not soon enough.

Sending love from both Micah and me, dear sister.

Love,
Maggie xx"

Katie let the thin paper drift to her lap and sighed.

"Bad news from home, Queenie?" Ruby asked, as she looked up from her nails. She was trying a new pink nail varnish called Pretty and Poised.

"No, just feeling sorry for myself, luv. I wish I hadn't missed my sister's wedding. Even though it was a small registry office affair, it's tugging on my heart to know I missed such an important family do."

"I understand. If we counted up all the birthdays, anniversaries, weddings and funerals that we've been forced to forego, we'd all be crackers."

"I know, Rubes. But some days, it's harder than others to put on a brave face and pretend I don't mind." *What I would give to be home just now, with Mum to fuss over me, and Tillie to laugh and have a lark.*

Ruby gave her chum a sharp look.

"Any other reason for your blue mood? Are you missing a certain Irish parachute jumper?" Ruby attempted to jolly her mate out of her glum state of mind.

Katie picked at a thread on the coverlet.

"I haven't heard from Ciaran since he left on D-Day. I can't help fretting – where is he? Has he been injured…or worse? Is he behind enemy lines? Why hasn't he written?" Katie had spent hours worrying about these questions. *Where are you, Irish? Why haven't you written to me?*

Ruby moved from her bed to sit beside her.

"I wish I knew. It's the waiting and uncertainty that chafes. Despite my best efforts, that Irish bloke got to me. Somehow, he has wormed his way into my heart. And now I can't stop thinking about him. Damn him."

"Katie, why are you fighting this so hard? He seems a decent chap. He obviously fancies you. He's been glued to your side since the day you two met. I saw how he looked at you. He's mad for you. What's the problem? He's not married or anything," Ruby finished with a flippant chuckle.

Kate jumped up, almost knocking over Ruby's nail tray.

"Why did you say that? Do you know something I don't? Ciaran's not married. He can't be."

The freckles on Katie's face stood out against her pale skin, her eyes wild.

"Darling, of course he's not. I was just teasing. Why are you so cross?"

"Don't say that. I can't let that happen again. I won't fall in love with a married man again. I won't."

CHAPTER SEVEN

"Easy, easy. I'm not saying anything. But maybe you should start talking. Sit down, please."

Katie sat, trying to catch her breath. Bloody hell. How had she gotten herself into this? *I swore I'd never confess my grubby secret to anyone. And now I've given myself away. What am I to do now?*

"Oh Ruby, I don't even know where to start." Dammit, her voice was breaking.

"Take a breath and start at the beginning. When did you meet a married man?"

"It was just after my probationary training," Katie confessed miserably, staring at her toes. "I was posted to HMS Flowerdown in Hampshire. It was a lively base – loads of dances, plays, shows, and the like. I joined up some sports teams – tennis, everything really. Even though it was a squash bunking in the Nissen huts, it was all jolly fun, if I'm honest." A ghost of a smile lit her face at the memory.

"Many of us girls were new in the Navy, so we helped each other figure things out, get accustomed to living away from home, you know."

Ruby nodded. The comradery amongst the Wrens was widespread and kept morale high.

"It was my first time away from home, and I loved the freedom – dances, plays, sports matches – all of it. I threw myself into naval life whilst I was finding my feet as an interceptor." Her voice sped up.

"There were loads of men. Not just active sailors, but many sent for rest and recuperation. We even went to the American dances, too. It could proper turn your head – all those servicemen vying for the attention of a few young Wrens. You know. It was exhilarating." Katie looked up, then down, examining her fingernails.

"I met him at a dance. Oh Ruby, he was handsome. Blond, with piercing blue eyes and a mustache. And a smashing dancer. At first, it was just a couple of dances on a Saturday night. Then, he would seek me out and I couldn't believe he would be interested in someone like me."

Ruby had to interject.

"Stop. What do you mean someone like you? Why must you always put yourself down?"

Katie shrugged and went on dully.

"Well, why would he, Ruby? There were so many beautiful young women. Why me? But I didn't stop to think, really. I just enjoyed the whirlwind of the moment.

"After a few Saturday nights where we would dance the night away, he asked to take me to dinner off-base. Ruby, I was that excited that I could hardly sleep or eat. I really thought I was in love. All the girls helped me to dress, sharing their bits and bobs so I could be presentable. It was a cool night, but I felt my whole body was on fire.

"He took me to a little restaurant in nearby Westchester. He even wangled the use of someone's car. It was so glamourous and magical. We chatted easily all the way there, and over dinner. Imagine Ruby – a real steak."

Katie's eyes sparkled.

"Oh my. That was a special night."

"I know what you're thinking. That he ravished me. But he didn't. He was the perfect gentleman, asking all about life in London, the family, my hopes and dreams." She choked a little. "He kissed me at the end of the night, and my whole body melted. I was sure Ralph was the one."

"Ralph?" Ruby pounced.

"Major Ralph Buckley, to be precise," Katie spat. "I will never say his name again."

"What happened next?" Ruby asked gently, a frown furrowing her forehead.

"We continued to see each other whenever we could. He was dreadfully busy, of course. As a junior Wren, I couldn't manage much time off. But for two glorious months, we met up, walked, and talked for hours."

"Sounds like a dream, darling. A beautiful dream."

"It started out as a dream and ended as a nightmare. He was shipped to another base for a fortnight to assist with training new soldiers. I missed him awfully."

Katie stood up and paced the tiny cabin. *This is so much harder than I thought it would be. Dredging up those times that I've forced myself to forget. Why was I so naïve?*

"One morning, I found a note – anonymous, of course – under my pillow. It was short and blunt. Ralph was a married man and lived in Norfolk with his wife and son. That he had a history of being vague about his past to seduce young Wrens, WAAFs, ATS, anyone really who fell for his charms.

"At first, I didn't quite clock it, Ruby. I couldn't. But it haunted me. I had to know the truth. As soon as Ralph returned, I confronted him, and he confessed. Blubbered like a baby. Professed his love for me, said he didn't care for her, promised he would leave her after the war. Wanted me to wait for him – the cheek. I went from wretched to cross in about ten seconds flat."

"What a bloody coward," Ruby burst out, despite herself.

"He was. Weak as water, a liar, and a cheat. I was that thankful that we'd only shared a handful of kisses and embraces. He'd pressed for more, but I always resisted. I felt ghastly for his poor wife. Married to such a rotter. I tell you, Ruby. I fell out of love in an instant. I told him I never wanted to see him again. He begged me to reconsider, but I was resolute. He transferred to the training base a few weeks later, so I didn't have to run into him. It was bloody awful. He didn't even have the decency to be a man about it all. He kept writing to me. I couldn't bear it. I was that relieved when he left. But I couldn't help thinking that everyone on the ship was laughing at me behind my back, saying how daft and foolish I'd been. I was miserable." Katie's voice broke, and tears spilled down her cheeks. She sat back down.

"I felt low about myself before, but then I felt like the gum on someone's shoes. How could I be involved with a married man? With a child? I didn't deserve any man. I swore off any involvement with anyone – at least for the duration of the war." She angrily wiped away the tears. "I also vowed I would never cry over that cad again. And I won't." She looked over at her mate.

"My poor Katie. How awful for you – the way he treated you. But you mustn't take this on. It wasn't you. He was the liar, cheat, cad, and coward. You said it yourself. You are better than ten of him, no – a hundred of him," Ruby protested loyally.

Through a watery smile, Katie regained her composure.

"Thank you, luv. That means everything to me. I know I'm better than the likes of him, but an experience like that – it really shakes you. And your confidence. And I was only twenty-one. Such a baby."

"Now you are the grand old age of twenty-three." Ruby couldn't help but laugh.

Katie gently punched her arm and snuffled.

"Give over, Ruby. You're only twenty-four yourself. But thank you for helping me through this. Being transferred to Capel Le Ferne was the best thing that's happened since I joined up. Meeting you, Jinks, all the others who know naught about my humiliation at HMS Flowerdown. A new start, you know?"

"A new start, indeed, luv. And remember – it was that gormless Ralph's humiliation, not yours."

Katie nodded, trying to take it on board. It was so much easier said than done.

"I really want to believe that. I do. And it gets easier each day. I've been jolly enough throwing myself into my work – keeping away from men of all ranks, sizes, and shapes. Until…"

"A certain Irish soldier appeared," Rubes finished for her.

Katie hugged her chum and dried her eyes.

"You're a dear mate. Let's not speak of this again. Let's look to the future – this war must be ending soon, and we can start to really live."

Ruby took the hint. Confidences had finished.

"Where do you think we'll be posted next, Queenie? Now that we've taken back French shores from the Germans, there's little need for us here on the coast."

The girls had been transferred back to the Y-Station at Cape Le Ferne, but watches were quiet indeed.

"I really don't know. There can't be much interception work with the fear of invasion fading. How these new doodlebugs will affect our work is anyone's guess. We'll just have to wait for our next orders."

"I suppose you're right. Are you ready to head over to the station? It's near time for our next watch. You know naval time is always—"

"Five minutes early," Katie finished with her. "I just need to fix my face, Ruby. And ta ever so much." She grinned, feeling lighter than she had for weeks. Mum was right. A trouble shared was a trouble halved.

* * *

"There's one more cup in the pot, Shirl. Will you have it? I have a slice of carrot cake to go with it. I daresay we have time before our WVS shift."

"Ta, luv. That would be a treat." Shirley smiled at her sister. "The house is quiet for a change. Where is everyone?"

The sisters sat in the Kingston kitchen on an overcast, muggy morning. Both women wore light cotton dresses, with the windows open, hoping for a breeze.

"Walter is at the office, of course. Tillie has taken Jamie over to Isla's. You know she has a flair for sewing. She is going to measure up our young lad for some new clothes. He's growing like a weed and she means to cut down some of Trevor's old shirts for him."

"And with Hannah off on an air force base, that's three girls away in service. However do you manage, Alice?"

"I hate it, if I'm honest. Maggie is being transferred back to a London gun site. Did I tell you? Katie is still down Dover-way, albeit she's proper fuzzy on her Wren duties. You don't suppose she is a spy, do you?" Alice whispered, leaning forward.

"I rather doubt it, but you never know. She's clever and quick. Maybe some type of Special Forces work?" Shirley sipped her tea.

"I just hope it's not too dangerous. Of all my girls, Katie is the one I worry about the most. Too brave by half, and sometimes doesn't think before she acts. And she's younger than the twins. I hope she doesn't rush into anything foolhardy."

"Remember that time she ran into the street to save a dog from being hit by a car? Didn't mind herself at all. Luckily, the man stopped, blared his horn, and she escaped without a scratch – she and the dog."

The sisters laughed companionably.

"That's our Katie. She has a big heart, though. Maybe after the war she'll find a husband. Tillie and Maggie have both been so lucky with their men. It's her turn next."

"And young Kenny, too. Any recent word from him?"

"I got a letter just the other day, Shirl. He couldn't say much about the D-Day offensive, but he and his naval mates were in the thick of it. I'm just that comforted that he's safe. We've lost so many."

The women sat in silence for a moment, each of them thinking of young Geoffrey gone before his twenty-third birthday.

"Five years, sis. This war has raged for almost five years."

"On September third, it will be. When will it end? Dare we hope by this Christmas?"

Alice shrugged.

"I don't even want to try to predict any longer. We just have to get stuck in, and hope the Allies will go from strength to strength and finish it."

"Speaking of getting on with it, I suppose we'd best get moving ourselves. We don't know how the buses will run today and we don't want to be late for our shift." Shirley stood up, taking her teacup to the sink. She peered out the window. "I hope it doesn't rain today."

"Let's bring our umbrellas, just in case. My hat is upstairs. Shall we go?"

The two women could almost have passed as twins. Short, a little round with middle age, a few wrinkles revealing the scars of extended worry, but with warm smiles for family and neighbours alike. Bustling with energy, they led their families admirably in these trying times.

Waiting at the bus stop, they chattered along.

"Not a breath of air, Alice. July is always so stifling."

"At least we're not standing in queue today. Let's be grateful for that."

"Too right, sis. And look, here's the bus. Only fifteen minutes late."

They climbed aboard and took a seat near an open window. The bus was half-full, and the driver waved a cheery hello.

"Good morning, ladies. Plenty of room today."

The bus lumbered on, picking up a few passengers. The WVS office was near Piccadilly Circus, near an hour's bus ride from their homes at Earl's Court.

"We'll stop at the shops later, Alice? I'm hoping to find a bit of bacon for Thomas's tea. I haven't had much energy lately to try any new recipes. Maybe a cold supper tonight."

"I know. Who wants to cook in this heat?"

A loud buzzing was suddenly heard through the open windows. The sound was deafening. Shirley stared, frightened, at her sister.

"Is that a doodlebug?" shouted a young mum, clutching her baby. In the dead silence that followed, all that could be heard was the loud buzzing drawing nearer. The baby started wailing.

The driver halted immediately, screeching the brakes, forcing everyone forward, hitting seats in front of them, and dropping handbags and shopping parcels.

"Everyone off. NOW! Run for cover!" The bus driver stood, motioning wildly for his passengers to disembark. Sweat soaked his uniform.

It was mass confusion. Everyone rushed the aisle, heaving towards the front of the bus. People pushed and shoved as they climbed over seats and each other to reach the open door.

Shirley and Alice were near the back, and could hardly move with all the heaving bodies pushing past them.

"Come on, Shirl. We've got to get off!"

Alice sucked in her breath, knowing they had seconds to spare.

Shirley was terrified, pupils wide. All the blood had drained from her face.

"There's no time. We don't have enough time. We've only got fifteen seconds," she babbled.

"Come ON, Shirl. We must," Alice yanked her sister's arm.

Suddenly, the buzzing stopped. The sisters looked at each other with horror. Alice shuddered.

"Quick, Shirl – hide."

She pushed her sister under a seat and crouched next to her. She reached for her hand....

And then a massive explosion. Everything went black.

* * *

Covered in dust, Alice opened her eyes. Somehow, she had been thrown to the back of the bus, facing backwards. The bus had spun around and jumped the curb, narrowly missing the taped-up windows of a local shop. She heard persistent moaning. The smell of cordite filled the air. A siren sounded in the distance.

Alice felt her face. It was mucky with dust and wet with blood. She looked stupidly at her hand. What had happened? How did her hair get so matted? She idly picked chunks of brick dust out. And why won't someone shush that baby? Someone coughed. Who was that?

Feeling dazed, she heard someone calling for help, and remembered that Shirley was with her. They were going to be late for their WVS shift. Coming into herself, she looked around the smoky bus, tilted at an odd angle.

The V1. Memory rushed in and Alice felt cold. *Shirley*. Where was Shirley? She could barely make out shadowy figures in the dust and smoke-filled air. She removed a man's hat from her lap – how had that gotten there? – and brushed away more dust. Where was her sister?

"Shirley, luv. Where are you? Are you hurt?"

She didn't recognize her own raspy, weak voice. She tried to stand, but something heavy was pressing on her lap. She tried to lift it, but it wouldn't move. As she tried to shift it, a burning pain in her side ripped through her. She was trapped.

Over and over, she screamed for Shirley, but heard nothing.

The pain in her leg was excruciating. Mercifully, she blacked out again.

CHAPTER EIGHT

"Aunt Shirley killed in V1 attack. Mum is injured and in hospital. Come soonest. Pops."

Katie's First Petty Officer silently handed her the telegram. Katie re-read it three times, and sunk to her chair. Aunt Shirley was dead. No, it couldn't be true. Laughing, helpful Aunt Shirley who'd already suffered so much? No. *No.* Poor Mum. What was happening in London?

"I'm very sorry, Kingston. Tough news. You've been given forty-eight hours' compassionate leave. Your transport will be here in an hour." She was left alone.

She felt numb, weightless, disembodied. Gazing out the window, she saw a bird flying over the cliffs. Skylark, she thought idly.

Ruby, Jinx and Edi were nothing but kind, as they clucked over her, helping her throw a few things into a holdall, and walking her to the lorry that would take her to the train station.

Katie couldn't think, daren't think. She put one foot in front of the other, willing herself to live minute to minute until she got home to her family.

The trip to London passed in a blur. Katie bought her ticket and stared out the window from Dover to Victoria Station. She'd asked not to be met – the trains were habitually delayed. With all the turmoil at home, she didn't want to be a bother.

Reaching London, Katie wearily lifted her bag to her shoulder, barely noticing the sights and smells of the hectic railway station. It was a warm day, and she longed for a cool drink. The train had stopped several times in the middle of nowhere with no explanation, and was an hour late. Placing her hat on her head, she stepped down from the train to the platform.

Pops was there.

Katie ran to him, tears streaming down her face, as she gulped for air. Heedless of the surrounding crowds, he held her close, stroking her hair.

"Shhh, Katie. It's alright. You're home now. Everything is going to be alright."

"How can it be, Pops? Aunt Shirley is gone forever. Nothing will ever be the same. How will we cope?" Katie's uniform front was wet with tears. Her body heaved in convulsions. She gasped for air.

"Take a breath, poppet. We're taking a taxi home."

Pops fished in his pocket for a handkerchief. Lifting her bag, he gripped her elbow tightly and pulled her towards the exit. He flagged down a black cab and swiftly ushered her in.

"How did you know, Pops? How did you know I needed you? I didn't even realize it myself." Katie was mortified at her outburst, and fought to regain control. She hiccoughed; her throat was raw from crying. *What a spectacle I've made of myself. Calm down, girl.*

He patted her hand and looked out the window – giving her a moment to compose herself.

"I didn't know, Katie. I just didn't want you to be alone any longer than you had to be." His gruff tone belied his own raw emotions.

"Thank you, Pops. I'll be fine now. Really. It was just seeing you – it brought on the tears I didn't know I was holding back. How is everyone at home? How is Mum?"

Back on even footing, Pops filled her in on the horrendous last few days.

"Everyone is home or expected today, save Kenny, who is too far away to sort leave. Hannah will be the last – around half-past five tonight. Mum is still in the hospital. She's broken her leg in two places. She also bruised three ribs and suffered a lot of cuts on her hands and neck from broken glass." He glanced at his daughter. "She's in and out of sedation, which is probably for the best right now. She's in a lot of pain, and wakes up hysterical, calling for her sister. It will be some weeks yet before she's home, poppet."

Katie gasped.

"Poor Mum. Is she at St Mary Abbots?"

"No," Pops replied shortly. "There was a V1 attack there last week and they transferred patients to St. George's. Because Mum and Aunt Shirley were on their way to Piccadilly, the ambulance transported her to the London Hospital straightaway after the explosion. They are taking excellent care of her, Katie."

Katie bit her lip. Every fibre of her being longed to rush to the hospital and stay at her mother's side, nursing and caring for her until she was healed. With just a 48-hour pass, she could hardly see her, let alone look after her in the weeks ahead. Bloody war.

"I know you want to see her, but let's get you home first. Trevor arrived last night, and Maggie this morning. They're all waiting for you."

Katie nodded.

"How is Uncle Thomas? Will he be there?"

"I expect so. He's being stoic, as always, but he's devastated. First his son, now his wife. He's been working non-stop since the accident. It's his way of getting through, I daresay."

"So, what happens next, Pops?" Katie asked. She felt lost and grief-stricken. Mum and Aunt Shirley were the backbones of the family. What to do now?

"There can't be a funeral, because there is – was – no…" He hesitated. "No body to bury," he finished slowly.

Katie gasped again, pressing her fingertips to her temples. Her head ached.

"Of the twenty-three people on the bus, only six survived – including your mother. The others died instantly, with little or nothing left to identify them. Do you want to hear more?" He paused.

"No," Katie replied shortly. "Surely, there will be a memorial."

"Yes, in due course. Thomas wants to wait until your mother is well enough to attend. I concur. To answer your question, I suppose we just carry on. Loads of neighbors and Shirley's WVS friends have been bringing food to the house, and helping to watch young Jamie. The rest of us are just there for each other, providing whatever small comfort we can. Tillie has been talking about a candlelight vigil tomorrow night – just for the family."

"That seems like a good idea, Pops. We need to show our respect for Aunt Shirley – and Uncle Thomas."

They rode the rest of the way in silence.

Pulling up to #40, Katie found the familiar sight of the white townhouse with the steps leading to the black-painted front door oddly soothing.

Jumping out of the taxi, Katie rushed up the steps, eager to reunite with her sisters.

She opened the door and ran upstairs to the drawing room. They were all there – Maggie in uniform with Micah, Trevor in his RAF dress with Tillie, and Trevor's mum, Isla. Jamie was nowhere to be seen, so likely napping. Uncle Thomas was likewise absent.

Tillie and Maggie sprang to their feet at the first glimpse of their younger sister. The three embraced, alternately crying and hugging.

Words spilled over themselves, as the Kingston sisters tried to make sense of the insensible.

"What a ghastly tragedy. I hope she didn't suffer."

"Poor Uncle Thomas. How can he bear it?"

"I miss her so, already. She was always in my corner."

"This family won't be the same without her."

"What do we do now?"

"Girls, let Katie sit. Will no one offer her a cup of tea?" Trevor asked. No one laughed, but the mood broke.

"Darling, of course. You've had a long and trying journey. Sit, and I'll brew a new pot," Maggie put in, leading her sister to the sofa.

"I'll do it," Isla volunteered. She picked up the empty tea tray and headed downstairs to the kitchen.

Everyone sat down.

Katie gazed at Tillie and Trevor, clutching hands. Micah stood next to Maggie, his hand on her shoulder. Mum and Shirley's absences were palpable.

"When can I visit Mum?" Katie addressed her father.

"She's only allowed one visitor at a time – for thirty minutes at most. You may be refused entry if she's asleep or in distress." He glanced at Tillie. Alice had been frantic the last few times she'd woken.

"I still want to see her," Katie said.

"Hannah and Uncle Thomas will be here for supper. You can go directly after that."

"What else needs to be done?" she asked, desperate to do something – anything – to help.

"Nothing, luv," quieted Maggie. "Let's get you settled, shall we? As always, it's rather a case of musical beds. Tillie and Trevor are in our old twin room. Micah and I have taken over Kenny's third-floor room. You and Hannah have the small boxrooms next door. I trust that will suit you?"

"Of course, Maggie. And thank you. I can kip down anywhere."

Isla returned with a loaded tea tray, which Trevor helped her settle on the sideboard. After a refreshing cuppa with rock buns brought by their next-door neighbor, the three girls retired to freshen up. On the way to the third-floor boxroom, they stopped at Tillie and Maggie's old bedroom.

"Robbie has been sleeping with me whilst Maggie has been away. I'm sure he wants to say hello."

Katie sank onto the double bed, cuddling the smoky bundle of fur, finding reassurance in his purr.

"She was like a second mum to me. I miss her so, already," Katie whispered into his soft neck.

"And she loved you dearly, darling. She spoke often of the times you spent with her after Geoffrey's death. You brought her a great deal of comfort with your daily visits, poring over the photo album with her over and over, making her tea, and bringing her little gifts. It meant the world to her, Katie," Tillie shared.

"It was no trouble at all. You and Maggie always had each other. I naturally gravitated to Aunt Shirley. We had so many fun times together." Katie's tone was wistful, but she was proud not to break down again.

"She saw you as the daughter she never had," Maggie put in gently.

"But I hardly saw her in the last couple of years," Katie said bitterly. She held up her hand. "And don't say it was the war. Even before I signed on to the Royal Navy, she would ask me to go to the shops with her, or even shelter with her at night. And I did – sometimes. But I was too involved in my own life, meeting my friends. I should have spent more time with her. She needed me."

Tillie and Maggie exchanged a glance.

"We know you feel wretched, darling, but you mustn't wallow like this. Aunt Shirley never said a cross word about you – quite the contrary. She cherished every moment you spent with her, making her laugh, and taking her mind off Geoffrey and his horrible death on the Dunkirk Beach. She knew you had your own life to lead." Maggie was gentle, but softly chided her sister.

"You're right, Mags. I mustn't be selfish. What's important now is helping Uncle Thomas and Mum."

After a quiet family dinner, Katie went to the hospital with Hannah. Mum was awake, and the nurse kindly let them both in for a brief visit.

Katie was shocked at the bruised and weakened state of her mother. Her leg was elevated in a contraption meant to prevent further damage to the cast. Her hands, arms, and neck were covered in multi-coloured bruises, cuts, and marks. She looked completely wiped out.

"Mum, the lengths you'll go to avoid making supper," Katie joked as she leaned over to kiss her on the cheek.

"Katie, darling. I'm so happy to see you. And Hannah," she seized both their hands. "Please stay. I get so lonely here on my own," she pleaded.

"We'll stay as long as the charge nurse will let us, Mum. And we'll be back first thing tomorrow. I brought you some chocolate from the NAAFI."

"My hand-picked flowers don't compare, but I'm relieved to see you, Aunt Alice," Hannah said shyly, presenting the small posy.

"How kind of you both." But she made no move to touch the gifts. "Is it a bad dream? Is my sister really gone?" she asked, her voice cracking.

"Mum, I'm sorry, but she is. Now you need to concentrate on getting better. And we'll all help you."

"But it was my fault. How can I rest? I pushed her under the seat. She's dead because of me," Mum's voice rose, and she plucked at the crisp, white sheets.

"Mum, shhh. It's not your fault. It was a hideous, terrible accident. If you want to blame anyone, it should be Hitler. And whatever evil generals or other Nazis conceived the ghastly buzz bombs. You must believe that, Mum."

"Hitler didn't push Shirl. I did. I did," she shrieked, as she pushed herself up on the bed.

Hannah looked at Katie, panic-stricken. Katie nodded furiously as she pressed her mum gently back into the pillows.

Hannah rushed from the room, bringing the nurse back with her straightaway.

"Mrs Kingston. What's amiss here? Remember, we talked about raising your voice and making yourself upset? It doesn't help, and you're disturbing the other patients." The nurse's matter-of-fact manner aimed to soothe.

"Stop. Stop. Don't you hear the buzzing? It's stopped. The bomb is going to drop on us," Alice's eyes were glazed and she screamed at the top of her lungs.

Another nurse burst into the room, carrying a small metal tray with a syringe.

"Steady on, Mrs Kingston. You'll feel better after a good night's sleep. It's been a trying day." She deftly injected the syringe into Alice's arm. Mum fell limp immediately.

"Try not to worry about her. She's still in shock and in a lot of pain. That's not her speaking. Just give her time," the nurse said. "She'll sleep now. You can return tomorrow at regular visiting hours."

Katie and Hannah kissed Alice's cheek. Katie gave her hand a squeeze and left with a heavy heart, chancing a backward glance, slightly – but only slightly – cheered to see her mother sleeping peacefully.

CHAPTER NINE

September 1944

"Have you finished packing, Queenie? One last knees-up at The Valiant Sailor tonight – we don't want to miss that." Ruby's bed was scattered with navy-blue clothing, toiletries, and old magazines.

Katie and Ruby dressed in casual navy uniform – jerseys and wide bell-bottomed trousers.

"Almost, Rubes. I can't believe I've just one last watch here at Cape Le Ferne. And I wouldn't miss the party for anything. It's strange to say during wartime, but I've enjoyed my time here. We've made some good friends, haven't we?"

Katie was feeling a little blue. The Wrennery was being disbanded, and all the girls separated and given orders to ship out to new locations. Katie and Ruby were being sent to bustling Portsmouth. Katie was inordinately pleased they'd been posted together.

"Lifelong mates, indeed. It's not Hellfire Corner any longer. More like a ghost town," Ruby agreed. "With all the troops and battalions being shipped out, there's no need for us anymore. Only the ack-ack batteries will stay back to defend against the doodlebugs."

"What do you suppose they'll have us doing at Portsmouth?" asked Ruby, shoving her sponge bag on the top of her holdall.

"'Administrative duties' is rather vague, isn't it? I suppose they'll have us typing or some such. They may post me doing accounts, given my background at Pops' office. One thing is for sure – no more Y-intercepting for us."

They both looked a trifle glum at the prospect.

"Why didn't you consider any of the overseas jobs, Ruby?"

There'd been recent postings for Wrens needed in telegraphy in Singapore and ports east. Neither Katie nor Ruby had applied, but Jinx had, and was already off to Malaysia.

"This probably sounds daft, but I just didn't want to leave England. With the war winding down, it seems frightfully more dangerous."

"I know what you mean. I couldn't bear to bring Mum any more pain, so I'm staying on dry land. You know the Wrens' motto – Never at Sea. I'm taking that to heart."

"How is your mum getting on? Happy to be home?"

"She is overjoyed to be back at Number Forty. It was a long go of it in the hospital, but she's walking now with the aid of crutches. She will make a full recovery, but it takes time. She's pretty much back to her old self, but more subdued. I doubt she'll ever get over the loss of her sister." Katie sighed. "I'm proper relieved that she was much improved than last time I saw her. She really terrified us there for a time."

"I know it's ghastly to watch a loved one go through so much suffering. I'm sure you and the family are a great comfort to her."

"When we're there. Which is rarely," Katie replied grimly. "That's another reason I'm not signing up for overseas. As soon as this damn war is over, I want to be back home. I don't want to sign on for another two years in the Royal Navy." *You needed me, Mum, and I wasn't there. I'll make it up to you someday.*

"Too right. But I wonder, is there another reason you want to remain on British soil? Could it have anything to do with an Irish soldier?" Ruby asked with a straight face.

"Sod off," Katie replied, throwing a pillow at her chum. "You know I haven't heard from him since June. It's been three months with nary a letter. Either he's a cad and has forgotten all about me, or he's injured – or worse." Katie bit her lower lip. She had spent many hours anxious about Ciaran, wondering if he was safe. And if so, why hadn't he written? She woke up many nights feeling panicky, jerked awake with her fear for him.

Ruby sighed.

"I won't make excuses for the bloke, but you know loads of jumpers were injured or captured. If so, he may not even be able to write or find a way to post it. And you haven't seen him on any of the casualty lists. Don't give up hope, luv." She pasted an encouraging smile on her face.

"Did someone say post? Kingston, I have a raft of letters here for you. Someone is popular today," a Wren dropped a packet of letters on Katie's bed. She snatched them up.

"Oh, one from Kenny. And Maggie. How marvellous. But what's this pile? Oh heavens. Look Ruby!" Katie's mouth cracked to a wide smile as she held a stack of blue letters aloft – all with the same bold, slanted handwriting.

"They're from Ciaran. In France. There are…" She started counting. "Five, six, seven." She clasped them to her breast. "Ruby, he's alive. Or was when he wrote these."

Ruby jumped up and hugged Katie, who was busy sorting the letters by date. *You're alive, you rotter. Ciaran, you made it.*

"Smashing, darling." She checked the time. "And you have thirty minutes before watch. I want a full report on what your young man has been doing."

Katie wanted to correct her, but was too gleeful. He was not her young man – at least not yet.

"I'm going out on the cliffs to read them in private. Fetch me when it's time." With that, she grabbed her hat and ran out of the cabin.

It was a windy autumn day, but Katie was well used to weather on the cliff. She found a rock, sat, and sorted the letters in date order. The first was dated June 21, 1944, from 'Somewhere in France.'

"Dear Katie,

Firstly, I apologize for not writing sooner. Don't fret, but I'm in hospital. The landings went as well as could be expected, but we lost too many good men. My jump was blown far off course because of the poor weather. I'm alright but I've smashed my right hand in seven places (lucky number 7, I reckon). They have me fixed up pretty well, but I'm writing this with my left hand. Don't worry about me, I'll be grand.

I expect my writing is almost illegible, but I promise I have been practicing. This is the first effort that is decent enough to send you.

I'll be here for another few weeks. They haven't quite decided what to do with me. Once the breaks have mended, I'm to be re-assigned to a defence position here or perhaps shipped home. As much as I long to see you, this war is far from over and I want to be of use.

I miss you, my sweet mavourneen, and trust you are keeping busy with the rest of the girls on base.

I'm tired now and will write more later. This letter has taken more time than I care to admit.

May the saddest day of your future be no worse than the happiest day of your past.

Fondly,
Ciaran xx"

A smashed hand. Poor Ciaran. No wonder he hadn't written. Her heart burst with relief and pent-up emotion. She wondered if he had other injuries that he hadn't disclosed.

Quickly reading the rest of the letters, she got a sense of his life in France. He had landed off-course, buried his parachute as he had been trained, and walked until he located his battalion. From there, he'd been hospitalized, had two surgeries, and was recovering.

His letters got longer and longer – and the writing more legible. They also increased in ardor – with Ciaran proclaiming his powerful feelings for Katie, and assurances that they would be together after the war. She cherished every word.

The last letter was dated August 26th – three weeks ago. He couldn't say much, but his battalion, and others from Holland and Belgium, had pushed back the German troops almost into Germany. The mission being complete; they were now being sent home. Home. Ciaran would travel separately once the medics had given him the all-clear.

Katie couldn't help herself. She jumped up and screamed hooray into the wind off the cliffs. He was just there – across the Channel – and was coming home to her soon.

She saw Ruby waving from the Y-station, clutched the letters and ran.

It was a jubilant celebration at The Valiant Sailor that night. It had been the home of many fine get-togethers over the last year, but this one was bittersweet. They'd gotten to know Peter, the pub owner, and all the barmaids.

Over a pint, Katie filled the girls in on Ciaran's news. They all congratulated her and drank to them both. A few of the remaining soldiers and sailors drifted in, and they danced with the Wrens to the accompaniment of an out-of-tune piano in the corner. As the evening drew on, the pints streamed forth, and the crowded pub almost overflowed. As Peter called for last orders, someone shouted for The White Cliffs of Dover just one more time.

There'll be bluebirds over
The white cliffs of Dover
Tomorrow, just you wait and see.

There'll be love and laughter
And peace ever after
Tomorrow, when the world is free.

The shepherd will tend his sheep
The valley will bloom again
And Jimmy will go to sleep
In his own little room again.

There'll be bluebirds over
The white cliffs of Dover
Tomorrow, just you wait and see[1].

The room fell silent, but the cliff gales whistled through the pub, reminding them of good times past, and uncertain ones ahead.

Back at the Wrennery, the girls made a cuppa in the galley, but Katie excused herself to read Kenny and Maggie's letters. And also, to re-read Ciaran's, if she were honest.

---
1   The White Cliffs of Dover lyrics © Gannon & Kent Music Co., Reservoir Media Management Inc.

She was a little tipsy but couldn't wait for the morning, when they'd all be up early for transport to Portsmouth.

"Dear Katie,
I'm not sure who is a worse letter-writer – me or you. It's been weeks since I've heard from you. But I understand, sis. The heat of the battle and all. It's been feverish here, but we're all that chuffed that we could protect our boys during the June invasion. We lost some good mates, which is harsh under any conditions, but we press on.

You asked in your last letter if I'm seeing anyone special. I have been, but you mustn't tell anyone. It's early days yet, but perhaps after the war, I'll introduce you two. She is loads of fun and I'm sure you would like her.

I'm on night watch shortly, so I'll sign off. Both of us in the Royal Navy, sis. Who would have bet on that?

Your rascally brother,
Kenny xx"

Katie dropped the letter. He sounded bright and breezy, but she knew more than anyone that you could fake anything in a letter. You never wanted to worry anyone back home, so you swallowed the harsh times and put on a brave face. What intrigued her more was that he mentioned a girl. This was a first! She hoped it was a love match and could withstand the trials and separation of war.

Next, she opened Maggie's letter:

"Dearest Katie,
How are you getting on? We are all fine here, especially now that the V1s seem to have slowed down. What an immense relief. I'm proud that our anti-aircraft guns are doing their jobs, along with the barrage balloons. Our fighters have had to learn how to combat all over again, but I think (I hope) we are besting these rockets once and for all.

Mum is doing much better. She's really got the knack for the crutches and can beetle up and down the stairs quicker than you can imagine. We planned to make a bedroom for her on the first floor, but she insisted she could manage, and wouldn't hear of anything but sleeping in her own bed. And she's coping beautifully. Isla has been a godsend. She's practically living here and doing most of the cooking and shopping. Between her and Tillie, the house is running pretty smoothly, albeit I expect Pops is glad that Tils is keeping away from the stove.

Jamie is growing by leaps and bounds. I know he misses his daddy, but Trevor was recently transferred to RAF Henley in London, where so much of the doodlebug action is happening. We all fret over him fighting aircraft fires with all this bombing, but we are on cheerful form for Tillie's sake.

Uncle Thomas seems lost, but is burying himself in work. We see him at least once a week for supper, but even that takes coaxing. He near bit Tillie's head off the other week when she offered to help him clear out some of Aunt Shirley's things. She was only trying to be kind, but I suppose it's just too soon.

Micah is getting stronger all the time. He keeps busy working at the Jewish Refugees Committee, which helps refugees who arrive here daily with practically nothing. He finds them temporary housing and clothes, arranges ration books for them, and even tries to source jobs for the men, who are desperate to work and look after their depleted families. It's so sad, Katie, to see physicians and solicitors taking on jobs as cooks and laborers just to get their families on their feet. Micah feels he is doing his small bit in this important work.

As for me, I have a bit of news myself. Micah and I are expecting a baby. It came as rather a shock – especially so soon after the wedding – but we are delighted. A little boy or girl cousin for Jamie. I'm feeling pretty good most days, but rather tired, and sometimes my breakfast comes up almost as soon as I get it down. Tillie assures me this is all normal. She's been a tremendous support to me. I should think she even guessed I was expecting before I knew it. Twin forces, I suppose. The baby is due in mid-to-late April, so I'll have to give up the guns before that. I want to stay on as long as I can, but I'm sure the ATS will have something to say about that – particularly as I have such a demanding position.

I suppose that's enough news for now, dear sister. I think of you daily, and hope you are keeping safe. Is it still as arduous as ever, now that the big push is over? Do tell us how you are coping with it all.

Love,
Maggie xx"

Katie couldn't believe the news. Maggie – having a baby. How wonderful! All in all, it had been a brilliant day. She quickly washed, donned her pajamas, and crawled into bed, where she re-read Ciaran's letters through twice more. The feelings she had been pushing away were growing every day, despite her best intentions. And the letters had made them swell tenfold. She'd be seeing him again soon.

CHAPTER TEN

October 1944

"Bloody hell, I'm going to be late," Katie muttered to an empty cabin. She had overslept and felt utterly rotten. Her head ached, she felt warm, and her arms and legs felt as heavy as tree limbs. And she had a cough. Just brilliant.

And today of all days. After months of waiting and wondering, she was meant to see Ciaran today. Back on British soil, he had returned to service even though his hand wasn't totally healed. He'd been re-assigned to intelligence work at Bletchley Park in Milton Keyes, Buckinghamshire.

Because of the June push causing all leave to be cancelled, Katie was now overdue a travel warrant and week's leave. She'd been saving it for a reunion with Ciaran, and to spend time at home with Mum.

After her watch today, she was meant to take a train to London to meet up with her Irishman. And now she felt under-the-weather.

Rolling her wayward curls into Kirby grips at the side of her face and tucking her bun under her hat, she set her mind on besting this cold.

I'll not be put off by a headache and sore throat. I just won't. She donned her stout black shoes and scurried to the office building, hoping no one would notice her tardiness.

Both she and Ruby had been lucky enough to secure permanent day watch schedules – she in the Admiralty office writing and answering letters, and Ruby as a telephone operator. It was nowhere as exciting as intercepting messages. But then again, that had too been dead boring many a time. At least there were no more four a.m. watches, and Portsmouth was a pleasant change of scene.

She managed through the morning, but felt progressively worse as her watch crawled by. By lunchtime, she knew she had a fever, and could manage naught more than a few sips of tea.

By three p.m., Katie realized she was seriously ill. She couldn't concentrate, and almost fainted when she stood up to deliver a muddled letter to the in-tray. Her CO insisted on sending her to sick bay, despite her shaky protests.

"Measles?" She exclaimed thirty minutes later. "I can't have the measles. My train leaves at 1700." She felt faint.

"You're not going anywhere, Miss. You'll be staying here in sick bay where we can keep an eye on you. Once you are past the contagious phase, you can reschedule your leave and finish recuperating at home – London, is it?" The doctor looked out over his spectacles at Katie, now lying in bed between crisp white sheets.

"Yes, London," Katie replied miserably. "I'm meant to meet my boyfriend and see my parents."

"We'll send word, my dear," a nurse said briskly, but not unkindly, in a voice that floated somewhere over her head. "This is the best place for you at the moment. We'll take proper care of you."

Katie tried to protest, but found she simply didn't have the energy. And the cool sheets felt heavenly against her hot skin.

"That's right, dear. Just rest. Don't try to talk. Let your body work fighting the measles."

But Katie didn't hear this last. She had drifted off to blissful sleep.

* * *

The next few days, Katie mostly slept, and ate a bit of toast with broth or tea. The nurses worked round the clock to keep her fever down, which was dangerously high at times. Not much could be done save for applying cool cloths or flannels, which only provided mild relief.

Five days later, the fever broke, by which time Katie had spots on her face and upper neck, which looked to be moving down towards her hands and feet. Calamine lotion provided some relief for the itching, but the patient was crabby and out-of-sorts.

"No one even to visit me," she moaned as she sat up in bed, trying not to itch. "With Ruby taking her overdue leave, and not knowing anyone here on the base, I'm left to my own devices all day."

"It sounds like you're feeling better, dear," smiled the day nurse. "And your CO has been in every night to look in on you."

"Oh," Katie felt foolish. She hadn't even remembered her Petty Officer's visits.

"When can I go home, please, Nurse?" Katie tried for a conciliatory tone. After all, it wasn't Nurse's fault Katie had missed her leave, and laid up sick here.

"Let's not get ahead of ourselves, Miss Kingston. That will be up to the doctor to decide. But most likely another five or six days. You wouldn't want to go on the train with all these spots, would you? Nor would you want to infect anyone else, I expect?" Katie felt properly chastened.

"Of course not, Nurse," she replied quietly.

"But I have some post for you. Perhaps that will cheer you up a little." She pulled a light blue letter from her pocket.

Katie crowed in delight. A letter from Ciaran.

"*Mavourneen,*

I was more than distressed to hear of your illness. I've asked to see you, but have been told by a lovely but firm Nurse that you were too unwell for visitors. That has me more than concerned, but she advised that within a few days, you'll be on the mend.

You are young, strong, and the most determined woman I know, so you'll be laughing and back to yourself before you know it.

I was able to cancel my leave and return to Milton Keyes, so don't fuss about any inconvenience on my part. I'm that relieved to be back on British soil that an extra train journey is naught to me.

I'll be ringing every day to check on you. Soon enough, you'll be able to take my calls, and Nurse Harsh-and-Mighty will put me through. I long to hear your voice, Katie.

Once you are well enough to convalesce at home, I'll be on the first train down to Portsmouth to collect you and escort you home. I won't take no for an answer.

Our leave won't be quite as we planned – but is life anymore? We must just take it day by day until you are well again.

'Til I see you again, be well and don't push yourself. A good laugh and a long sleep are the two best cures, as we always say. I'm sure you are chafing at confinement, but it's all for the best to get you back on your feet in good time.

Love,
Ciaran xx"

Katie smiled for the first time in days.
"Nurse, may I have a mirror, please?"

* * *

In the event, it was five more days until Katie was declared fit for travel. Albeit she'd had no personal visitors to lessen the chance of contagion, Katie had been flooded with calls, telegrams, and letters from her family, Ruby, and Ciaran. She still felt weak as a newborn kitten, but was feeling stronger each day. She couldn't wait to see Ciaran, but hoped the spots would disappear by the time they were reunited. She was feeling well enough to have some vanity about how dreadful she looked.

The morning he came to fetch her, she dressed and waited impatiently, more than a little nervous.

She needn't have been. Ciaran was relaxed and ever so kind to her.

"I'm not made of glass, Irish," she teased him, as he practically carried her onto the train and settled her in with a blanket. He'd somehow sorted a car to transport them to the train station, so she'd hardly had to move. Admonished by Nurse to take it slow and not flit around London, Katie snorted. She had no intentions of rushing around town.

"Perhaps not, but whilst your tender self is under my care, I intend to treat you as such. I wouldn't want to answer to your father if something happened to you." He tucked the blanket round her, and barked at anyone who came near the carriage wanting one of the empty seats.

"I've brought a flask of tea and a few sandwiches. Do you fancy fishpaste or cheese and pickle?" He looked so young and eager to please that Katie couldn't help grinning.

"I'm not hungry just yet, but I could manage a cuppa, ta."

He carefully poured her a mug, which she cupped in her hands. The carriage was a little chilled, and she was glad of the warmth of the hot drink. She wouldn't admit it, but the trip had already been wearing.

"Sit, Irish, and tell me what's been going on in London. All I've seen these last several weeks are years-old magazines."

Ciaran raked a hand through his auburn hair and sank down next to her.

"Would you like the good news or the bad?"

"The good news," Katie replied promptly. "That will sustain me through the bad."

"It appears we've seen the last of the V1 rockets, and all. Our RAF boys and ack-ack gunners like your sister sorted how to combat them. The last few attacks were either completely shot down or re-routed to non-inhabited locations. The last assault was earlier this month – at least we hope so." He wiggled his eyebrows.

"On the seventh of September, the Minister of Works Duncan Sandys famously proclaimed that the Battle of London was over. They've done so much damage, Katie. Don't ask me how I know this – but something like two-thousand doodlebugs have landed within Greater London, causing thousands of fatalities and serious injuries." He looked grim.

"Is that the bad news, then?" Katie leaned forward.

Ciaran laughed shortly.

"No. I wish that was all of it. But it's not. The day after the grand proclamation, an enormous explosion blasted Staveley Road in Chiswick, killing three people and injuring another seventeen. But it was a new type of bomb – not a doodlebug. They are calling it the V2. It's mysterious and deadly." Ciaran looked out the window.

"Oh dear. That sounds despicable. Another new weapon from Hitler. How much can we endure?" She sat back, feeling ill in her stomach. "Tell me more," she whispered.

"There is no sound, no warning," he replied dully. "Because the huge bomb is supersonic, and travels faster than the speed of sound. They are ballistic missiles which are launched into the atmosphere, and then bounce back to their targets. You don't hear the roar until the explosion has already wreaked its damage. Sure, and they are unstoppable, mavourneen," he halted and took Katie's hand. "We'll immobilize these new rockets – just like we did the buzz bombs. We have incredible minds working on it." He gave her an encouraging smile.

"And the mood in London?" she asked, brown eyes meeting green.

"I won't mislead you. It's grim. People are not just despondent, they are terrified. Nerves are frayed, and well – I suppose that's the gist of it."

"We must get home. Mum must be proper panicky. And after all she's been through." She rose as if to make the train move faster.

"Sit down. London is not on fire. This is just another trial for us to overcome. And we will do."

"I'm sure you're right, Irish. And thank you for telling me the truth – hard as it was to hear. It's easier than half-truths and my own wild imaginings."

She braved a small smile.

"I'll have one of those cheese and pickle sandwiches, if they're still on offer."

"That's my girl," he kissed her on the cheek and produced a slightly wilted sandwich wrapped in greaseproof paper.

Pops and Tillie met the train, which was only three quarters of an hour behind its time. After introducing Ciaran to them, Pops enfolded Katie gently in his arms, and eased her into a waiting taxi, Tillie fussing around her. In no time, they arrived at the Longridge townhouse.

Only Mum and Isla Drummond were on hand to meet them – the rest of the family could not get leave. When Katie embraced Mum, she felt wobblier than expected, and a little tearful.

"Darling, I'm glad to see you. I've been that anxious about you, contracting measles, of all things. Do sit down. Was the train ghastly?"

Mum looked frail, but a little better than the last time Katie had been home. Her once-round figure was gone, leaving a tiny bird-like frame. Even her movements were light and frantic, like a small sparrow.

"Not too wretched, Mum. Ciaran has been most kind." She introduced him round.

"I've made tea," Isla Drummond said as she brought in a loaded tray. "It's just the thing after a long train ride. I'll be mother, and then I'm off. Jamie is still sleeping, so I'll leave you to enjoy your tea in peace."

"Thank you, Mrs Drummond," Katie gratefully accepted a cup. "Ciaran, please sit."

"Thank you, I'll leave with you, if that's alright, Mrs Drummond. Katie has had enough excitement for one day and needs to rest. I'll call back tomorrow." He raised an eyebrow in Katie's direction, as he gulped the hot tea.

"No need to rush off, Irish. We just got here." Katie was loath for him to go.

"Mr McElroy is quite right, luv. Thank you for so kindly accompanying my daughter home. You are welcome here anytime. But now, we must get Katie up to bed. You're looking a little done in, luv," Mum declared.

Katie suddenly felt drained, and nodded.

Ciaran kissed her on the cheek and looked her in the eyes.

"Till tomorrow, mavourneen," he whispered.

She smiled and gave herself up to the loving care of her mum and sister.

CHAPTER ELEVEN

"Katie, it's done Mum a world of good having you to look after and fuss over." Tillie patted her hand. "It's stopped her from reliving the bus accident over and over again in her mind."

"Pleased to be of service, sis." Katie saluted, as she sat up straighter in bed.

It was her fourth day at home and Katie was bouncing back quickly. The spots were fading and her energy returning.

"And thanks to you, I've gotten a twenty-four-hour pass." Maggie entered the room, wearing her ATS uniform.

"Maggie!" cried Tillie and Katie together.

"I've brought you some chocolates a Yank gave me. You're looking well, luv." Maggie kissed her sister on the cheek.

"Ta, Mags. But I wouldn't go that far. I'm meant to go for a short walk with Ciaran this afternoon. I'll need a bit of lippy to perk me up."

"Are you certain you're up to it?" Tillie asked, with a frown. "You've only just been home a few days."

"I'm not only up to it, I can't wait," Katie replied. "Ciaran has been so kind, visiting me every day, looking after me, bringing me little gifts. I've seen such a gentle side to him."

"It sounds serious, Katie," Tillie probed. "I've never heard you even talk about a man before, let alone praise him."

"Nor have I," echoed Maggie. "It's wonderful to see." She gave her younger sister an encouraging smile.

Katie gazed from one beautiful blonde twin to the other, just so happy to be with her sisters.

"Is it serious?" Tillie continued. "Is there another Kingston wedding coming during this war?"

Maggie looked at Katie, but said nothing.

"Maybe. I'm not sure. But give us a chance. It's only been a few months, and I've hardly seen him – we've been separated more than together."

Maggie threw her twin a meaningful look. This was serious.

"We'd all be delighted if it works out that way, luv, but there's no rush. From what I've heard, he seems like a decent chap. I never knew you fancied Irishmen," she teased.

"Neither did I," Katie said, fluffing her brown curls. "And it's so brilliant to see you both. It's been so long since the three of us have been together in somewhat jolly circumstances." She sighed.

"Well, it's almost Christmas and the war won't be over this year, but I'll bet a penny that by this time next year, we'll all be together for good," Maggie breathed. "Everything I see and hear on the base convinces me of that."

"And your baby will be here then, too," Tillie piped in. "The Kingston family just keeps growing. And if you are in love with this Irishman, and he with you – what a better way to end this war than with another wedding? It would cheer Mum up no end."

"How is Mum? Truly? Has she left the house since she's been home?" Maggie's golden brows raised in concern.

"Sadly, no, Mags. She's still too fearful. The doctor said to give her time, but we all hate to see her jump at every noise, and panic when the air raid siren goes off. I'm not sure when – or if – she'll ever be back to her old self."

The three sisters sat in silence.

"If you're right about the end of the war, Maggie – and I truly hope you are – we'll all be home for good before long, and can properly nurse her back to health. You know how often she laments that her four children haven't been together in years. Surely, once the war is over, and Kenny and I are demobbed – Mum will rally?" Katie asked. *Please let things get back to the way they were before the war. Please let everyone in the family return safely. We've suffered enough.*

"Her body is recovered. It's her mind and heart that need mending. She misses Aunt Shirley dreadfully. I should think the family being back together will help. Other than that, who can say for sure?" Tillie shrugged.

She'd been the daughter who'd seen Mum's terrors up close – running to her bedside when the nightmares made her scream, and urging her to get out of bed some days. Pops also offered quiet comfort. It was a slow process.

"This damn war," muttered Maggie.

"I'll do my best to get another pass and travel warrant to come home for Christmas," promised Katie. "We need to make it festive for Mum."

"So will I," Maggie said. "Being based back in London, I should be able to manage it."

"And I'll still be here," Tillie said wryly.

The girls broke into a fit of giggles, breaking their gloomy mood. They spent the next hour catching up on Maggie's pregnancy, young Jamie's latest antics, Kenny's last letter, and Katie's description of how she met Ciaran at Dover Castle. In no time, Katie was ready to meet him for a walk in the neighborhood. Tillie lent her younger sister a precious lipstick, and Maggie brushed her hair till it shone. By the time Ciaran arrived at half-past one, the small tin of chocolates had disappeared.

***

"Are you quite certain you're up to it, and all?" Ciaran came to collect her, and stood in the Kingston front hallway, twisting his cap. "You could rest and we can try again tomorrow?"

"Nonsense." Katie pulled on a cardigan and picked up her hat. "I've been bedridden far too long. It's a lovely autumn day – probably one of the last. Besides, I've been given the all-clear by the doctor. So, what are we waiting for?" She gave him her brightest smile.

"How can I resist a pretty lass like yourself, then? Come on, mavourneen." And he gallantly swept her out the front door on his arm.

"I love this time of year, Irish. The crisp air, the changing colors of the leaves, wearing warm cardies. And I can finally be out again to relish it." She scooped up a handful of leaves, dropped them over Ciaran's head and ran ahead of him.

"Steady on, Katie. You're just out of your sickbed. Take it slow," he called after her as she sprinted into the park. Smiling wide, he shook the leaves free, and raced after her.

He caught up with her and the couple strolled from Nevern Square, turning into Philbeach Gardens. The afternoon autumn sun warmed their faces. Katie felt young and alive again and was grateful for it.

"Ciaran, thank you ever so much for taking such marvellous care of me this past week. It's meant the world to me." She looked up at him with a broad smile.

"I'm just that relieved you are feeling more yourself. Sure, and the doctor in Portsmouth had me rather anxious. Contracting measles as an adult can be proper dangerous."

"Poppycock. I'm right as rain, and ready to get back to the ship. But not before you and I enjoy some time together, so I can show you my London."

"All in good time." He spied a bench. "Shall we sit for a few minutes?" He didn't want her to overdo it, but was reluctant to fuss over her.

"Yes, let's." Katie didn't want to admit it, but she was feeling weary. Perhaps her energy hadn't bounced back in quite the way she had hoped. "And I'll be fine, Irish. Just a few spots, is all."

Ciaran raised an eyebrow. The Portsmouth doctor had told him that Katie's temperature had got alarmingly high, and she had been put in isolation with round-the-clock nursing until it was brought down. But he would not tell her about that.

"Of course, you will." He sat back, closed his eyes and soaked up the sun. "You'll be grand."

"And your hand? How is it healing? All the attention has been on me. I'm an idiot – or should I say eejit – for not asking after you before now." She gently picked up his right hand. It was warm and dry. A shiver ran down her back. He felt it too.

He took his hand back and flexed it.

"Sure, and it's mending slowly. It's not quite back to full strength, but getting there. And I've sorted writing with me left hand – it's almost as legible as the right one."

Katie picked up his hand again and examined the scars which ran from his knuckles up beyond his wrist – top and bottom. She traced a finger up each one in turn, feeling the raised skin and pockets of swelling. She raised his hand to her lips and started kissing the marks.

He moaned. Katie's head snapped up and their eyes locked – mossy green burning into chocolate. He leaned forward as she dropped his hand. Closing her eyes, she lifted her face for the kiss she knew was coming. And had longed for.

His warm lips pressed into hers, softly at first, then with insistent pressure. He pulled her closer and deepened the kiss. She groaned and put her arms around his neck, taking in his outdoorsy scent. Oh, how she'd missed his embraces. She felt the tingling hum from her lips heating her entire body – all the way to her toes. She gave herself in to him, the feelings, the experience, the moment.

She felt his lips leave her own and nearly whimpered in disappointment – until he started kissing and nuzzling her neck. Delicious ripples feathered through her. She could hardly stand it. Hungrily, she pulled up his face to reclaim his lips. *More, more.*

"Katie, you taste so sweet. I've missed you so." He almost pulled her into his lap.

Katie registered this in her sensual haze, and abruptly sat back.

"Whoa, Irish. We're in the middle of a park in broad daylight, you daft brute." She was a little breathless.

"Sorry, so sorry. I let meself get carried away, and all. But I won't apologize for being in love with you." He stopped.

Had Katie heard right? Had he just declared his love for her?

"You…you…what?" she stumbled.

"I've rather surprised myself too, luv. But now that I've said it, I find it's true. I am in love with you, Petty Officer Wren, Katherine Kingston." He kissed the freckles sprinkled across her nose and upper cheeks.

"I…I…I think I'm feeling slightly ill, Ciaran. I'm sorry."

He was instantly solicitous.

"Bloody hell. I knew this was too much for you. And I've gone and ruined the afternoon." He raked a hand through his thick hair. "I'll take you home straightaway."

"You haven't bodged the afternoon at all. It's been pure heaven to be out in the fresh air – with you. And I heard what you said, Irish. I just need time. I'm rather overwhelmed, is all." She pleaded with her eyes, hoping he'd understand.

He'd said the words that she'd longed to hear from Ralph – and never did. What she would have given to have had her love returned so easily back then. But a married man couldn't profess his love, could he?

She shook her head. Why was she thinking of Ralph when a caring, kind, and undeniably gorgeous man had just laid his heart out for her?

"I understand completely. It was wretched of me to put that strain on you when you are early days in your recovery. Forgive me?" He looked like a sad puppy.

She stood, pulled him into her arms, and kissed him.

"Naught to forgive, Irish. But we'd best be getting back. Mum is having the whole family for supper, and they'll be having collywobbles about me being out so long."

They held hands and made their way back to the townhouse, speaking of just today and tomorrow – making no plans for the future. Yet.

December 1944

In the event, everyone but Kenny was able to get leave for a short Christmas at home. Katie, Maggie, Hannah, and Trevor all made it to the townhouse for at least twenty-four hours. Even Ciaran stopped by for a flying visit before travelling to Ireland to spend a few days with his parents.

Albeit the Christmas table was filled with family, including Uncle Thomas, a reunited Micah and his sister, and Isla Drummond; Aunt Shirley was sorely missed. Alice did her best to make it a festive occasion, but her eyes were always a tad too bright, her speech a little too quick, and her manner rather frenetic.

Young Jamie saved the day yet again. At nineteen months, he was a going concern. Barely sitting still, it took both grannies, parents, and assorted aunts to keep track of him. He loved the makeshift decorations, and couldn't stop putting his hands all over everything, despite protestations of "mustn't touch." He loved to laugh, and to be tickled and chased by his daddy.

The men were all talk with the latest news that the Home Guard was being stood down – a sure sign that the war was, in fact, winding down – slowly as it might seem.

At dinner, Mum hovered over Maggie, who was already as a big as a house.

"Mum, I'm fine. Please sit and enjoy your meal," Maggie chided softly. She looked over at her husband and nodded.

"Maggie and I have a spot of news about the baby," he began.

"Everything is alright?" Mum's eyes darted to her daughter.

"More than alright, actually. We've just found out that we are having twins," Micah announced in his quiet voice.

"Twins! Another generation of Kingston twins – how marvellous." Mum's voice broke.

"Darling, that's brilliant." Tillie jumped up and hugged her sister. "More twins in the family! How fantastic. Double the cousins for Jamie, too."

The family chorused their congratulations. It was a Christmas moment to treasure. Finally, some good news as this wretched war lingered on and on.

Trevor exchanged a look with his wife and cleared his throat.

"It seems this Christmas is full of surprises. Tillie and I also have some news to share." He placed his hand over his wife's.

All eyes turned expectantly in their direction.

"Come June, Jamie will have a little brother or sister. The Kingston family seems to be expanding at an ever-increasing rate."

Mum welled up and Katie rushed to comfort her.

"Mum, it's good news. Don't be sad," she urged.

"I'm alright, it's just the shock. Happy tears, really." Alice attempted to regain control. "Oh my, what lovely Christmas gifts. Two of my girls having babies, and another set of twins at that. I don't see how Father Christmas can top it."

After a simple dinner of two small chickens, and a table full of veg, the family crowded round the wireless to hear the King's Royal Christmas Message, which they all found stirring.

"His Majesty has a way with words," Pops said contentedly over a cup of tea and a slice of Christmas pudding made from makeshift ingredients.

"I especially liked the passage when he said, 'The lamps which the Germans had put out all over Europe were being rekindled and were shining through the fog of war.' Quite eloquent."

"Just so, Walter," Thomas agreed. "1945 is looking to be the year of victory for the Allies." He nodded to his brother-in-law, who rose along with Trevor and Micah.

The men retired to the library for pipes and brandy.

This suited the women just fine. There were three babies to plan for, weren't there?

CHAPTER TWELVE

January 1945

"Thank you for the lift. It's frightfully cold this morning." Katie shivered as she and Ruby climbed aboard the lorry. It was no warmer on the transport, but at least there was no wind. Their navy greatcoats gave them protection, but Katie was grateful not to have to walk from her lodgings at the Red Lion to the naval base.

"They are saying it's the coldest January in fifty years – even Big Ben's clock hands have frozen. Blimey. I've heard that Canadian troops have built ice rinks around London. It seems they miss ice-skating." The driver was a fount of news.

"Bloody hell," said Ruby, pulling her collar close around her neck and face. "Who would choose to stay out in this cold longer than necessary?"

"It's not that bad, Rubes. It keeps you alert and fresh – ready for the watch ahead."

"Hah," replied her chum. "We need something to keep us awake. The watches here are dead boring compared to our work at Dover or Capel Le Ferne. But there are plenty of men around – that's something, I suppose."

Ruby had been in great demand since their transfer to this coastal base. As a major hub for Operation Overlord, military personnel of every service branch had swarmed the coast. Of those still in port, Ruby seemed to date a different bloke every Saturday, and frequented the local dances with no shortage of partners. Katie accompanied her sometimes, but found she didn't take as much pleasure dancing with random chaps as she had earlier in the war.

"Who's the lucky lad this Saturday? I can't keep track of all your boyfriends, can I?" Katie teased.

"I haven't quite decided yet. Either Angus or Alistair. Can't quite make up mind if I fancy a Scot or a Brit."

"You're incorrigible, luv. But why not? You don't have any ties. Might as well live it up."

Ruby smiled in return.

"How do you like our new digs? It's not quite as squashed as Abbot's Hill. Those cabins were chock-full of Wrens of every shape and size. The queue for the loo was absolute madness."

"Too right. I don't mind being overtop the pub at the Red Lion. Everyone is proper friendly. And we only have two other Wrens to share the bathroom." Katie had bounced back from her bout with the measles and was her cheerful and optimistic self again.

"It's a going concern at nights, though. Sometimes it's rather loud when trying to get some kip."

"I suppose we all have to make do with whatever quarters the Women's Royal Navy puts us up at. It could be worse. I've heard some of the girls whingeing about old farmhouses with no heat, or cabins with a lecherous old coot skulking round." Katie shrugged. "And no more hill to climb up after watch."

"True that. And there's always a cup of tea on offer. Or something stronger."

"Ruby, I saw a notice asking for volunteers at St. Mary's Hospital. They are looking for Wrens to sit with some of the serious burn patients, read to them, help them write letters, take them for a turn in the garden, and so on. What do you reckon?"

"Not sure, Queenie. My evenings are pretty engaged."

"Sod off, Ruby. You can spare a couple of nights a week. Think of those poor lads here for months, suffering through painful operations to try to repair the skin and minimize the scars. It's the least we can do to sit and cheer them for a couple of hours."

"You're right, luv. I was just having you on. Count me in."

"I'm glad you said that – because I already signed us both up. We're expected there tonight." Katie grinned triumphantly as the lorry bumped its way to the harbor.

"Come on, then. Let's see if there's a cuppa going before watch." Ruby clambered out of the chilly lorry into the freezing air.

"Righto, and thanks. I knew you'd want to help out."

* * *

After a busy day, the pair met up again in the canteen.

"How was your watch, luv? Ready for some shepherd's pie with nary a sheep in sight, or sausage and mash with the merest hint of meat in it?"

"I'm betting on fish pie, Ruby. Which is never a bad thing. At least we know what's in it." Katie stood in queue with her chum. She didn't mind much what she ate, as long as there was loads of it. She always had her thoughts on the afters. Her sweet tooth had suffered mightily throughout this war. With sugar, butter, eggs, and pretty much anything delicious on the ration, puddings were usually a major disappointment. Katie thought longingly of their old housekeeper, Faye, and her mouth-watering confections. She wondered idly if she'd be back after the war. She sincerely hoped so. The Kingston women weren't known for their cooking.

"You were right, Queenie. And look – peach custard. What a treat."

"That's jolly good. Let's tuck in."

The girls joined a table of four other Wrens where girl chatter abounded. The sisterhood of Wrens had made the new transferees feel welcome. There was a bond of loyalty that pervaded any group of Wrens. Maybe it was because the men on base often outnumbered them, and they felt the safety of sticking together. Or the long watches where bonds were built, and lifelong friendships formed. Or just the camaraderie of young women away from home, being lonely and in need of companionship. It was beyond reassuring to walk into a new group of Wrens and be instantly accepted. There was always a snooty girl or two, or someone who kept to herself, but on the whole, Wrens welcomed their own with open arms.

After finishing their tea and custard, the girls walked to the hospital and waited in the lobby for instructions. They were joined by a handful of other Wrens. After a few minutes, two nurses in pristine white uniforms entered the lobby. One was clearly in charge. She had blonde-grey hair pulled tightly into a bun, and a brisk manner.

"Girls, come together," she clapped her hands. "I'm Matron, Nurse Cox. And this is Nurse Gibson. Thank you for volunteering your time to help these injured servicemen. These brave men have been severely wounded – most from D-Day operations last year, but we get new cases all the time. Most are burns, but some are also temporary blindness, memory loss, and other serious or chronic ailments. These men struggle with what they've seen and experienced. Some of them have nightmares and anxious episodes, others refuse to speak, or have other nervous conditions.

"You'll each be assigned to a specific patient. Nurse Gibson has the tick list. I encourage you to spend two hours with each one. Simply talking, mainly listening, is likely what will make the most difference. Some men will want you to read to them or help them write letters home. You may simply sit there, quietly keeping them company. It may be possible to walk with them to the garden, but not tonight. First, try to establish a friendly, cheery rapport with them. But remember, you are professionals, so don't let the situation become personal.

"You'll be visiting the same patient each time. If there is a problem with a particular serviceman, please report it immediately to Nurse Gibson. If a patient asks to switch to another visiting companion, please do not take it personally. We strive to find good matches based on age, home county, etc. but it is mostly just chance.

"It's splendid of you to offer your time. You may feel you are not making a difference, but rest assured, you will make a significant impact. These men are alone, and our nurses are run off their feet, and can't spend much individual time with each patient. Thank you and good luck. Any questions?"

Matron looked around expectantly.

"What if the men get violent?" asked a tiny Wren tentatively.

"We don't expect this to happen. We are only assigning you to non-violent patients. However, if you are at all uncomfortable, find a male orderly straightaway. They are always on the ward. Then report to me. We will re-assign you to another patient. Anyone else?"

No one dared.

"Excellent. Nurse Gibson?"

The tall, brown-eyed nurse consulted her clipboard and called out the names of the Wrens and their assigned servicemen.

"This way, girls. Ellis, Kingston, Winston-Hodgson – you're on the burn ward. Farnsworth, Langford, Pigglestone, and Rhodes – you'll be in post-surgical and chronic care."

Katie was ushered to a ward with eight patients lined up in beds, four to a side. They were all dressed in hospital gowns; some had bandages on various parts of their bodies. Curious, most of them looked up when the women entered the room. A couple were asleep or pretending to be.

"Petty Officer Kingston, this is Lieutenant Christopher Payne. He's from London, isn't that right, Lieutenant?"

Katie tried not to look shocked. It was impossible to tell the age or much else about this patient. The entire right side of his face and neck was scarred and red with burn marks. In some places, the skin was puckered and looked extremely painful. The scarring may have continued down his chest or further, but she couldn't tell because of his hospital gown. His right arm was bent at a strange angle, and he was missing two fingers. *The poor man.* What on earth had happened to him? It must have been just awful.

He tried to smile, but his lips twisted into an ugly grin because of his disfigured mouth.

"Hullo Miss." He didn't extend his hand for a shake, and Katie was relieved, but in a guilty way.

"Good evening, Lieutenant. It's very nice to meet you. I hope it's alright if I sit with you for a little while?"

He shrugged.

"If you like."

Katie pulled out a chair and sat down. *What have I gotten myself into? Whatever am I going to say now?*

"You're from London, Lieutenant? My family has a home in Earl's Court."

"I'm originally from Stratford," he replied in the same flat voice.

"Lovely," Katie said, unsure whether to ask after his family. Surely, he would be at home being cared for by loved ones if there was anyone to look after him.

She looked at the small table next to his bed. It was cluttered with empty paper cups, books, and a stack of letters. Not knowing what else to do, she tidied up.

Picking up the letters, she noticed they hadn't been opened.

"Would you like me to read your letters for you, Lieutenant?"

With his uninjured left hand, he snatched them from her.

"No," he replied tersely. "I know what they say. I don't need to read them."

Katie sat back down. *Now what?*

"I'm sorry, Miss…?"

"Kingston. Katie Kingston."

"I'm terribly sorry, Miss Kingston. My manners aren't up to par these days."

"That's quite alright, Lieutenant. I'm sure you're in quite a difficult circumstance." She felt her words were inadequate. Utter rubbish.

"Quite," he almost laughed. He seemed to take pity on her.

"You could read my book to me, if you don't mind. My one eye is near blind, and it's tiring trying to read."

"Yes, of course. This one?" She held up a worn edition of Treasure Island.

"Yes, thank you. My mother sent it to me. She thought it might cheer me to revisit a childhood favorite."

Katie opened to the bookmarked page and began reading. Before long she was absorbed in the story.

"Very good, Miss Kingston. You may go now. Visiting time is over." Nurse Gibson appeared at her elbow, startling her.

Katie couldn't believe two hours had passed. She stood and placed the book back on the table.

"Will I see you again, Miss Kingston? I shall try to be in a better mood."

"Yes, of course. I'll see you Thursday at the same time."

"Goodbye."

Katie met Ruby in the lobby and they set off for their billet.

"How did you get on, Katie? They paired me with a nice young man with some type of nervous condition. He was twitching from his eyebrows to his toes and fidgeting constantly with his hands. I wrote a letter home to his sister for him. It was a bit of alright."

"Mine is a Lieutenant. He's been terribly burned, Ruby. I don't know how. But his face is a mass of scars. He was quite low. He has a load of unopened letters, but he wouldn't let me touch them. I'm sure it would lift his spirits to hear from home. Someone cares for him; I just know it. I'm sure I can help him."

"Hopefully, you can, Katie. But remember what Matron said. Don't get personally involved."

"I won't," she promised. "I just can't help thinking of my brother, Kenny. When he was MIA earlier in the war, he was taken in by a fisherman and his wife and nursed back to health. It could be my Kenny in a bed like this. I need to help this poor soldier. You see that?"

"Yes, I do. How thoughtless of me – sorry, luv. And I'm sure you will do him a world of good. Just take it slow. If you can," she smiled into the dark night.

"Blimey. It's even more frigid now than this morning. Let's move a little faster. I'm gasping for a cup of tea and a bikkie at the Red Lion."

"Or even a gin and tonic, if we're lucky?"

"On a work night? You are daft, girl." Katie shook her head in the darkness and blew on her fingers.

In no time, they found the pub in the blackout, pointing their torches down to find tiny lights on the unfamiliar streets.

"Well done, you," Katie sighed as they opened the door to the warm pub.

"And you, Queenie," Ruby beamed.

CHAPTER THIRTEEN

"Dear Katie,

How are you, sis? Tillie wrote you are now in Portsmouth. I reckon that will be my port of arrival when I finally get demobbed.

Wouldn't it be brilliant if you were still there to meet my ship? That's a homecoming to look forward to. But Hitler is not quite finished with us yet. We have more work to do to get rid of that bastard.

What do you reckon with three babies on the way? #40 is going to burst at the seams. There won't be a place for you and me when all this is over. Seriously, I'm chuffed for the twins and their hubbies.

Do you have any plans with Ciaran for the future? I know it's early days yet, but from what I hear, he's a decent bloke. Still, I will have to give him the brotherly once over when I return to ensure he's good enough for you.

I must dash. I just heard the horn for dinner, and I won't be giving that a miss.

Love from your wayward brother,
Kenny xx"

Katie smiled. She could picture her tall, lanky little brother rushing off to eat. It was always reassuring to hear that he was alive and well. Or at least alive. One could never really tell how loved ones in service were getting on. They minimized health issues or terrifying experiences. No one wanted to worry loved ones at home more than they already were. She hardly said a word about what life was really like on base herself. Not that she could. The threat of the Official Secrets Act loomed over her like the Sword of Damocles.

She opened the tiny drawer to the table next to her bed and placed the letter on top of the others. The family was terrific in writing to her – Mum and Pops, Tillie, Maggie, and Hannah. She felt a pang of guilt about not writing more and determined to spend this Sunday catching up on her correspondence.

Catching sight of Ciaran's letters, she couldn't help but pull them out and re-read them. The last had arrived just two days ago.

"Dear Katie,

I'm sitting here in an overcrowded hut with men sitting on their bunks, smoking, reading, and writing letters. It's bitterly cold, and most of us are wearing all the clothes we brought with us.

The park is large, but it's just a short walk from my sleeping hut to work, so I'm grateful for that. I imagine you walking from your digs to watch each day in this cold, and wish I were there to warm you.

It was grand to meet your entire family last autumn and at Christmas. They were kind to this Irish stranger, and I see why you care so much for them all. It's quite a gang. I told my parents all about them (and you) whilst home at Christmas. It's my heart's desire to take you to Ireland when this war is over. I know Ma and Da would love you dearly.

You understand I can't tell you about my work, but it is looking quite promising that it will be ending soon. There's a sense of humming excitement about it all that fills the air.

Mavourneen, I realize I rushed you with my hasty declaration last year. I'm sorrier for that than you can ever know. The last thing I want is to scare you off or have you finding me an unwelcome suitor. I don't take back what I said, though. My feelings are still just as deep for you – probably deeper as time passes. As sure as eggs are eggs, I believe you will come to feel the same, my adorable little Wren. But there's no rush. Our time will come.

I've put in for a 48-hour pass to visit you. As soon as I hear whether I get it, I hope you'll be able to wrangle one, too. You can do anything when you put your mind to it. It would be a delight to just walk and talk with you around Portsmouth. I'm sure I can catch a bunk nearby.

My fingers are blue with cold, so I'll stop here. I'm ever so glad you are back to your bouncy self. I can't wait to see you again.

May the roof above you never fall in, and those gathered beneath it never fall out.

Love,
Ciaran xx"

"Mooning over Ciaran's letters again, Queenie? When will you just admit to yourself that you've caught feelings for your handsome Irishman? I can see it as clear as day."

Ruby plunked onto her own narrow bed next to Katie's.

"I never said I didn't have feelings for him. I'm just not sure that it's love, you daft cow."

"Rubbish. You keep denying this to yourself. You're the daft one."

Applying a scant coating of pink lipstick, Ruby fluffed her fringe and picked up her coat.

"You can mope about. I'm off to a date with a Yank."

"Give over, luv. I'm not moping at all. Who's the Yank, anyway? Someone new, or are you giving a chap a second chance?" Katie sidestepped the issue.

"A new one. His name is Larry something. Ta ra for now." With a backward smile, she was out the door in a flash.

Katie looked around the empty cabin, feeling a bit lost. And she did mope about. She filed her nails, straightened up her messy drawer, and even tidied under her cot.

She considered washing her hair, but it wasn't her night for the bath, so she gave it a hundred brushstrokes instead. It made her think of her sister, Tillie, who unfailingly gave her golden locks the same treatment each night.

Her boots needed polishing, so she attended to that. She had a shirt to press, but was disinclined to haul out the iron. It was one of her most hated chores. Listlessly, she picked up a book and put it down after re-reading the same page three times.

In a fit of fury, she threw it against the wall.

Damn that Irishman. He's creeping into my heart and mind – despite my best intentions.

She threw herself back on the bed, sinking her head into her pillow. *Alright, girl. I suppose you need to give this a proper think.*

Whenever she had been uncertain about a decision, Mum taught her to make a tick list – what she liked about the idea, and what she didn't. It usually helped to clear her mind and settle.

She pulled out a piece of paper and pencil and considered. What did she fancy about Ciaran, and what was making her uneasy?

First, he was a gorgeous lad. She knew that was small-minded, but it was the first thing that came to mind. Next, he was kind. He'd looked after her properly when she had the measles and been nothing but tender and sweet. She smiled. That counted for loads. Third, he was a decent chap from a good family. He worked hard and was brave. Well, that's probably three, four, and five. Six, he was constant in his attention and love for her. Seven – and this was a big one – he wasn't married or attached. Eight – he had the most endearing Irish sayings. She crossed that out – it didn't really count for much.

Katie chewed the end of her pencil. Now for the hard part.

What made her so hesitant about letting go, and really loving her tall Irishman? First, second, third, fourth, and 100th – she didn't deserve him. He was miles above her level. He deserved someone far more worthy of his love.

Seeing it in black and white made her feel more miserable. How could she ever think of a life with him, a love? She hadn't been wanted as a child. How could an honorable man like Ciaran truly want her? Was it possible?

She felt a flicker, like a candle flame as it caught on a match.

Should I believe what Ciaran is saying? Could I? He was steadfast, sincere. Maybe I should stop questioning myself and just believe? I wish I could talk to Tillie. She always makes me feel strong and better about myself.

Sighing, she went back to her list. Ireland. He lived in Ireland on a farm with elderly parents who needed him. If she considered any kind of life with him, she'd have to move to Ireland. *How can I move to a different country away from my family and everyone I love? Mum and Pops, my sisters, their babies. It's what I know and love. And what I've been waiting for these long war years.*

She didn't know. She just didn't know.

***

Over the next several weeks, Katie grew to know Lt. Payne a little better. She'd insisted he call her Katie, and he reluctantly gave her permission to call him Chris. It was probably against regulations, but Katie was determined to break through his shell. Even if he said little, she could tell he was pleased to see her when she turned up. He'd taken to brushing his hair and wearing a clean gown.

"Hullo, Katie. Are you okay?"

Katie had brought cigarettes from the NAAFI. He gave her his half-smile, half-grimace.

"I'm brilliant. The weather is warming up. From a frigid January, February is a treat."

"Why are you here on a Saturday? Not that I'm whingeing, mind you."

"I won't be able to come Tuesday next. My boyfriend is popping down from north of London on a twenty-four-hour pass." *How did that pop out? I'm calling him my boyfriend now?* Somehow it fit. And felt good.

"Oh, you've got a boyfriend. What's his name?"

"Ciaran. And he's a lieutenant in the Army." She leaned forward. "Special forces. Shhh." She put a finger to her lips.

"I see," Chris said, his distorted features expressionless.

"Righto, shall we get on with Treasure Island? I wonder what adventures Jim is up to today." She reached for the book.

"I suppose," he replied dully.

Katie took a chance and closed the book.

"Have you had any more letters from home?" she asked softly, settling onto the hard chair.

"Maybe one or two." He didn't meet her eyes.

"From your mother?" Katie held her breath. Had she gone too far?

"Likely. Or my sister, Mavis."

"Shall we have a look, Chris?" She itched to open the ever-growing pile of letters.

After what seemed like an eternity, he responded.

"Perhaps one from Mavis," he said finally.

"Brilliant." Katie reached for the stack. Rifling through, she looked for a letter posted from a Mavis. She noted a few from what looked like Chris' mother, and several from someone named Violet. She wisely bypassed these and plucked the most recent letter from Mavis.

"May I read it?"

Looking out the window, he nodded.

"Dear Chris,

How are you, dear brother? I understand you may not be well enough to write back to us, but it would do Mum no end of good to hear from you. She worries about you so, and longs to visit. Please, can you let us come?

Pleading aside, we are well. The V2s are trying, and we pray Hitler has no other vengeance weapons in his arsenal. Please, when will this war end?

The boys keep me hopping. Every time I turn my back, they are fighting or getting into a scrape. They miss their dad, I suppose, which is bringing out the worst in them. I'm doing my best to bring them up on my own, but it's not always easy. Enough moaning.

Please reconsider your orders for no visitors. Mum, Violet, and I would dearly love to see you – no matter how you look, or the injuries you have sustained. You are still our dear Chris, and we miss you so.

All my love,
Mavis xx"

"She's always known how to push my buttons. Older sisters can be so bossy."

"Indeed," Katie replied. Should she probe further?

She glanced out the window. The sun was shining, and it was a crisp February day.

"Shall we be naughty, and have a sit in the garden? I saw a pushchair in the hall. I'm sure no one would mind if we nicked it for an hour."

His face lit up.

"That would be cracking, Katie." The smile almost reached his eyes.

It was progress, she told herself. One step at a time.

***

"Katie, thank goodness you've come. You've had a telephone call from home." Ruby's forehead creased. She'd been waiting in the pub for Katie's return from St. Mary's.

"A telephone call? It must be serious. Pops must have called from the phone box down the street. Damn him, why won't he modernize and fix one up at the townhouse?" She twisted her fingers with mounting nerves. "What was the message?"

"He said he'll ring again at half-past four. It's near that time now."

"What could it be, Ruby? Someone must be hurt. I hope it's not Mum." She'd gone white. Was it Kenny? Or Maggie at the ack-ack site? Or something amiss with one of the coming babies. Oh dear.

They sat at the bar and had a weak cup of tea, waiting for the telephone to ring. At precisely half-past, it rang. Katie rushed to answer it.

"Katie, it's Pops. Are you alright?" She strained to hear with all the popping and crackling on the line.

"Pops, I'm fine. What's happened? Is it Mum? Maggie?" She clutched the receiver for dear life.

"We are in good health here at Number 40. But I'm afraid I have bad news. Be strong, poppet. It's Trevor. He's been seriously injured in an explosion at the RAF airstrip. We're not sure of the extent yet, but he's been blinded. Tillie's gone to nurse him at a London hospital. He's been severely burned. There's no way to soften this, my dear."

CHAPTER FOURTEEN

"Pops, no." Katie didn't realize she was shouting until Ruby shushed her. "Is he going to be alright? When is he coming home? Oh dear, poor Tillie." She knew she was rambling. It must be shock.

"Details are muddy at the moment, but I knew you would want to know. And before you say it – please don't put in for leave. Trevor isn't immediate family, so you likely won't get it on compassionate grounds. In the event, we don't know exactly yet where he's being transferred to in London. Mum and I will keep you apprised of his progress. To answer your other question – Tillie is doing as well as can be expected. She's being stoic – calling on her ambulance training, I should think. Isla is in pieces, as you can imagine. None of us are quite sure what to do."

Pops sounded a trifle lost, which frightened Katie even further. He was always the rock of the family. Was this the crisis that was going to strain the Kingston family beyond repair?

She murmured words of comfort and they said their goodbyes.

"I just don't believe it, Ruby. Trevor is so big and strong. He's been fighting fires throughout this entire war, and was a fireman before that. I can't bear to think of him maimed, blinded, or worse." Her mind went to the disfigured young man at St. Mary's Hospital. Was that Trevor's fate? How could Tillie bear it?

"I expect you need something stronger than tea, Queenie. Charlie, can you muster a gin and tonic for my friend here?"

The pub owner nodded and brought two drinks in no time.

"Take a breath, Katie. Don't get ahead of yourself. You have no way of knowing how serious Trevor's injuries are. Let the doctors do their work. Sometimes these situations don't turn out as grim as originally thought."

Katie tossed down half the drink in one gulp. Her panic ebbed slightly.

"No doubt you are right. Pops sounded so dreadful. And he said Trevor was blinded by the explosion. How ghastly for him."

"Katie. You mustn't agonize until you have more facts. Give it some time. Your family will keep you informed as they hear more from the doctors."

Katie nodded and finished her drink. She couldn't wait for Ciaran to arrive on Monday. She really needed him. More than she thought possible.

"Thank you, luv. I think I'll go aloft to our cabin. I need some time to myself."

"Absolutely. I'll look in on you in a little while."

* * *

Katie hung on for Ciaran's arrival on Monday. She yearned for his calm presence, twinkling eyes, and reassuring smile.

Mindlessly, she got through her Monday watch, and rushed to meet Ciaran's train at the end of her day.

She only had to wait three quarters of an hour, and the fair weather held, so she wasn't too frigid. His train pulled in, and as soon as she spotted him on the stairs, she raced over and practically threw herself into his arms, fighting back tears.

"Shhh, mavourneen. Don't cry." He held her, stroking her dark curls, crooning until she stopped crying.

"I'm so sorry, Irish," she wiped her face. "I never meant to lose myself like that. And I've gone and drenched your overcoat." She attempted humour to hide her embarrassment.

"Never apologize for being you, Katie. You've gotten a grave shock. It's only natural to let go when you see a loving face." He wiped a tear from her cheek and kissed her.

He was right. It was a tremendous relief to surrender to his steady strength. It almost didn't register, but it had. She was growing attached to this remarkable Irishman.

"I'm starving. Where are we going to eat?" Ciaran hoisted his bag over his shoulder and adjusted his cap.

"Do you fancy The Nut? It's close by." Katie struggled to regain her equilibrium.

"The Nut? What's that when it's at home?" he joked.

"The Keppel's Head Hotel. I've booked you a room there as well. But if that's too fancy for you, Charlie said he can set up you up with a room at The Red Lion. So many of the hotels and buildings in Portsmouth have been bombed. We're a constant target for the Luftwaffe. We've been hit sixty-seven times up to D-Day. They can't resist our dockyards," Katie reported matter-of-factly.

It was true. Portsmouth officially suffered 67 air raids between July 1940 and May 1944, three of which had been major attacks. During one of the heaviest air raids, approximately 300 German aircraft dropped 350 tons of high explosives and 25,000 incendiaries. The impact was shattering – 171 deaths, 430 injured, and 3,000 made homeless. Portsmouth Guildhall was virtually destroyed by fire when hit by incendiaries, the water mains damaged, making firefighting near impossible.

During the four-year period of the Portsmouth Blitz, 930 people were killed and thousands more injured. Something like ten percent of the city's 63,000 homes were destroyed, and thousands more sustained some level of bomb damage.

Locations such as the naval base, military installations, and factories were undoubtedly the primary targets although the aerial targeting was not particularly accurate, especially at night. Consequently, large numbers of civilian residential areas were hit.

Other damage included thirty churches, eight schools and one hospital, with another severely ravaged. Prime shopping areas such as Commercial Road and Palmerston Road were virtually obliterated.

Much of the destruction could still be seen wherever you looked. Portsmouth would need major rebuilding after the war.

"The restaurant is open to all navy personnel, so I've booked us a table."

"Grand. Lead on."

The pair lingered over a delicious dinner of ham, winter veg, and a couple of glasses of wine – a rare treat. The treacle tart was delicious, if a little shy of sugary sweetness.

They spoke of Trevor's condition. Nothing new was known except that Trevor had been fighting to put out a Hurricane fire from a V2 bomb, when it blew up. The explosion had thrown him back, causing burns on his hands and forearms as he protected his head. He would survive and recover, but the most alarming injury was the blindness caused by the explosion of light so close to his eyes. Whether it was temporary or permanent, the doctors couldn't say. For now, he was in a dark room covered in bandages, and wouldn't be coming home for several weeks.

"It sounds extraordinarily serious, but thankfully, his life is not in danger. You must be so relieved." He sipped his tea whilst scraping the last of the treacle from his dish.

"I am, Irish. But I'm gutted about his sight – will it come back? And will he regain full use of his hands? How will he cope? Will he be able to manage with an active youngster and a new baby on the way?" *Stop babbling, girl. Get a hold of yourself.*

Ciaran reached across the table and put a finger on her mouth.

"I wish I could stop your brain as easily as your beautiful lips. Sure, and didn't your mum always tell you that eighty percent of the things you worry about never happen?"

Katie was gobsmacked. When had he tucked that information away?

"Yes, she does," she replied slowly. "I suppose you're right, Irish. It's just that I've seen firsthand the ravages of burn marks with this soldier I'm visiting. My heart aches for Chris, and I don't want that life for Trevor. Or my sister."

"You are a sympathetic soul, Katie. I suppose we'll just have to wait and hope for the best."

The rest of their leave passed by far too quickly. The next day they walked round the docks and town, and viewed the German wreckage for themselves. After seeing so much destruction over the last few years, they were rather numb to it. Buildings and houses bombed out, neighborhoods destroyed, churches decimated – it was all too miserably familiar.

Stopping for lunch at a small café, the couple warmed up over tea before ordering beans and spam.

"Even though it's a small farm, it's getting to be too much for Da and Ma to manage. They had me so late in life, and they set such store on me, I daren't let them down." Sipping his tea, he carried on the conversation they'd been having on their walk.

"What animals do you raise? I'm a city girl. You'll have to help me understand." She raised her own mug to her lips and drank deeply. The warm tea seeped into her, warming her from the inside out.

"Chickens, cows and a few pigs, a horse and cart. We used to have sheep, but Da had them slaughtered early in the war."

"What's the horse's name?" Katie asked, nibbling a stale biscuit.

Ciaran laughed, his eyes crinkling in amusement.

"Leave it to yourself to care more about the horse than the farm. His name is Keegan – it means little fire, feisty and spirited. Just like you and all. He's an Irish draught horse and has been taking us to the Friday market every week for years." He wiggled his eyebrows. "Enough information for you, luv?"

"Plenty," she replied. "He sounds enchanting. What do you sell at market?"

"Eggs, milk, and whatever preserves Ma is making at the moment. That's for the people. We also grow oats and barley, and sell it for cattle and pig feed. It's not much, but we get by. We barely make ends meet most of the time. Honestly, it's a tough life, and all."

It was hard for Katie to understand. She knew she lived a privileged life in London. Pops owned his own accounting firm, and the business had thrived, even throughout the war. Their lifestyle was not lavish, but they had everything they needed and more. Their townhouse was in a fashionable part of town, and was well-appointed and comfortable, albeit not sumptuous.

In the Navy, she'd seen women from many walks of life. A high percentage of them were from the upper classes, even aristocratic. Considered the high end of the services, the Women's Navy was an exclusive branch. Katie had worked watch with more than a few toffee-nosed ratings and Wrens that had never washed a dish, tidied their own things, or cooked a meal in civilian life. It had been a rude awakening for these snobby girls, and many struggled.

It was a novel experience for her to be around a proper working man, someone who worked with his hands and wasn't ashamed of it.

"Sounds like honest work, Irish. You should be proud of your parents. They've been toiling a long time to make a good life for you."

Ciaran placed his hand over hers. It was warm and brought the delicious shiver she had come to crave.

"They have, and I owe them a lot. I could never leave the farm, and if I'm honest, I don't want to. I love the work — being outside, besting the elements, working with the animals, and in the fields. It's satisfying — even on our small level. And it's time for Da and Ma to take it easy. I worry about it all the time. The long days and heavy work are too much for them. They had a laborer, but he left for a better paying factory job in Liverpool." He paused as the waitress brought their food and placed it in front of them. They both tucked in hungrily.

"Could you fancy life on a farm, Katie? It's honest work, but not easy. The animals need to be cared for morning and night, three-hundred-and-sixty-five days a year. No break on Christmas Day or Easter. It's physically tiring. And sometimes heartbreaking — when you lose an animal, or a crop is washed out because of constant rain. But I can't wait to get back there, mavourneen. After the cruelties of war, and everything I've seen, I crave the open air, the simplicity of farm life and its pleasures. I can't imagine a different life, and I don't want to, and all. Could you see yourself there?" His eyes bored into hers.

Katie took a mouthful of beans to buy herself a little time. She didn't quite know what to say. It did sound appealing, making a life with Ciaran on a small Irish farm. She was young and strong. She wasn't afraid of hard work. But it was so far away from home — in London. And her sisters, nephew, and more babies coming. And Mum and Pops. She had never thought ahead to leaving the townhouse, let alone her country. Her head was spinning.

She gave him an encouraging smile.

"Ciaran, I never thought I would ever consider such a life. Honestly, it's never entered my mind. But hearing you talk about it, I need to weigh it up. The farm life sounds like a wonderful existence after living on top of each other these last few years. I don't know if I'd be good at it, or total rubbish, but I might give it a go. The idea of you and I getting stuck in together on the land draws me."

Ciaran was watching her intently, with a small smile playing around his lips. She held up her hand. Here comes the hard part.

"Nonetheless, to be so far away from home is a huge step, and one that would be bloody hard for me. I need to think about it, Irish. You must give me time. That's the best I can do at the moment." Her brown eyes pleaded with him. Could she really leave her beloved family – and country – to live with virtual strangers? This would not be easy. Would she be disappointing either her parents or Ciaran? She felt a little sick.

"I can live with that, Katie Kingston. But I won't stop asking. And the next time we can both sort a seventy-two-hour pass, can we visit my folks in Ireland?" He held his breath.

Katie leaned forward.

"I can't wait to meet them," she mustered a smile. "And Keegan, too. Somehow, I should think we'll be fast friends."

CHAPTER FIFTEEN

March 1945

In London, V2 rockets were still firing, causing havoc with Londoners' sleep and nerves. The New Cross disaster in November 1944 had been a horrific attack. Woolworths in the southeast borough of Deptford had been chock-full of women and children in the pre-Christmas rush. The force of the explosion had flung customers and outside pedestrians into the air and tossed them great distances. It took Civil Defence personnel three days and nights to locate and extract all the bodies and remains; those that still existed. The final toll was 168 dead, and 123 seriously injured. It was a tremendous blow.

The British people received a positive sign when the government asked the Civil Defence force to gradually stand down, signalling the end of the war surely coming.

However, more V2 attacks over the Christmas week had seen the Prince of Wales pub on Mackenzie and Holloway Roads bombed on Boxing Day. Revelling patrons in the cellar had been trapped after a fire started. Another 71 Londoners were killed, with 56 severely burned and injured.

Since the new year, there had been a further 67 incidents, the misery being compounded by the return of several V1 attacks. Deptford and Smithfield Market were hard hit, bringing dozens more casualties, and seriously harmed.

London was battered, but not broken. Londoners headed back to the underground shelters night after night, weary but determined. They queued hour after hour, hoping for a bit of bacon or cheese. Paying close attention to Allied movements across Europe, they felt the stirrings of hope that it might soon be over, really over.

The Ardennes offensive looked to be a last major enemy assault – an unsuccessful attempt to recapture the port of Antwerp, cutting off the Allies' ability to re-supply the Army. Lasting from December 1944 to January 1945, it had been a profitable operation for Germany, even though it fell short of its aims. Thwarting the Allies' preparations, it inflicted considerable damage, but Germany paid a heavy price. They lost 120,000 men (to the Allies' 75,000), and stores of material that it could ill afford to replace. Germany had thus forfeited the chance of maintaining any sustainable resistance to a renewed Allied offensive. It was, therefore, only temporarily successful in halting the Allied advance.

In February, the controversial bombing of Dresden, Germany, killed tens of thousands of civilians. It was considered one of the world's most beautiful cities because of its architecture and art treasures. Some said that the military value of the bombing did not justify Dresden's near destruction, and that the city could have been spared.

The American invasion of Iwo Jima began on February 19, 1945, and was still raging. Known as Operation Detachment, it was charged with the mission of capturing the airfields on the island for use by P-51 fighters, and rescuing their own damaged heavy bombers. Some of the fiercest fighting so far marked the battle. The Imperial Japanese Army had fully fortified their island positions, and the soldiers defended them tenaciously. The Japanese lost 90% of their soldiers, and many were taken prisoner. On the fourth day of the battle, the Americans took Mount Suribachi. The papers had been full of the photograph of six Marines raising the American flag on the peak. It was an enormous triumph for the Allied forces.

Berlin suffered its worst air raid of the war when 1,500 American bombers dropped over 2,000 tons of bombs on the city. On March 7th, British and American troops crossed the Rhine. The tide was turning against the Germans.

Britain began to see the light at the end of a long tunnel. The Allies were going from strength to strength. Pathe News reels showed good news in the cinemas. Everyday citizens crowded the train stations, cheering on returning soldiers. Even the glummest of citizens felt a sense of hopeful expectancy.

* * *

"Darling, today's the day. It will be wonderful to have you at home. Jamie can't wait to see you," Tillie burst into Trevor's hospital room, arms full of his civilian clothes, shoes, and overcoat.

"Good afternoon, luv. I've been waiting for you all morning. Give us a kiss, then." He reached his bandaged arms toward his wife's voice.

Tillie happily obliged, dumping the clothes on the bed and diving into Trevor's waiting arms.

His arms and hands were slowly healing. A full recovery was expected, albeit he'd have permanent scars. Yet, his eyesight hadn't returned.

In the weeks he'd been in the hospital, he'd learned how to wash, comb his hair, and dress himself. He still needed help to shave, but was fiercely independent, and hated being reliant on anyone for even the simplest tasks.

His mood was cheery, albeit he had low days, and lashed out in frustration. He refused to believe his sight wouldn't return and insisted on planning for a future where he was fully recovered.

After dressing, all that was left was to wait for the hospital discharge papers. In no time, the couple were on their way, Trevor adamant in hoisting his own bag.

"Remember, Tils. Walk slowly, and let me hold on to your arm. Don't guide me. Just tell me if there's a step up or down, or an obstacle."

Tillie bit her lip, relieved that her husband couldn't see her frown. Trev had bluntly rejected the white cane offered by the nurses. He refused to be identified as a blind man and was confident it was just a matter of time until he was fully sighted again.

"Of course, luv." They made their way slowly to the main hospital doors. "There are several steps, Trev. Stop, let me count. It looks to be about eight or ten. Can you manage?" She tried not to fuss.

"Yes, yes. I can get on just fine," he said shortly.

Tillie had been firm about taking a taxi home from the Princess

Beatrice Hospital, even though it was just a few minutes' distance from the townhouse. Trevor had fumed, but understood he needed to take things slowly.

"Daddy," cried Jamie after the pair had navigated the townhouse stairs and entered the home.

Trevor stood in the centre of the hallway, trying to place where his son stood. He didn't get the chance. A small bundle of Drummond launched himself into his father's arms, almost knocking Trevor down.

"Whoa, son. Easy does it. I missed you, my boy." Trevor softly caressed Jamie's face, tracing his features with his bandaged hand.

"Daddy, ball," he wriggled out of Trevor's grasp, and ran to fetch his red ball. "Daddy, ball," he repeated.

Alice strode into the hallway and took the ball from her grandson, pausing briefly.

"Granny will play ball with you in a bit, Jamie. Daddy needs to rest. Let's go to the kitchen and have some milkie. Granny has some nice bikkies. Welcome home, Trevor," she added.

Tillie threw her mother a grateful glance.

"Ta, Mum. Jamie, go with Granny." He obediently took his granny's hand and toddled to the kitchen stairs.

"Trev, let's get you settled. I'll bring Jamie back to see you once he's had his snack. Would you like to lie down?"

"Useless. I'm a useless father," he said, standing still as a statue. "And how am I meant to help you with a new baby when I can't even play ball with my two-year-old son? And I don't want to lie down."

"Darling, you are not useless. It's just a matter of adjustment. You can do plenty with Jamie."

"Like what, Tillie? Read to him? Feed him? Give him a bath?" he asked bitterly.

"You can cuddle him, love him, tell him stories. And once your eyesight is back, you'll be chasing him around in no time, playing Big Bad Wolf again. And rocking your new child. In no time, Trev." She almost shook him.

"I rather think I am tired, Tils," he snapped. "Perhaps I will rest for a while."

Tillie offered her arm, and the couple turned to the stairs.

* * *

"How do you feel giving up the service, little one?" Micah rubbed his wife's shoulders. "A bit wobbly?"

"Yes and no, luv. It's hard to leave my chums, and I've loved doing my bit working the ack-ack guns. But I'm worn out lugging these babies around, and it's time to rest." She gave a wan smile and sunk heavily onto the bed.

Maggie was due in just over a month, and she was a shapeless mass of unborn babies.

"You have more than done your bit. Even these last several weeks, with the administrative work you've been doing since you haven't been able to work the predictor machine any longer. You've earned a few weeks' respite. Life is bound to get proper busy before long." He removed her shoes and rubbed her feet.

Maggie moaned.

"Thank you, luv. That's heaven. And what you really meant is since I've been big as a house. When I couldn't see my feet to tie up my shoes, that was a clear signal that my time was up. I'm sad to leave Pip and the others, but I'm that relieved to put up my feet a tad before the twins make their appearance. Just my luck, though, that as I'm getting released, Princess Elizabeth has joined the ATS."

"Hard cheese, Maggie. But she won't be operating ack-ack equipment. Isn't she training as a truck mechanic or some such?"

"I believe so. She is taking driving lessons, private instruction, map reading and so on. It will be wonderful to see her in the ATS uniform. She'll do us proud, I've no doubt." She brightened.

"I'm sure she'll be splendid. Can I change the topic? Are you still resolved to move into my parents' house before the babies come?" he asked with a frown. It seemed too much for his weighty wife.

"The house is bursting now – Trevor and Tillie need our room. And I really must set up house before my time. It's only a few streets away. Have you booked the removal van yet?"

Micah's parents had leased their London house when they'd left for

France early in the war. A few weeks ago, Micah had approached the renters, and was chuffed to find out that they were planning to move to the country. The V2 attacks had frightened the elderly couple, and they were miserable in London. Micah and Maggie were moving within a fortnight, and much of Micah's family furniture remained there.

"Certainly, the house is full. And I am content to move back to my childhood home, Mags. It feels right, somehow. Even though my parents will never return, we can make it a happy household again. You and I, Hannah, and our babies. And yes, I've booked the removal van for Saturday next." His smile was bittersweet as he remembered his parents. A shadow passed over his face, briefly aging him.

Along with the rest of the world, Micah and Maggie had been shocked when they'd heard the news that Auschwitz, Birkenau, and Monowitz concentration camps had been liberated. In mid-January, the soviet army entered Auschwitz and found horrendous, inhumane conditions – 7,000 emaciated prisoners, most of whom were ill or dying.

It was later discovered that as Soviet forces approached the Auschwitz concentration camp complex, SS units forced nearly 60,000 weak and dying prisoners to march west from the Auschwitz camp compound. Many died along the route. Before the death marches began, thousands had been killed in the camp's gas chambers. The Nazis scrambled to murder as many Jews as possible to conceal the horrors they had inflicted on those remaining.

Numbers were still murky, but it was looking like at least a million people had been executed in Auschwitz alone since 1940. It was unfathomable.

Samuel and Ruth Goldbach had been two of the people killed at the Auschwitz camp – simply for being Jewish. Micah had been searching for them since they had been deported from Drancy in France. He had finally received official confirmation that they had died – from typhus, it was reported. The overcrowded, unsanitary conditions, compounded by starvation rations, resulted in a multitude of infectious diseases that had taken many lives.

For weeks, he had been silent and detached, trying to make sense of the insensible. Maggie coaxed him back to life, reminding him that his parents would have wanted him to live and take care of his sister, and now his unborn children. He still carried an air of sadness that would likely last a lifetime.

"Do you reckon there's a cup of tea to be had round here? I'm longing for one," Maggie asked gently. She hated to interrupt his reverie.

Micah shook his head as if to clear it.

"Yes, little one. Forgive me. I was woolgathering. I'll fetch it for you straightaway. Unless you want to come down?"

Maggie sank back into the pillows.

"I couldn't get up, even if I wanted to. Which I don't. Ta, luv." She closed her eyes.

* * *

Aboard HMS Implacable, Kenny Kingston sat on his bunk, penning a letter to his sweetheart. Implacable was an aircraft carrier, originally assigned to the Home Fleet, attacking targets in Norway in 1944. Kenny had been transferred once the ship had been built. It had since been re-fit and assigned to the British Pacific Fleet, with upcoming missions attacking Japanese naval bases.

"Dear Astrid,

It seems an age since I've held you in my arms. I miss you desperately. Miles of land and water separate us, but I left my heart behind in Norway. I hope that doesn't sound too rubbish – it's not like me, but I can't stop thinking about you, and the too-short times we've spent together.

I meant what I said, dear Astrid. Once this war is over – and it will be soon, of that I'm quite certain – I aim to bring you back to London. For good, I hope.

It's nearly over, my dear. Then I have a VERY IMPORTANT question for you. Our time is coming, dear one. I must stop now. It's time for our weekly tot of rum, and I don't want any of my mates to nick my ration. Write back soon, and sending you all my kisses.

Love,
Kenny xx"

As he folded the letter, he conjured up the tall, blonde beauty with icy blue eyes that had captured his heart completely. Grinning, he snatched up his cap and headed aloft.

CHAPTER SIXTEEN

"Good evening, Chris. How are you getting on? Why are you sitting here in the dark?" Katie breezed into the hospital room and switched on his lamp. Taking in his appearance, she fought a wave of dismay. His hair was mussed and greasy, he hadn't shaved in some time, and judging by her nose – he hadn't bathed recently either. Not to mention the glower parked on his face. She stopped mid-stride.

"Has something happened?"

"I opened Violet's letters. That's what's happened," a sullen voice emanated from the bed.

Katie pulled up a chair, sat down, and put her hands in her lap.

"And what did she say?" she asked simply.

"Just the usual. She still loves me, is begging to come and see me, you know."

"And that's the big catastrophe? Your girlfriend still loves you – even though you've been ignoring her for weeks?"

"Fiancé. Violet is my fiancé. And that's not it." He stared at the wall.

"Fiancé? I see." She ached to shake him, to make him see he was loved, and to seize it. But she paused. Maybe blustering in was not the way to go here. She sat back.

"So, what is it then, Chris?" she asked softly.

He turned in her direction and saw only compassion in her big brown eyes.

"I don't want her to love me. I want her to forget me. That's the kindest thing I can do for her now." His eyes were dull, and she strained to hear him.

Katie considered.

"Is that for you to decide? Or Violet? Shouldn't you at least give her the chance to see for herself and decide if you have a future together?"

"Ha, that would tear it. She'd run away screaming if she caught sight of me."

"You can't possibly know that, Chris. Give her a chance. At least, do her the honor of breaking it off with her in person. Don't you owe her that?" she pleaded.

"I suppose." He was still gazing at her, a grimace in place.

Katie caught a sudden inspiration.

"Why don't you tell me about her, Chris? What's she like? Violet is such a pretty name."

"I've known her for an age. We went to school together."

"And...?" Katie pushed, but just a little.

"She's a tad taller than you," he started slowly.

"Isn't everyone?" Katie encouraged.

His lips twitched.

"She has blonde hair and hazel eyes. She lives just round the corner – or did, before the war. She's a nurse now, and training to be a midwife." He turned his gaze to the window. "Violet has a heart of gold, and is always taking in stray dogs and cats and..."

The air raid warning sliced through his words, startling them both.

"Bloody hell. Not another one. When will this ever end?"

Katie stood and turned about.

"What are we to do? Where is the shelter?"

"In the basement. Come on, chaps, here we go again," he called wearily to the six other patients in the ward.

Katie looked around her in confusion. All of these men were to evacuate to the shelter basement – three floors below? Thank goodness they were ambulatory.

Springing into action, she aided Chris and the others as they shuffled into their slippers and dressing gowns and lumbered down the hallway towards the stairwell. Clearly, they had done this many times before. An orderly rushed in and guided several of the patients who were slightly unsteady on their feet.

Chris waited until the room was empty before leaving.

"Come on, Chris. It's our turn now." Katie steered him out of the ward to join the queue of men in various states of undress.

It was a slow descent to the shelter, with the piercing sound of the siren ringing all around them. Nurses and orderlies assisted injured patients that could still walk. More than once, Katie lent a hand to a chap who stumbled on his way down. By the time they got to the basement, she was sweating and more than a bit anxious.

How would the really sick patients be transported down the staircase to safety?

Finally reaching the bottom, she and the orderly shepherded their little group to the basement room that served as shelter. The orderly turned around immediately to help other patients, so Katie settled the newcomers onto the crowded benches.

Like any basement shelter, the surroundings were grim. In order to provide adequate protection, it was windowless, with cement floors and walls. A bucket in the corner served as loo, albeit a small measure of privacy was provided by a makeshift curtain. Benches lined the walls, and lighting was supplied by hanging bulbs. A table with a tea kettle offered a glimmer of comfort to an otherwise dreary and airless room.

After five years of war, no one expected anything different. Resignation and fatigue lined most of the faces. At least it wasn't the middle of the night – or not yet. The frustration of shelter life was made up of three parts: ceaseless boredom, waves of fear, and the aggravation of not knowing how long the confinement would last. Sometimes, after relocating all but the sickest of patients, the all clear would sound. Then, everyone would troop back upstairs grumbling, and resettle into the activities that had been interrupted. In other instances, they'd be stuck below ground for hours, never knowing when release would come.

A natural camaraderie emerged. Men chatted in small groups, smoked, and played cards. Singalongs were not unheard of either, and of course many of the patients slept – albeit fitfully. A cheer would inevitably erupt once the all-clear sounded, and the day could return to normal.

"This silence is ghastly," moaned a Scotsman in the corner. His right arm was in a cast, and he had purple, yellow, and blue bruises across his neck and on one side of his face. "With the Luftwaffe bombings, we could hear them coming, and brace ourselves. Or not, if we heard them split off. With these blasted V2s, there's no sound to warn us. Just a sudden explosion, and you're meeting your maker. Bloody bastards."

A chorus of murmurs echoed agreement.

The V2s had proven stealthy and lethal. Fewer than the V1s, they were more deadly. The missile's penetration and concentrated blast caused much greater destruction at the epicentre than the V1, particularly given its lack of warning. It could create a crater almost ten feet in depth, causing an earthquake effect which cracked washbasins a quarter of a mile away. Floorboards shuddered, window frames shook, and clouds of soot blew out of fireplaces miles from the explosion.

Hitler's revenge weapon was frightening indeed. And caused even further strain and frayed nerves in the city shelters that Hitler had targeted.

These and all Britons were well used to and entirely fed up with shelter life.

"Are you alright, Chris? I must help the others."

It never occurred to Katie not to jump in and do whatever she could to transport vulnerable patients to safety.

Chris waved her away, taking a cigarette from a patient next to him.

Katie ran back to the staircase, where she thankfully spied Nurse Gibson.

"Where are the patients who need to be helped, Nurse?" she asked, breathless.

She gave her a grateful smile.

"We've cleared the third and fourth floors, P.O. Kingston. We have transported most of them to the east shelter. How full is this one?"

"Nearly," Katie calculated rapidly. "But could probably take a few more." How did she know? But she wouldn't be party to turning anyone away.

"The second floor is almost clear. We could use your help on the first floor – where most of our most serious cases are located. I'll fetch you an orderly to assist you. Do what you can to carry injured patients to the shelter. Use whatever stretchers and push chairs you can find. For those attached to machines or too ill to move, try to shift them under their beds. Do your best."

Katie nodded and turned to race up to the first floor.

"And Katie," Nurse Gibson shouted after her.

Katie paused and turned back.

"Bless you, dear."

Katie darted away. There was no time to waste.

A quarter of an hour later, most of the patients had been transferred and were accounted for. The air raid signal continued to blare, insisting there was still danger nearby.

Katie lost track of the number of times she and Frank had run up and down the stairs, bearing patients on stretchers. The burliest of staff bumped and jostled unfortunate souls down the stairs to safety.

"This ward is clear, Frank. Now where?" Katie pushed a damp curl from her forehead and took a breath. She didn't stop to think. She couldn't. It was already too long moving these poor men to a secure location. The siren blared mercilessly.

"Just one to go, P.O. Kingston. Where the most severely injured patients are – some are in comas, others are heavily sedated for their pain. If we move them, we will have to be awfully careful. Matron has been there since the start of the raid, so with a bit of luck, there should only be a handful of patients remaining. If we can't move them because of their injuries, we'll be forced to shift them under their beds."

Katie nodded and the pair dashed through the empty halls to the Critical Conditions Ward. Frank was right – Matron was there directing two orderlies and a nurse, patient-by-patient.

"Easy, Steven. Lieutenant Florham has just come out of surgery, poor dear. Be careful."

Two orderlies painstakingly lifted the Lieutenant onto a canvas stretcher and practically tiptoed down the hall with him.

"Right. One more down. Three to go. Frank, do you think you and Petty Officer Kingston can manage this midshipman? He's unconscious but stable. He has a head injury, but has been placed into a medical coma until we are certain there is no swelling of the brain."

Katie swallowed hard.

"We'll keep him safe, Matron. Won't we, Frank?"

"Yes, Ma'am."

The duo carefully slid the patient onto the stretcher, with Matron's help. She laid his morphine bottle, which was still attached to his arm, across his chest, and wrapped it in linen.

"Off you go, then."

It seemed to take an age, but Katie and Frank carried the still-unconscious midshipman down the short staircase and onto a waiting gurney, where a nurse guided him the rest of the way to the shelter.

Katie chanced a quick smile at Frank, who nodded. Sweat poured down her back and between her breasts. Her arms ached, and her legs felt like lead. These patients were bloody heavy. And she was hungry.

"Almost there, Frank. Shall we get on with it?"

He grunted.

Back in the Critical Care Ward, only one patient remained, all by himself. Matron had apparently accompanied the next-to-last man to safety.

The patient lay silent on his bed, attached to his intravenous drip.

"Do you know what's the matter with him?" Katie whispered.

Frank shrugged.

Katie looked in vain for a chart or note or something to guide them. Nothing. And they were out of time. The crashing sounded nearer.

"I suppose we'll just do it again, Frank. Let's load him onto the stretcher and make a go of it."

She sounded more confident than she felt.

"I'm not sure, P.O. Kingston," he wavered, unsure if he should take the word of a volunteer.

"What else can we do, Frank? We can't leave him—"

BOOM. An explosion shook the floors and rattled the medications on the shelves. A flash of light illuminated the sky through the window.

Katie was thrown to the floor near the door, landing hard on her bottom. The lights flickered and went out.

"Frank, are you there? Where are you?" Katie called into the darkness, rubbing her sore behind.

Silence. Damn it. Where was he?

Crawling around, Katie encountered broken glass from toppled bottles, but ignored the pain to her palms and knees. She had to find Frank. After what seemed like hours, she found a leg. Feeling slowly, and calling his name constantly, she concluded he still had all his limbs. What a relief.

"Frank, are you alright? Answer me. Wake up, Frank. I need you." She wanted to shake him, but didn't dare.

Feeling gently around his face, her hand came away wet with blood. There was a huge gash on his head. From what, she couldn't tell, but he was out like a light. Without thinking, she dragged him by the leg, huffing and puffing, until she felt the edge of an empty bed. Pulling him under, she hoped that would be enough to protect him.

Going by memory, she stood and counted the beds until she found the remaining patient, who was still out cold. Plaster had rained all over him, and Katie brushed it away as best she could. Should she try to move him? What to do? It was pitch black except for the random flashes of light from nearby bombs.

Listening for any help to steer her, she heard nothing. She was on her own. The sweat that had been drenching her back turned cold.

She pushed another hospital bed next to her patient, who she was calling Horace in her head. *The stretcher.* Where was it again? By the door? She felt her way over to retrieve it and laid it on top of the empty bed. Inch by inch, she squirmed and wiggled him onto it, pulling his IV bottle onto his chest, as she'd seen Matron do earlier. Feeling around the base of the bed, she hoped for a handle to lower the bed – even a few inches. There was nothing on two of the sides, but her hand felt something on the other one. Turning the knob slowly, the bed lowered bit by bit until the resistance told her it was as low as possible.

There was nothing for it but to pull him onto the floor and hope for the best. Her hands had stopped bleeding but were still slippery. Wiping them on her skirt, she used the back of her hand to wipe away the sweat that dripped into her eyes. Heart racing, she started at the end with his head, and gently pulled him onto the floor. He bounced, but only a little. He slid down the stretcher a bit, so she quickly lifted the bottom half of the stretcher onto the floor. *Thud.*

With her last remaining strength, she pulled, shoved, and pushed the stretcher under the bed. Plonking herself under the one next to it, she pulled Horace's blanket higher and took his hand.

"Come on, Horace. You have to make it. I've got you as safe as I can. We're in this together. Please fight."

Another boom sounded, but this one was further away, and Katie dared to breathe. Was it almost over?

She kept talking to Horace, telling him about her sisters, Kenny, Jamie, the new babies coming, even about her feelings for Ciaran. Anything to penetrate the silence and will a sense of life into the still man. Time ticked slowly by. She called to Frank regularly, but there was no response. Sitting alone, Katie realized how thirsty she was, and dammit – she needed to use the loo.

About twenty minutes later, the lights flickered again, and stayed on. Someone must have got the generator going. Immediately after, the all-clear sounded. Katie almost wept in relief.

She looked at her patient, who still had plaster dust on him, and blood smearings from her hand. She put her head to his chest. Still breathing.

"You did it, Horace. Well done you."

As she scrambled to her feet, she heard feet running down the hall, as she put her hand to her own head. The room was spinning.

"Well done you too, Kingston," a faraway voice mumbled, as she felt strong arms load her onto one of the hospital beds.

She must have fainted, because when she came to moments later, Matron was applying a cool cloth to her forehead, as the room came alive with nurses and staff returning patients to their wards.

Katie sat up, but too quickly, and felt a little dizzy again.

"Not so fast, P.O. Kingston. You've had quite a shock with your heroics, and you've lost blood from your hands and knees."

Another nurse was cleaning her wounds, and the iodine stung like mad. Dressings and plasters were applied, as Katie sat there docile, trying to come to terms with what had just happened.

"How is Horace?" she burst forth. Looking around the room, she couldn't see him.

"Who is Horace, dear?" asked Matron.

"The patient I helped. Under the bed. Is he alright?" Katie couldn't have borne it if he had perished.

"Lieutenant Bickerton? His name is not Horace. But he's going to be fine. At least, he's no more injured than he was. Thanks to your quick thinking, P.O. Kingston."

Katie gulped for air; she was that relieved.

"What about Frank? I think he hurt his head." *Please let him be alright.*

"He's being seen to at the moment. He may have a concussion and need a stitch or two, but he should be fine." Matron paused. "Do you think you can walk, dear? I'd like to take you to my office for a drink of something a little stiffer than tea."

Katie nodded, and after a quick trip to the bathroom, Matron showed her to her office where two large brandies were produced.

"You were exceedingly brave, P.O. Kingston. You helped save many patients by taking them to the shelter. Not to mention your superhuman efforts to protect Lieutenant Bickerton."

Katie took a small sip of the brandy. Its warmth burned her throat and warmed her straightaway. She found she was shivering – shock, she supposed.

"Was anyone hurt? What happened, Matron?"

"V2s," confirmed Matron grimly. "An office building two streets over was obliterated. Not sure of the casualties yet. But everyone here at the hospital is safe. Thanks to the likes of you and the rest of the staff. We are immensely grateful."

Katie took another sip. She didn't know what to say. She was half-embarrassed. Anyone would have done what she did.

Matron wanted her to spend the night in hospital, but Katie insisted she was fine and had to get back to digs. Matron agreed only if she could put Katie into a taxi. They struck a deal. Katie was to ring Matron the next day and stop by in two days for a dressing change. If her wounds didn't improve, she'd need to see the doctor at the docks.

Katie agreed, eager to go back to her billet, her bed, and a night of oblivion. And a proper wash-up wouldn't go amiss either.

CHAPTER SEVENTEEN

"And how is Horace doing now, luv? Have you seen him since the blast?" Mum hovered over Katie, home with a short pass to fully recover from her injuries. Alice held the teapot aloft, offering her daughter another cuppa.

"No thanks, Mum. I'm floating already." She laughed. "And his real name is David, but he'll always be Horace to me. He isn't out of the woods yet, but he's awake and alert. Matron thinks he will recover, but it's going to be quite some time before he's well enough to be released. He wants me to sit with him now, too. But I'm fully occupied with Chris, albeit he's probably going home soon."

Katie was pleased to see the light behind her mum's eyes again – if it took worrying about her youngest daughter to help her heal, Katie was all for it.

"That's wonderful. You must have really helped him loads."

"I'm not sure about that. But he's finally agreed to visitors. His mum and sister came last week, and it did him no end of good. I even convinced him to see his fiancé, Violet. I'm ever so happy about that. Hopefully, his heart will melt when he sees her, and the scars and burns won't matter. Isn't that the way of true love? Sweethearts all over the country are coming home with limbs missing, scars and burns, and even nerves or anxiety. We welcome them with open arms, and cherish them all the more. That's what I'm banking on, in the event."

Katie's hands and knees were healing well, but she looked worn out. Alice resisted telling her so, and focused on giving her youngest daughter loads of love and nourishment – as much as she could in the short time Katie was home.

"Splendid, darling. You've really made a difference with that young man. Perhaps he's turned a corner in his recovery."

"I hope so, Mum. He's also said he's now open to more surgeries – including skin grafts – to help the healing and make him look more like his old self. He has a long recovery ahead of him, but with the support of his mum, sister, and fiancé, his future is looking a little brighter." Katie turned a weak smile towards her mother.

Alice took a sip of her tea.

"You've neatly changed the subject of the V2 explosion night, luv, but you've glossed over your part in the safe evacuation of all those patients. It must have been frightening."

"You know, Mum – I didn't even stop long enough to be scared. Not until the end, at least. I was just that intent on getting those men to the shelter, that I didn't even consider how dangerous the situation really was."

"That's my Katie – rushing in headlong without a care for your own safety," Alice tutted. "I trust you won't be trying that again anytime soon. You're too precious to us."

Katie let that slide off her, discarding the compliment. As always. Anyone would have done what she did. She was nothing special.

"I have no plans to, Mum," she replied with a raised eyebrow.

"You must have impressed Matron no end. What you did was so brave, luv."

"She thanked me over and over. It was a bit too much, really."

What Katie didn't tell her mother was that Matron said she'd talked to her CO about recommending Katie for some type of bravery commendation. It would probably come to naught, but she was chuffed with the praise, nonetheless. No point saying anything to Mum or Pops unless it came to something. Which it likely wouldn't.

"We're dead proud of you, Katie. Pops and I – well, all of us, really. We're having a family dinner tonight with a double celebration – your upcoming birthday and your acts of bravery."

"We certainly are, young lady." Tillie breezed in, Jamie in tow. "We couldn't be prouder of you, sis." She hugged Katie carefully, as Jamie climbed into his auntie's lap.

"Shhh, Jamie. Auntie Katie has been hurt. Come down this instant." Tillie reached for her son.

"He's no bother, Tillie. I've missed this little tyke." She nuzzled his neck. "And let's have a look at you. How is that baby growing?"

Tillie groaned.

"Faster than his or her brother, that's for certain. I have months to go, and I don't know how I'll bear the summer heat with this big tummy."

"You look marvelous, Tils. As always," Katie reassured her. And she did. Her tall, willowy figure hardly showed the baby. Her golden hair shone and her skin glowed. Being a mum certainly agreed with her.

"Ta, darling. You are kind, if exaggerating just a tad. How are you feeling? Let me see your hands."

Tillie had driven an ambulance during the first part of the war, and was the household nurse when needed. She took both of her sister's hands in her own, examined them closely, looked at her knees, and pronounced Katie on the mend.

"It was just a few cuts, nothing really. The doctor on base said they won't even scar. I'm still feeling a bit tired, that's all." The shadows under her eyes gave it away.

Tillie patted her hand.

"It's likely a bit of delayed shock, luv. You'll be yourself in no time. But for now, let us spoil you a bit. It's not every day that you turn twenty-four."

This brought a gale of giggles from her sister.

"That's a lark, Tillie. Twenty-four is not much of anything."

"Leave off, Katie. Every birthday is special. And this one is superb – you survived your ordeal, and will be good as new before you know it," Mum persisted.

"Alright, Mum. I know when I'm beat. Who else is coming?"

"The usual gang," Tillie jumped in. "Trev is upstairs resting, and Pops will be home from work soon. I'm not sure if Uncle Thomas can make it, but Micah, Maggie, and Hannah are expected. If Maggie doesn't deliver those twins before supper. You won't believe it when you see her."

"I can't wait," Katie replied simply.

The evening was a smashing success, with loads of laughs and the best food that Mum and Tillie could muster on rations.

"It's delicious, Mum. Much better than what's on offer at the mess on any given night." Katie dug in with her usual gusto.

"Soon enough, even rationing might be a thing of the past," Tillie said, shoving a spoonful of mash in the general direction of Jamie's mouth.

"I doubt that will be anytime soon," Trevor objected, feeling around his plate for a piece of bread. Tillie, next to him, watched whilst chewing her lip. Should she help him? She decided against it, knowing how touchy he could be when he tried to fend for himself.

"Anything's possible now that the blackout's been lifted," Walter added mildly.

"That alone is worthy of celebration," Katie raised her glass. "It feels decadent, somehow, having the lights on at night with nothing to dim them."

"Churchill wouldn't have allowed it, if things really weren't winding down," Micah said. "It's a brilliant sign for our future. Our children won't need to be afraid." He gazed at his wife, who smiled gently.

"Cheers to that." Trevor felt around for his wineglass, found it, and gratefully lifted it in the general direction of the lot of them.

"Cheers," they chorused together.

"Cheese," Jamie sang from his high chair.

Everyone dissolved in laughter.

Isla Drummond brought a lovely carrot cake into the dining room for the birthday girl.

As they were singing Happy Birthday, they heard a loud knock downstairs. Before Katie blew out her candles, a tall Irishman appeared at the door of the dining room, a large, wrapped gift in hand. He motioned the others to be quiet as he came up behind Katie and chimed in his baritone as they finished the song.

Katie jumped up, turned around, and shrieked.

"Ciaran, you're here! Now it's the best birthday ever." Heedless of her whole family watching, she threw her arms around him and kissed him on the lips.

"Will you be blowing out the candles, then?" Isla asked dryly.

Katie giggled, leaned over, and blew out the six candles that Mum had kept back.

"Why six?" asked Ciaran curiously.

"2 plus 4 of course," Mum answered matter-of-factly. It made perfect sense to her.

"Of course," replied Isla, smothering a smile.

Everyone enjoyed a sliver of Isla's delicious carrot cake, save Maggie, who claimed to be full. Mum kept an eye on her – she was worried about her very pregnant daughter.

After dinner, they played a game of charades in the drawing room. Maggie excused herself early, saying she was falling asleep on her feet. Micah escorted her upstairs.

Tillie was next to turn in. After putting young Jamie to bed, she helped Trevor with his nighttime routine before laying her own weary head to rest. This new baby was taking more out of her than she cared to admit.

One by one, the drawing room emptied, leaving just Katie and Ciaran.

"Don't stay up too late, luv. You need your rest," Mum bade a soft goodnight.

"Finally, we're alone. I need to examine your lacerations meself, mavourneen." He tenderly unwrapped the bandages from her hands, touched the healing gashes, and kissed each palm before re-wrapping them.

"I'm fine, Ciaran, really." Yet Katie was touched to her core.

He repeated the process for her knees, insisting on kissing them, which embarrassed Katie greatly.

"Ciaran, stop. You're tickling me, you brute."

Despite her exhaustion, she found Ciaran's compassionate touch arousing. He seared her skin everywhere he touched her. Her lips longed for the touch of his own.

Settling her back on the sofa, he leaned in, eager for the taste of her as well. He pressed his lips on hers, setting off the heat that they both craved.

He paused for a moment and wiggled his eyebrows.

"Is yourself healed enough for an embrace?"

In response, she pulled him down by the collar and kissed him deeply. He returned the kiss and tightened his hold on her. As he pressed his upper body close to hers, she felt a delicious thrill course through her.

What would it feel like to press her naked flesh against hers? She shuddered in anticipation.

He halted instantly.

"Are you alright? I haven't hurt you, have I?"

"No, Ciaran. Albeit I am a little tired. But what I really want is to see what's inside that gift. You've kept me dangling since you brought it." She gave him a mischievous look and lunged for it.

But Ciaran was quicker and nabbed it.

"Not so fast, Katie Kingston. First, promise me something." He held the package too high for Katie to reach.

"What is it, Irish? You're not asking me to compromise my good name, are you?"

"Not at all, me darling. Nothing near so sinister. I need you to promise me the next time you have a seventy-two-hour pass, yourself will come with me to Ireland to meet me folks. With the blackout ending, and no sign of a V2 rocket in weeks, this war is surely about over. It should be safe enough to travel, and it's time for us to plan for our future, and all."

Katie was flustered and thrilled at the same time.

"Of course, I'll come with you, Ciaran. I'm that eager to meet your ma and da myself. I promise I'll put in for leave, but I probably won't get it for a bit given I'm away on a sick pass at the moment. Satisfied?" She reached for the package again.

"And our future?"

"Plenty of time for that once the war really is over. But yes, Irish. You and I just might have a future together."

He lowered his arms in disbelief, and Katie pounced on the package.

"Got it," she cried in triumph. Seeing his crestfallen face, she kissed him on the cheek. "And I meant every word."

He brightened as she pulled the ribbon and paper off the box, and lifted the lid. Unfolding the paper that surrounded something soft, she plucked out a thick white jumper.

"Ciaran, it's beautiful," she murmured, rubbing the soft wool against her cheek.

"Me mam knitted it for you. She said to tell you it will be welcome on a cold winter's night at the farm."

"I love it, Irish. Please give her my warmest thanks. No, I'll write her a note." The jumper was lovely.

"There's more." He grinned, taking joy in her youthful exuberance.

She dug back in and removed a small box. She opened it and squealed.

"A necklace! It's beautiful, Ciaran." She gave him a dazzling smile as she inspected the gold chain with a sparkle of green at the bottom.

He took it out of the box and undid the clasp.

"I thought maybe you needed a little protection when I'm not around. See, here is an emerald four-leaf clover. It's just a small one, but perhaps it will keep yourself from jumping headfirst into danger." He fastened the slim gold chain around her neck.

"It's smashing, Irish. I absolutely adore it. And perhaps it will become my lucky charm. It's so thoughtful. Thanks ever so much." She babbled as usual when she was nervous or excited. Had she been expecting something else? A ring? No, this was just brilliant.

She reached over and kissed him.

Inside, she was happy and relieved. She wasn't ready for an engagement ring – not yet anyway. If Ciaran had presented her with one today, she would have been proper confused. Her feelings were growing stronger for him every day, but she wasn't quite ready for an engagement and marriage. She definitely saw a future with this tall, kind Irishman, but the events of the past few days had taken a toll on her, and she simply wasn't ready. Her heart swelled knowing that he understood this, too. Maybe he really was the one for her.

"Ciaran, this means the world to me. It's like you can read me like a book, and know exactly what I would have wanted. It's so special. I'll treasure it always."

She stood, knocking the empty box to the ground.

Reaching up, she put her arms around his neck and pulled him down for a long, lingering kiss.

"My sweet girl, my mavourneen. I love you so. Happy Birthday," he murmured when they broke, both of them breathless.

The clock in the hall struck 11:00.

Ciaran ran a hand through his auburn hair, kissed the tip of her nose, and sighed heavily.

"As much as I would love to stay and caress you longer, I fear I'm already in trouble with your mum. She said you needed rest, and here I've kept you up later than I'm meant to. I'm sorry, but it's just so hard to let you go."

"Will you be back tomorrow?" Katie asked, eyes wide.

"I can see you in the morning for a couple of hours, before I'm due back at Bletchley. Luckily, it's a short train ride from London."

"That would be grand, just grand," she imitated his Irish lilt.

A discreet cough announced someone at the doorway. Ciaran and Katie looked over to see…Micah.

"I'm so sorry to trouble you, but everyone else is asleep. I'm afraid that Maggie is about to have the babies. She's had indigestion for hours and hasn't been able to sleep. The indigestion has turned to pains, and she's in rather a bit of discomfort. I suppose perhaps it's time we took her to the hospital?"

"Bloody hell." Katie turned to Ciaran. "The best birthday ever. Time for some twins."

CHAPTER EIGHTEEN

"Aren't you the clever girl having the babies whilst I'm here?" Katie bounced upstairs and into her own room, where Maggie rested, looking drawn and pale.

Ciaran had gone to the corner box to ring for a taxi.

"I'm sorry to be a bother, Katie. I only meant to have a lie-down before going back to ours. But the indigestion seems to have progressed to labor pains."

With that, she grimaced and clutched her belly.

Katie sat on the bed and held her sister's hand.

"That was a bad one," Maggie gasped after a couple of minutes, finally releasing Katie's hand from her tight grip.

"Should I wake Mum?" Katie had no experience with childbirth. She was feeling panicky, if she was honest.

"No, I don't want to disturb her. It could be hours yet."

"Tillie?"

"Yes please. I need her right now."

"I'll just be a tick, darling."

She left Maggie in Micah's capable care and dashed quietly down the stairs to Trevor and Tillie's room. The house was dark and silent, and she didn't want to wake anyone unnecessarily.

"Tillie," she whispered, as she knocked lightly on the bedroom door.

"Is it Maggie?" Tillie appeared straightaway, and was already half-dressed.

Katie nodded.

"How did you know?"

"She's my twin," Tillie replied simply. "I just felt something was off with her at supper. I've been keeping a close eye on our quiet girl. How is she getting on?" She'd already finished buttoning up her cardigan and softly closed the bedroom behind her to leave her husband and son undisturbed.

"She's having pains, and looks a bit washed out. Aside from that, I do not know. She was asking for you, Tils. I'm sure you will ease her mind, if not the pains."

"Righto, what are we waiting for?" Tillie was halfway up the staircase already.

Maggie was in mid-pain when the sisters pushed open the door to the bedroom. Micah looked on helplessly as his wife battled another contraction.

"Darling, I'm here. No need to be brave. Shout if you want to." Tillie rushed to her sister's side.

"But everyone is asleep. Well – most everyone," Maggie grunted.

"I'll wait for the taxi with Ciaran. I'll fetch you when it's here." Katie left. She was in over her head with baby matters. Best to leave it to the expert – Tillie. Was she awful to want to escape the childbirth ordeal? Running down the stairs, she didn't much care. She was relieved to escape.

Within a quarter of an hour, the taxi had arrived. Between Micah and Tillie, they heaved Maggie down the stairs and into the waiting cab. Mum had woken up and fussed around her laboring daughter. She wanted to come to the hospital with the little group, but Tillie insisted she stay home to look after Jamie when he woke up. Trevor was a terrific daddy, but it was challenging for him to manage the day-to-day care of his son with his blindness. Tillie assured her that between Micah, herself, and the doctor and nurses, Maggie would be well taken care of. Mum was torn, but reluctantly agreed.

"As soon as I can call round Isla's tomorrow to drop off Jamie, I'm coming to the hospital, and you can't stop me." She kissed her daughter on the forehead as Maggie huffed and puffed her way out the front door, down the front steps, and into the night.

"That's fine, Mum," Tillie called over her shoulder. "Maggie is doing brilliantly. The babies will be here before you know it."

In the event, it was almost two days before the twins were born. By then, Maggie was so exhausted that she didn't know how she would carry on, but Tillie never left her side and kept her spirits up.

"Darling, you're doing so well. Not long now," Tillie encouraged.

"You've been saying that for hours. Why don't you just shut up?" Maggie snapped.

Tillie shared a smile with the attending nurse. This was all to be expected – especially with a long labor. The mum-to-be would often take out her frustration and pain by lashing out in anger at those closest to her.

"I'm sorry, luv. I know it's hard. But just think about these two beautiful babies that will be here soon. You just have to work a little harder, a smidgen longer until you can hold them in your arms."

"Your sister is right," the nurse replied crisply, as she straightened the rumpled sheets and picked up the empty water glass. "You're nearing the end. Brace up, dear. I'll fetch you more water and be back to check on you straightaway."

"She can go to hell, too," stormed Maggie as another pain overtook her.

"That's right, Mags. Let it out. Yell as loud as you like. It's hard work birthing one baby, not to mention two."

The contraction passed, and Maggie grabbed for her sister's hand.

"I'm sorry to treat you like rubbish, Tillie. It's just that I'm so tired, and these babies aren't coming. I've seen two sunsets and two sunrises, and they still aren't here. Why Tillie, why? Is something wrong with them?" Maggie's hair was plastered to her head from the sweating and exertion. Her beautiful brown eyes were filling with tears of exhaustion and frustration. She looked pale and wan. She'd hardly slept the last two nights, and had eaten little.

"There's naught wrong with them, darling. If there was, the nurse would be bustling around, rather than bossing you about. And the doctor would be here, tut tutting and telling you that everything will be alright. And no need to apologize, Mags. You've been working for hours – of course your temper is frayed."

Tillie was completely knackered. She'd been with Maggie for two days, only leaving her sister's side for tea and an occasional sandwich.

Being pregnant herself, it was taking a toll on her, but she couldn't be convinced to go for a rest. Micah paced the halls, constantly asking for news of his wife. Mum kept him company, trying to distract them both.

Hours ticked by. Finally, it was time for Maggie to push. At first, she was elated – at last she could help bring her babies into the world. But it was exhausting work. And she'd had barely any sleep in the last two days.

"I can't do it, Tillie. I can't push any longer. I just can't," Maggie wailed again. She had been pushing for two hours, and was completely spent.

Tillie leaned over her sister, looked deeply into her watery eyes, and almost shook her.

"Yes, you can Maggie Goldbach. And you will. You are stronger than you think. Look what you've done already. You've carried these babies for nine months, hardly slept these last few weeks, and when was the last time you've seen your feet?" Tillie's eyes locked with her sister's. Maggie merely nodded.

"Here's another one," she gulped.

"Right, Mrs Goldbach. Give me an enormous push this time. You're nearly there," the doctor urged.

With a guttural groan and a mighty push, Maggie finally delivered a tiny baby girl, who entered the world with a thunderous cry.

"You've done it, Maggie. She's here. Aren't you marvelous?"

The nurse deftly wrapped the baby in a towel and briefly showed her to Maggie.

"She's beautiful," sobbed the new mum. "She has Micah's mouth."

"Right, Mum. We need to pop her into an incubator in the special nursery to keep an eye on her." The nurse was all business.

"Is she alright?" fretted Maggie.

"She looks healthy, indeed. Just a little small – as we knew she would be," confirmed the doctor.

"Oh, alright," Maggie followed her daughter out of the room with her eyes. "Oh, OWWWW." Another wave flooded her body.

"Here comes the second one," the doctor reported.

Tillie grabbed Maggie's hand.

"Squeeze as hard as you like, luv. Bear down."

And like a flash, a second little girl slid into the world. As loud as the first one announced her arrival, baby number two was calm and quiet.

"Is she okay?" Maggie tried to rise on her elbows to see her second daughter. "Is she breathing?"

"She's just fine, Mrs Goldbach. Her color is excellent. She's a little smaller than her sister, but hale and hearty."

On cue, the baby cried, and Maggie sagged in relief.

"Can I hold her?" she asked through her tears. "My sweet girl."

The doctor nodded curtly at the nurse.

"Only for a moment, mind. We need to get her into an incubator like her sister."

Maggie carefully took the small bundle into her arms, and crooned in the way of new mums since the beginning of time.

"What a little love. You are so beautiful."

Tillie wiped a tear from her eye as she heard a ruckus at the door.

"I need to see my wife. Is she alright?" Micah's quiet voice was persistent indeed.

"My husband. I need to see him." Maggie looked up from the baby, who was being taken from her arms.

"I'll have a word with him, darling." Tillie rushed from the room.

The Kingston clan filled the hallway – Pops and Mum, Trevor and Jamie, Micah, and…Hannah. When had she arrived?

"Darlings, Maggie has just done the most incredible thing and had two perfect babies. They are both tiny, but healthy. They've gone to the nursery to be checked over, and will need to spend some time in the incubators."

"Is Maggie alright?" Micah seized Tillie's arm.

"She's exhausted and elated and already missing her babies. But she'll be just fine," Tillie smiled, feeling suddenly completely worn out. She pushed back a lock of her own damp blonde hair.

"When can I see her?" Micah and Alice pushed forward.

"That's up to the doctor. I should think it will be a little while until she's tidied up and ready for visitors."

"What did she have?" asked Trevor from the corner of the waiting room.

Tillie and Maggie had discussed this moment in advance.

"That's Maggie's news to share. You'll know soon enough."

A short time later, Micah was admitted to Maggie's recovery room.

"Little one, I've been so worried about you. Are you alright? It's been so long since I've seen you." He took her gently in his arms and placed a soft kiss on her lips.

"Better now, my love. I've missed you so, but I have been rather occupied."

"You look beautiful, Maggie. Glowing even more now that you were before they were born." He paused. "How are they?"

"Ruth is the larger of the two. She has your mouth, I should think. She's gorgeous."

"A girl," Micah exclaimed. "How wonderful." He stroked her cheek.

"Two girls, Daddy. Rachel is slightly smaller, but just as beautiful. She looks just like her big sister Ruth."

Micah gasped.

"Two girls? I'm the luckiest man in the world. You are a marvel, Maggie. I'm in awe of your strength and fortitude." He grinned from ear to ear. "Thank you for agreeing to name one of them after my mother. It means the world to me to keep her memory alive." His voice cracked.

"No need to thank me, Micah. I'm that tired, but I couldn't be happier. And the names we agreed upon seem to suit them. There wasn't any question of any others. I just want to hold them and count their little fingers and toes."

"The doctor said they may only be in the incubator for two weeks or so. As soon as they are five pounds each, they can come home with us. Ruth and Rachel Goldbach. I still can't believe it. I love you so, little one." Micah beamed.

"And I you, dearest Micah. Now we are parents. Our life is going to change in so many ways. With the war almost over, it's a new beginning for all of us. I'm that pleased that the twins will be part of this new era."

"When can I see them?" Micah asked, brown eyes earnest and serious.

"You can have a look anytime. I'm not certain when either of us can hold them. Would you look in on them now? I'm desperate to have you see them, talk to them – even through glass. I need to hear everything. I only saw them for seconds. I never even got to hold Ruth yet." She put her face in hands as the tears dripped down her cheeks.

"I will, darling, but I will not leave you like this." He held her until her tears were spent. He tenderly wiped her face with his handkerchief.

"I know you're tired, little one, but are you well enough for any visitors? Your mum is about to beat down the door – she's that eager to see you. And I have a surprise visitor for you as well."

"Yes, please. I want to see Mum. And who is here to surprise me? I can't imagine."

"The charge nurse is harping on only one visitor at a time. I'll do my best to bring them both in, but no promises."

"Alright, Micah." Maggie settled back into the pillows. "Do go and see the girls in the nursery whilst the guests are here. I'm longing for word of them."

"Of course, I will. I need to get acquainted with my daughters."

He strode to the door, opened it, and Alice burst inside. Behind her was Hannah.

They were allowed in for just a quarter of an hour. Tears, laughter, hugs, and words spilled all over each other. Hannah had secured a 48-hour pass from her WAAF duties, and had already spent a good deal of it in the waiting room, but was overjoyed to meet her two nieces. She'd have to go back tomorrow, but didn't regret coming for one instant. Mum couldn't stop touching her daughter; she'd been beside herself with worry for the last two and a half days, waiting and wondering what was going on in that little hospital room.

"Maggie, you gave us a fright. We didn't know what was going on. We're so thankful you are alright, and the girls, too. Imagine. Twin girls. It brings back such wonderful memories of when you and Tillie were born. You're going to be a brilliant mother. Twins are such a blessing."

Mum couldn't stop babbling and crying. She could finally let it all out. She was so happy for her daughter and son-in-law. It had been a long, hard road for them. They deserved this happiness, and so much more. She cried anew, thinking of her friend, Ruth Goldbach, who would have been a loving bubbee, but would never meet these two beautiful babies. And now, her life wasn't in vain. She could live on in her granddaughters – her namesake Ruth and her twin Rachel.

"Why is it babies bring out so many emotions in us?" She was embarrassed to be seen in a moment of weakness like this. She didn't even realize herself that she was also weeping for her lost sister, Shirley.

"There's an old Jewish proverb: 'A drop of love can bring an ocean of tears.' It's alright to cry, Aunt Alice." Hannah smiled sweetly.

"Thank you, luv. I couldn't have said it better myself." Alice tried to pull herself together.

The nurse bustled in, and ordered the visitors out, firmly but not unkindly.

"Our patient needs her rest. No more visitors today. You can discuss amongst your family who may come tomorrow. Only two of you. Mrs Goldbach has been through a lengthy ordeal, and will need all her strength to cope with her recovery and looking after those two lovely babies. Now – out you go. And remember what I said – just two of you tomorrow."

Maggie kissed them both goodbye and lay back, drained but comforted to have seen Mum and Hannah. She was impatient to have Micah back at her side, and to hear how the babies were doing. And she was starving. She'd worked up quite an appetite. But she would just close her eyes for a little whilst she waited. A wee nap only.

She drifted off instantly.

CHAPTER NINETEEN

"You'd think we'd be getting better at goodbyes by now, but each one is more wretched than the last." Katie hugged Tillie close. "Please rest a bit, luv, after that hospital ordeal. It took almost as much out of you as Maggie."

"As if," Tillie laughed. "I was just there for support. Just as she was to me when Jamie was born. And someday, it will be your turn," she added lightly.

"Sod off, Tils. Let's get your baby born first."

She embraced her sister one last time, picked up her holdall, and hurried to her track. The train station wasn't as busy these days. The war was definitely winding down. She saw a vendor selling union jacks – surely that was a sign that there would be something to celebrate soon?

As April progressed, the Allies were showing all signs of winning. Increasing numbers of Axis prisoners were being taken – in April alone, 1,5000,000 had been taken on the Western Front. German troops were captured – some said over 100,000 – in what would be the final Italian war campaign. Masses of German soldiers surrendered on the Eastern Front. Allied camps sprung up to hold hundreds of thousands of these imprisoned or surrendered Axis forces personnel.

Allied forces discovered the horrific scale of the Jewish persecution in concentration camps and forced labor compounds. As they advanced into Germany, the Allies were shocked and appalled by what they found. On April 15th, the camp of Bergen-Belsen was liberated, and 10,000 starving, seriously ill, and near-dead prisoners were found by the British 11th Armored Division. The dreadfully overcrowded camp where food, water, and basic sanitation were scarce, if not non-existent, fostered an environment where starvation and widespread diseases like typhus and dysentery were rampant.

Thousands of bodies were found unburied everywhere.

It was an insurmountable task to provide crucial relief. The first priorities were to bury the dead, contain the spread of disease, restore a water supply, and arrange for a reliable food stream.

Well-intentioned troops dropped canned foods, mainly spam and other high-fat products. Disastrously, many of the emaciated prisoners who scrambled for the first real food they'd had in months or years, perished within a few days as their bodies couldn't manage the fatty food after the starvation diet of filthy broth they'd endured as their once-daily rations.

The world took a collective gasp. No one could fathom that humans could be treated so horrendously, particularly hundreds of thousands of Jews. How could this have happened?

Just four days later, the American 42nd Infantry Division found the Dachau death camp. They tried to save as many of the mortally ill inmates as possible, but many were so malnourished, weak, and sick that they continued to die after liberation. It was appalling.

Other signs continued to prove the war would soon be over.

By the end of April, Germany had withdrawn all their forces from Finland. Then Italy was liberated and Italian dictator Benito Mussolini was captured and executed.

Amidst all the news came the shocking report from America that President Roosevelt had died suddenly from a cerebral hemorrhage. He'd been ailing for some time, but his death was a shock, nonetheless. Britons grieved for the prominent leader who had brought America into the war at a crucial time. It was well acknowledged that the Allies wouldn't be at the point of ultimate victory now without the invaluable leadership and support of the American forces.

***

Gratefully slipping into a window seat, Katie's thoughts drifted over the last few days. Maggie's twin girls were precious. Although tiny, they were strong and nursing well. It was likely they'd be home in a fortnight. Maggie was overrun with hospital visitors to where the nurse forbade everyone save Micah, so that the new mother could get the rest she needed to care for, not one, but two new babies.

Back at the #40 Longridge Road, the Kingston household was filled to bursting. Tillie and Trevor's growing family seemed to take over the townhouse. Once the war ended and Kenny came back, there wouldn't be room for her anymore. She always assumed that she'd simply return home, and everything would be the way it was before Herr Hitler had taken the outrageous idea that he could take over the world.

But it couldn't. Everything had changed. It wasn't just three sisters with a baby brother. Both Tillie and Maggie were married with families to look after. Kenny was now a grown man, with war wounds and scars that none of them even understood as of yet. Mum and Pops were steady, but Mum had been changed forever when her sister died. Nothing could ever be the same again. Was there space for Katie at home with all this post-war uncertainty? Would she even fit in anymore? They all had their own lives now. Oh, she knew she'd be welcomed back, loved even. But was that her place now? Was it where she should be?

Hearing the rumble of the train as it pulled into the next station, she looked out the window, not having a clue where she was. It would be wonderful to actually know where you were going again once the markers and signposts were back. Back home.

Home.

Ciaran.

A tremor went through her body. A small gasp escaped her lips.

Ciaran is my home. For now, and for always. Wherever he goes, I will go. Where we live just doesn't matter. As long as we're together, we will make it home together. This is my life now. My life with Ciaran. It's my turn for happiness. Hell, I'm going to become a farmer's wife. A laugh bubbled up through her throat. She giggled out loud.

"What's so funny, soldier?" A short, straw-haired Yankee raised an eyebrow.

"It's Petty Officer, actually. And it's a private joke." She turned back to the window, still smiling like a gormless fool.

How had this young Irishman crept up on her emotions like this? How had he become so important to her? Essential, even? He'd seeped into her heart and taken hold. And for the first time, she wasn't filled with panic. She wasn't afraid to be loved. And to love back with her full heart. She fairly pulsed with the joy of it. She couldn't wait to tell Ciaran how she felt. The future was bright and beautiful. The war was close to being over, and she was going to build a life with the most remarkable man she'd ever met.

"You look like the cat that swallowed the cream, Queenie," Ruby greeted her in Portsmouth. "Babies doing alright, then?" She kissed her mate on the cheek.

"Brilliant, ta. And how kind of you to meet my train." She gave Ruby an impulsive hug.

"What's put the smile on your face, then? Is it the fact that Berlin is surrounded by the Soviets? Or that Hitler is likely holed up somewhere, cowering?"

"Righto, that's something to celebrate, isn't it, Ruby? This ghastly war's end is within sight. It's wonderful to know that little Ruth and Rachel are being born into a new era. No bombs, no rationing, no queuing. By the time they are three or four, there might even be a choice of sweets for them."

"Yes, that is splendid, Katie, but you haven't answered my question. Does your ear-to-ear grin have anything to do with Ciaran?" Ruby teased.

"As a matter of fact, yes." Katie held her chin up proudly. "I've decided I rather fancy him."

Ruby was gobsmacked. Katie had been so evasive about Ciaran all along, and here she was making a grand declaration.

"All I can say is that it's about time. The man has the patience of a saint. He'll be that chuffed, I rather think."

The two linked arms and began the trek back to their digs.

After greeting the pub owner, the girls climbed to their room, where Katie chucked her bag on the bed. She picked up a letter from her nightstand. Her brow furrowed seeing the postmark from London with a royal seal.

"My word, whatever can this be?" She sank onto the bed, turning it over and examining the envelope. A Buckingham Palace return address. Bloody hell.

"You won't find out by turning it about. Open it. I'll admit I was tempted to peek. It's ever so exciting." Ruby sat on her bed opposite, eyes riveted to the envelope.

Katie glanced up with a question in her eyes, and carefully slit open the top. Her eyes widened as large as saucers. She read it aloud.

"Dear Petty Officer Kingston,

I am pleased to inform you that you have been awarded the George Cross by His Majesty, King George VI, for acts of the greatest heroism or of the most conspicuous courage in circumstances of extreme danger.

On the evening of March 29, 1945, your bravery resulted in the successful evacuation of several wounded servicemen at St. Mary's Hospital in Portsmouth. Your quick thinking and dedication resulted in many lives being saved during a V2 attack.

You will be awarded your medal at a service at Buckingham Palace at a later date. Congratulations.

Yours truly,

Peter Wooldridge Townsend
Equerry to His Majesty, King George VI"

"Katie, you're being awarded the George Cross! How wonderful. You're too brave by half."

Katie's face was a picture of emotions – disbelief, delight, pride, and then dismay. She threw it on the bed.

"What's wrong? Surely that's a staggering honor, Queenie?" Ruby was utterly confused.

"Oh, they probably pass these out to anyone who does a kind thing here or there," Katie dismissed the letter.

"Are you daft, girl?" Ruby almost shook her friend. "This is an extraordinary distinction. What's the matter with you?"

Katie shrugged.

"Perhaps it's a mistake, meant for someone else. I'm certainly not wonderful or extraordinary," her voice was all but inaudible.

Ruby paused and took a deep breath.

"Darling, whatever has gotten into you? Of course, this is meant for you, and you know it. What's really the problem?"

Katie tidied up the letter and busied herself unpacking her case and putting things away.

"I'm not a hero, Ruby. I just did what anyone else would do in that situation. I'm not worthy of any honor, especially from the King."

Ruby heard the words *I'm not worthy* and nodded her head. She'd heard this before.

She sat next to Katie and took her hands in hers.

"And why are you not worthy, luv?" she asked softly.

"Uh, I dunno." She shrugged and tried to extricate her hands.

"Yes, you do. But I don't. So, tell me."

"It's just that..." Katie stumbled. "It's just that I'm nothing special. Just the younger sister of the marvelous and beautiful Kingston Twins. Just the short, freckled, unremarkable younger sister, always getting into scrapes. Not marvelous or beautiful...or much of anything." She picked at a nail and tried to avoid looking at Ruby.

"Why ever would you think that, luv?"

"Why wouldn't I? Tillie and Maggie are gorgeous, talented. Everything always came easy for them. Now they have husbands and babies, and tremendous lives ahead of them."

"And?" Ruby prompted. She knew there was more.

"And I was meant to be a boy," Katie blazed, angry tears in her eyes.

"Rubbish," declared Ruby. "Your parents wanted and loved you – just for yourself."

"So then, why did they try again for a boy? They stopped after they had Kenny." Bitterness crept into her voice.

"Maybe they were so delighted with you, they wanted another child. Perhaps they were happy with whatever healthy baby was meant for them – boy or girl. Maybe, just maybe, they wanted a large family, and were thankful for all their children."

Katie didn't respond.

"Did you have an unhappy childhood? Did your parents favor the twins or Kenny over you?" Ruby was determined to get to the root of the problem.

"Noooo, not really. Mum and Pops treated us all pretty fairly. But the golden twins – everyone has always made a fuss over them. You can imagine – everywhere we went, people oohed and aaahed over them."

"Isn't that natural?" argued Ruby, pressing her point. "Twins are rather uncommon. Most people have never even seen them. And your sisters are lovely – not just in looks, but in personality. Is it their fault that they get noticed?"

"No, I suppose not." She considered for a moment. Tillie was kind and always thinking of others and how she could help them. And Maggie – shy and unassuming, but so thoughtful and sweet. Maggie hated all the attention that she and Tillie got – just for being identical twins. "Maggie hates being in the spotlight. She backs away at every turn."

"See what I mean? That must be ghastly for both of them – being lumped together like some kind of circus side show. Never being considered as individuals. Answering the same questions all the time from complete strangers. I don't envy them one bit." Ruby brushed her hair, keeping an eye on her chum.

"I never really thought about it, but I suppose you're right. It can't be much fun being the object of peculiar looks and odd remarks." Katie was seeing things in a new light.

"And Kenny? Has his life been a bed of roses with three older sisters lurking about, and likely telling him what to do?"

Katie laughed.

"Maybe not, but he is the only son of the house. No one can take that away from him. He and Pops are close and they have always spent masses of time together."

"Maybe to get him away from all the girl talk in the house?" Ruby observed.

"Perhaps. Pops and I have a special bond, too. He taught me how to ride a bicycle and encouraged me to play sports. And he gave me a job at his firm when I begged. He thought I was too young, but I knew I could do it."

"See what I'm saying, Katie? It's far from easy having glamorous sisters like Tillie and Maggie – but it takes nothing away from you. You are smart as a whip. Look how quickly you picked up intercepting. And brave – you rush into any danger, heedless of any risk to yourself – to save others." She waved the King's letter under her mate's nose. "You are the best friend a girl could have, and you have enchanted that Irishman with your charm and beauty – inside and out. I'd say you lucked out in the Kingston family gene pool. Your sisters and brother probably envy you."

"Do you really think so?" Katie asked, her eyes filling up with tears. She got a tingling feeling – could she have been wrong about herself all this time? Bloody hell. The way Ruby put it, she didn't sound half bad. A pretty good sort, really.

"I know so," Ruby said fervently, changing into her nightclothes. "And you do, too, deep down. You wouldn't be the woman you are without being a person of integrity and value. Do you get it, Queenie? Do you finally get it?"

A slow smile spread across Katie's face.

"You know, I suppose I really do. My fears have been getting the best of me." She held up her hand as Ruby opened her mouth to protest. "My old fears. I've sold my family short. Each of them has had so much to endure. They have been nothing but kind and loving to me. It's time for me to shed that old insecurity."

She snatched up the letter and spun around the room.

"Perhaps I deserve this award. I saved a lot of wounded patients. Or at least I helped. And I am lucky to have a man like Ciaran. And he's lucky to have me." She hugged Ruby. "Thank you, darling, for opening up my eyes. It's a new beginning for me, for us."

Shouts and cheers from the pub downstairs rose louder and louder. Someone banged on their door and thrust it open.

"You won't believe it, girls. Hitler has just killed himself. The war is all but over!" A young man left the door open as he continued down the hall with his astonishing message.

Katie and Ruby shrieked and hugged – tears mingling with whoops and hollers. Within moments, Ruby had dressed, and the two rushed down the stairs to be with the jubilant crowd.

CHAPTER TWENTY

"Dear Ciaran,

My darling, there's so much to tell you, but I must, must, MUST start out by saying that at last I've come to my senses. I'll say the words to you in person when next we meet, but my heart is full. I'm the luckiest woman in the world to have your love, and I promise I'm going to show you how I feel about you now and for the rest of our lives.

Are you falling over in a faint? Yes, I said the rest of our lives. I know we belong together. I'm not sure how, but we'll sort it as a couple.

What changed my mind? So many things. Seeing Maggie with her new baby twin girls – yes, more Kingston girls – was thrilling and heartwarming. They've named them Ruth and Rachel, and they are as cute as buttons.

On the train back to base, I suddenly realized that I want that life. A loving husband, a family someday, and building a life together. All of it. I hope that's still what you want, my dearest.

With everything ending, it's just a matter of time until you and I are demobbed. Then we can start our life together, Irish.

This is probably the longest letter I've ever written. But I just couldn't wait to tell you – I'm fair to bursting to see you. Can you sort a 48-hour pass? I'm desperate to hold you and say in person what I only hint at on paper.

Please, please come and see me soon.

All my love,
Katie xx"

* * *

Ciaran read the letter twice, raking his hand through his unruly hair.

"Bloody hell," he shouted. Grabbing his cap, he ran off to beg his CO for leave.

* * *

"Why do you reckon Hitler married Eva Braun before they took those cyanide pills?" Tillie asked her husband, as they passed through the gates of the London Zoo. As a wounded serviceman, they gave Trevor free entry.

It was a beautiful May morning, warm air pushing out the last remnants of a cool spring. Birds sang and the air was alive with promise.

"Maybe he vowed to wed her after the war? He claimed to be a Catholic, so he thought he'd make an honest woman of her before meeting his maker? Who knows what went on in his twisted mind." Trevor held onto Tillie's arm as Jamie scampered in front of them.

"It's hard to imagine he had a romantic turn of heart just at the end when everything was crumbling all around him. He was evil through and through."

"I won't disagree with you, luv. But let's not spoil the day talking about him. Tell me, what do you see?"

Tillie gazed at her handsome husband, staring blankly around him. His eyesight had still not returned, but he was optimistic that any day now, his perfect vision would be miraculously restored. The doctors said this was possible. There was also a chance that partial sight would return. Or he'd remain forever blind. There was no telling.

Tillie tried to be as optimistic as her husband. She longed to look deeply into his eyes and share the intimate love that had made her fall in love with him. She ached to see his joy in his son and how he'd grown. And of course, she wished Trevor could see their new baby, and enjoy every moment with him or her. She fought back a sigh.

"Monkeys, monkeys, Daddy," shouted Jamie, pointing madly at the monkey house.

Tillie grimaced. Each time Trev couldn't see what his son could see knifed him in the gut.

"Let's find some mummies and babies, shall we? Just like Aunt Maggie and her little ones," she said smoothly.

"Mummy and baby," Jamie cooed, enjoying the antics of the monkeys climbing around the monkey house.

"How about we wander over to the reptile cages? Perhaps you can pet a snake, lad." Trevor smiled.

"Snake, snake!" Jamie fell to the ground, mimicking a slithering motion.

"Darling, get up. The ground is still cold," Tillie tried to wrestle him up; no mean feat with a tummy full of baby. She was not quite eight months pregnant, and more than ready for this infant to be born.

"Listen to your mother," Trev chided young Jamie. "Perhaps there is an alligator in with the snakes."

Tillie huffed and puffed as she heaved herself up, struggling against a wriggling toddler.

"Are you alright, luv?" Trevor felt for his son, and expertly took him from his mother's arms, and hung him upside-down, holding his feet in the air.

"Now you're a monkey," he teased. Jamie giggled in delight.

"Could we sit down for a minute, Trev? I am feeling a bit winded. This baby is jumping up and down like a monkey in my stomach."

"Of course, luv. Do you see a bench nearby?"

Tillie led the trio to a nearby spot and sank gratefully onto the wooden bench.

Trev reached for her hand, as they wedged the wiggly two-year-old between them.

"Maybe this outing is too much for you. This baby is really taking it out of you," he said, as he stroked her hand.

"It seems so much harder than the last time, I'll admit that. Running around after Jamie is exhausting, and I can't just lie down for a rest whenever I like." She bit her lip. She hoped Trev didn't take this as a slight because he couldn't mind Jamie the way he used to. He was so touchy these days. "And today is wonderful, Trev. It's a joy to be out of the stuffy house and into the spring air."

"Soon enough we'll meet this young lad or lassie, Tils. What do you reckon we'll get this time?"

Tillie rubbed her back. It ached so much more this time.

"It's hard to see how we could manage another young boy with as much energy as Master Drummond here." She chucked the little boy under the chin. He was absorbed in the sights and sounds of animals all around. "But I suppose we'll sort that out if we have another baby boy. I would love a little girl though, if I'm honest. What a lovely companion for her two big cousin girls. And you?"

She looked at his face in profile. So handsome he still made her heart stop, even in her enlarged form. She missed him staring into her eyes. She longed for it.

"A healthy baby is all I want," he replied. "With everything we've all been through, good health is the most important thing. A boy or girl doesn't matter. Jamie will love either a brother or sister, I'm sure." He tried to smile, but it was rather twisted.

"What about names, luv? We've got to settle on something." Tillie snapped her fingers. "Why don't we each select a name? If it's a girl, it's my pick. If it's a boy, you get to choose." Tillie giggled.

"That could be dangerous. What if you name our beautiful baby daughter Gertrude or Mabel?"

"Those are perfectly respectable names," Tillie objected. "But I was thinking of either Victoria or Susan."

"What about Shirley after your aunt?"

Tillie went still.

"Trev, that is so utterly kind of you. What a brilliant way to honor my Aunt Shirley." She paused. "But maybe it would be too hard for my mum and Uncle Thomas to hear the name every day? Especially if she's getting a proper scolding? Maybe we should save that for a middle name. But I love you for suggesting it." She snuggled into him, causing a squeak from Jamie, who was getting squashed.

"Whatever you like, luv," Trev replied easily. "Victoria Shirley Redwood sounds rather majestic."

"I guess we'll have to wait and see." Trevor heard the teasing tone in her voice.

"Do you have any boy's names in mind?"

"I'm partial to either William or Peter. Could you live with either of those?" Trev found her lips and kissed her.

"They are both quite respectable. It will be down to you when the time comes – if it's a boy."

Trevor smiled and suddenly felt a sharp pain in his head, right behind his eyes. A flash of light passed before him, then he saw stars. He shook his head, trying to clear the dizziness. Then…all dark again.

"Are you okay, darling? Why are you shaking your head?"

"It's naught. I just felt a bit dizzy, is all."

"Penpen, penpen," Jamie shouted. "Me feed penpen."

Tillie laughed.

"Are you up for the penguins, darling?" Tillie heaved herself to her feet.

"Fishies for the penguins, Jamie luv?" Trevor took one of his hands, whilst Tillie took the other, leading the way to the new penguin pool.

"Princesses Elizabeth and Margaret visited this exhibit early in the war. It has open viewing and a revolving fountain. Very modern, I should think."

"It has been getting heaps of attention. You've been wanting to come to the zoo for some time, Tils. I'm glad we made the effort today, aren't you, young James?" Trevor pulled up his son with one arm, whilst Tillie plucked him up on the other side, swinging him between the pair of them.

"It is a lovely day, even if I could be mistaken for a beached whale," Tillie joked, patting her enormous stomach with her free hand.

"Rubbish. Don't talk about my wife like that." He stopped and cocked an ear. "What is all that racket?"

"It's the penguins. It's feeding time, and they are swarming around the keeper. My word, they can squawk."

Jamie started squealing too, seeing dozens of Humboldt penguins in the open viewing area.

"Crikey. Between the sound and the smell, I sure know where I am, luv. Where is the keeper? Can Jamie see what's going on?"

"He's enthralled, Trev. The keeper is just over there with his pail of fish, chucking them out to the penguins. They are fighting like cats and dogs over it. Or should I say, fighting like penguins?" She laughed at her own quip.

"You're a fine strapping lad. Fancy feeding the penguins?" The keeper held out the bucket to Jamie.

"You've got his hand, right Tillie?" She could hear the worry in Trev's voice.

"I do, luv. He's fine. A little shy, but proper intrigued."

For several minutes, the children crowded around the keeper, who let them each choose a fish from the bucket. Black and white flashed as the penguins noisily snatched their dinners from small, eager hands.

"Go on, Jamie. Give him your fish," Tillie encouraged as Jamie hung back.

Some of the bigger children crowded in, and the penguins screeched louder.

Tillie put her hand to her back again. The throb in her lower back was bothering her something awful today. She needed to put her feet up as soon as she got home.

"Mama." she heard Jamie shout. "Mama!"

Tillie pushed forward, realizing with a dreadful thud she couldn't see her son.

"Jamie, Jamie. Where are you?" She frantically searched amongst the children, who had parted to let her through. Where was her baby?

A loud splash caused everyone to turn to the sound in horror.

"A baby has fallen in!" someone howled.

"Mama, Papa!" Jamie's tiny voice screamed in terror.

"Jamie," Tillie pushed towards the edge of the pool.

She felt a large presence thunder past her, jump over the low ledge and plunge into the frigid thigh-high waters. Trevor.

Within seconds, he'd fished out his screaming and soaking wet son, dragged him out of the penguin pool, and carried him to a nearby bench. Tillie raced over to them.

"Jamie, darling. Are you alright?" She pulled him to a sitting position as he sputtered out freezing water, gulping and crying all at once. Once she saw he had stopped choking, she clutched him to her chest, tears threatening to break.

"My baby, my baby. I'm so sorry, Jamie. I just looked away for an instant. Are you alright?" She frantically checked his limbs, assuring herself that his arms, legs, and fingers were intact. Her heart still raced, but as Jamie stopped crying and hiccupped, she slowed down. As he calmed, she turned incredulously to her husband.

"Trevor, how did you do that? How did you find your way to Jamie? How did you…?" She broke off as he gave her a smile that split his face in two. He was looking at her.

"You can see?" she asked tentatively. "You saw him?" She didn't dare breathe.

"Yes," he said quietly. "I don't know what happened, Tils. As soon as I heard him shouting for help, I jumped up. I could hear the direction of his voice, so I started running. I saw stars in front of my eyes, and then some light flashes, and then blurriness. Then everything cleared, and I could see. The rest was just instinct. I ran to Jamie and jumped in to save him. Tillie, my son saved me."

He hugged them both tight, and the crowd burst into spontaneous applause before slowly dispersing.

"Me penpen," a small voice piped up. Slowly and proudly, Jamie pulled a small fish out of his coat pocket.

Tillie and Trevor burst into laughter.

"I should think we're done with feeding the penguins for today, little chap."

Trevor took the fish out of his son's hand and rose slowly to throw it to the approaching penguins.

"I'm so sorry, mate. I didn't see the wee lad put the fish in his pocket. I expect the penguins got excited and pecked at him to get the food. They can be rather aggressive, nipping when they're hungry. And your little boy is just the right height for these little scarpers. Between the penguins and the other children, somehow, he must have gotten pushed in. Is he alright, then?" The short, silver-haired keeper was the picture of contrition.

Trevor waved away his apology.

"He's fine. Really. No harm done. In fact, a lot of good has been done. Cheers mate." Trevor was all smiles.

The wet little family gathered their things and walked towards the entrance.

"Are you steady, luv? Do you need my arm?"

Tillie was still stunned. Trev could see again. How? What had happened? Would it last? Did she have her husband back?

"I don't need any help. I can see just fine. A little blurry, but I can see this lovely Mayday, my beautiful wife, and soggy little boy. Tillie, it's a miracle. Look how Jamie has grown. And you too, I might add. I've missed so much these last months."

Tillie gazed deeply into her husband's eyes.

"It doesn't matter, darling. We've always been here, and now our future is as bright as anything. You'll be able to see the baby when it's born. We can just go on from here."

"Me hippo," Jamie tugged at his father's sleeve, still shivering.

"I'm sorry, young man, but it's time for us to go home, and get you warmed up."

Jamie started wailing.

"Perhaps just an ice cream, luv? We're cutting his entire trip short." Tillie spotted an ice cream vendor.

"I suppose he rather broke off our day," Trevor replied drily. "But I couldn't be happier. Ice cream for everyone."

"And then we need to get you to the doctor's straightaway. This is an enormous breakthrough, Trev. You must get looked at – today."

"Me ice, me ice," chirped Jamie, right on cue.

"Yes, darling. We'll get you a lovely ice cream," Tillie promised.

CHAPTER TWENTY-ONE

"The doctor said that because Jamie was in danger and needed help, it was in some way responsible for Trev's vision coming back. They can't really explain it."

"What a remarkable turnaround," Mum exclaimed, pouring tea for the couple in the Kingston family sitting room. "I just don't believe it. And you had no signs?"

Trevor and Tillie sat side-by-side, gazing at each other like newlyweds.

"I had several episodes of flashing lights and seeing stars, but I didn't dare hope. Then when I heard Jamie in distress, and I knew Tillie couldn't jump in after him, I acted by instinct. I leapt to my feet, running towards the sound of his voice, and by the time I got to the water, I could see. It was murky, and blurry – but I could see my son."

Tillie reached over and pushed away a lock of his black hair.

"I couldn't believe it. I still can't," she said.

"What else did the doctor say?" asked Walter. "Do they think this is permanent?"

"They believe so, sir. I have one-hundred percent restored vision in my right eye, and about eighty percent in my left. Apparently, the eyes will adjust over time so that I will see pretty clearly overall."

"Splendid, Trevor. First rate." Walter smiled, wondering what this would mean for Trevor's firefighting career.

"I don't think I'll be back with the Fire Service after the war, though. Captain said they'd be glad to have me, but I expect it's time for a change. Besides, Tillie thinks it's too dangerous for a man about to be a father of two to fight fires day and night." It was as if Trevor had read Walter's mind.

"Absolutely right," she replied firmly. "There will be plenty of jobs for you, darling."

"Will you take on a desk job with the Fire Service?" Walter asked, tamping down his pipe.

"Perhaps. I'm not sure that's for me. I like to be in the action, not pushing paper around. I could take on training. Or I may leave the service altogether and do something completely different. I have spent a lot of time talking to Micah about the work he's doing with refugees. I like the idea of helping families reunite." He shrugged. "Let's get this war won first. In the meantime, I'll give it all serious thought. In between changing nappies and chasing young Jamie, that is." He beamed.

"And just in time," Tillie countered. "This baby will come before long. And as eager as I am to meet him or her, the idea of having a baby and a two-year-old is rather daunting."

"We're here to help, luv," Alice chimed in. "And Nana Isla is only too keen – it's pretty much all we talk about."

"Ta, Mum. We appreciate all you do to help. But you've got Maggie's two on your hands as well. There's never a dull moment in the Kingston family."

"We like it that way, don't we? I can't wait until Katie and Kenny are home. I want the house bustling and busy like the old days," sighed Alice.

But they all knew it would never be the same. They were five years older, each with their own scars from all they'd seen since 1939. And some people from around the table six years ago would never come home again. Tillie's first fiancé Colin, Cousin Geoffrey, dear Shirley, and so many other friends and neighbors who had lost their lives in bombings, explosions, and aftermath catastrophes.

And for the ones who had survived, they weren't without the marks of war – either inside or out. Years of fear, worry, rationing, waiting, and general disquiet had aged people prematurely, caused nervous health conditions, and left them weary and in varying degrees of discontentment.

Thanks to prolonged rationing, everyone in the Kingston family had lost weight, like many of the British people. There had been valid concerns that England would be starved out by German U-boats bombing the food supply. More and more foods had been rationed as war waged on. The Dig for Victory campaign had been a brilliant success in growing vegetables and precious fruits. Although the general population was heartily sick of the food on offer, no one had starved. Day and night dreams of unlimited butter, cream, sugar, fresh fruit, and even tea kept everyone going.

London looked quite shabby, but rebuilding carried on every day. With barrage balloons and sandbags disappearing, it was looking like dear old London again. The dreaded air raid siren system had been dismantled. Hopeful signs were everywhere.

"I can't wait for the good new days." Tillie sighed, shifting to find a comfortable position. "I hope this baby turns up before the weather gets too hot."

"Soon enough, darling," Mum soothed.

"It's warm for May, isn't it?" Tillie fanned herself. "I'm meant to pop over to Maggie's for tea and a peek at the twins. I'm not sure I'm up to it, if I'm honest."

"I'll take you over, darling. I'd like a word with Micah about these horrific reports from the camps and the inhumane treatment that's gone on there. It must be ghastly for him to think of his parents dying under those conditions."

They all fell silent for a moment, thinking of dear Sam and Ruth Goldbach, deported to Auschwitz and mistreated until death by starvation, disease, or both.

"It's almost unthinkable," Mum said.

"And that bastard Hitler will never pay for his heinous crimes," Walter hissed.

"Walter, language," Mum exclaimed.

"We're all adults here, Alice. And now we know what that monster has done."

"What an evil brute he was," Tillie agreed. "But others will pay – those that are still left." She checked her watch. "Crikey, I'd best be getting to Maggie's. I suppose she could use a bit of adult company."

"I'll watch Jamie if you two want to go on your own. That will make it easier on you, luv," Mum offered.

"That would be brilliant, Mum. Are you sure?"

"Of course, I'll give him his tea and put him down for a n-a-p," she said in a low voice. Luckily, Jamie hadn't heard and was happily playing at his dad's feet. "He's no bother."

Tillie laughed. "Spoken like a doting granny. Ta, Mum. We'll see you later."

In practically no time, Trev and Tillie were knocking at Micah's and Maggie's door.

Micah answered, a wailing baby in his arms. He grinned at the sight of the couple.

"How wonderful of you to come by. Trevor, you really are looking like your old self." He shifted the baby to his other arm to shake Trev's hand.

"Getting there, mate. Still a tad wobbly on my feet, but on the mend."

"Come in. Come in. Maggie is feeding Ruth. I'm trying to put this one down, but she's having none of it." Despite the crying infant, Micah was calm.

"Shall I have a go?" Trev asked. "I was rather good at rocking and off-key lullabies with Jamie. I need to get back into practice, pronto."

Micah handed Rachel over and led the pair to the sitting room. Their tidy living space was now overrun with baby gear times two. Nappies, blankets, and toys were strewn about the room. A basket of unfolded baby clothes sat precariously on the edge of a chair.

"Sit, please. Here, let me move that basket. Sorry about the mess. I can't believe how much two tiny human beings can produce. Tillie, how are you getting on?" He scooped it up and placed it on a nearby table.

"I'm alright." Her face was flushed. "I'm feeling as if I have twins in here, but the doctor assures me it's just one. A rather big one, I imagine." She sunk gratefully into the chair. "Shall I help with the folding?" She half-heartedly lifted a hand.

"No, leave it. I'll sort it later. Ah Trevor, you are a marvel. She's asleep. Bless you."

Trevor had been rocking and cooing at little Rachel. The cries had subsided to whimpers, and then nothing.

"I'll take her and check on my other two girls. It never ends round here." Micah disappeared with the baby into the bedroom.

"Shall I put on the kettle? I'm desperate for a cup of tea." Tillie half-rose.

"I'll do it," Trev offered. Since he'd gotten his sight back, he was helpfulness itself.

Tillie nodded. She was getting so tired all the time now.

"Darling," Maggie exclaimed as she came into the room. "I've just put Ruth down, so we may just have about fifteen minutes before one of them wakes up." She looked tired, but content. "How did Mum do it? What a load of work they are."

"I'm making tea, is that alright?" Trev called from the kitchen, as Micah rejoined the group.

"Yes, please," Maggie said. "There's half a custard pie left from your mum's visit. Could you fetch that as well, Trev?"

"Is this really just the four of us with no children crying or needing to be picked up?" Tillie asked, as the foursome looked at each in amazement.

"For now. Don't disturb the quiet though. No telling how long it will last." They all laughed – but softly.

Over tea and pie, they exchanged pleasantries, baby talk, and of course best wishes to Trev on his eyesight returning. Inevitably, the talk turned to war.

"It's near enough to being over. Strangely, it seems more nerve-wracking just waiting for the final announcement than living through the Blitz," Tillie complained.

"Surely not that worrying, but yes, I know what you mean," Maggie replied, sipping her tea. "When do you think Churchill will officially declare the end?"

"I should think a matter of days now. Germany is surrounded, and there's no hope of a rally."

"A few years ago, I should have thought we'd all be out there on the streets celebrating when the time comes. But we're in no condition to be roaring about Piccadilly Circus or Trafalgar Square, are we Tillie?" Maggie turned to her sister.

"No, I should think not. You with two tiny babies to look after, and me with this little one just about here. We'll have to leave the street parties to the younger generation." Tillie patted her sister's hand. Both knew they were happy just where they were.

"Hey, speak for yourself, Tils," argued Trevor. "I may just storm Buckingham Palace for a glimpse of the King and Queen."

"Alright, luv." Tillie shifted in her seat. "Just say hello for me, would you?"

"I suppose the prisoners of war will soon be released." Micah turned the talk to more serious avenues. "We'll be there to greet as many as we can and help them re-settle. I can only imagine how ghastly their condition may be. From what we've seen in Germany, the war horrors just keep on appearing. I'm sure you've heard the BBC reports and seen the newsreels at the cinema." His smile had turned grim.

"We have, and it's beyond belief. We're so sorry to hear what's been done to the scores of Jewish people, and so many others in these death camps, Micah," Trev said sadly.

"How can humans treat their fellow men, women, and children so abominably? It overwhelms me to think of it."

"And to think that for the last six years, no one knew what was going on." Tillie shook her head.

"Oh, people knew," Micah said shortly. "The British government knew. Most likely for at least the last several years. From my experience in France, I can tell you that the Vichy government knew what the Nazis were doing – the roundups, ghettos, deportations, and starvation camps."

"What about the German people?" Tillie whispered. "Surely they were aware of what was going on right beneath their noses?"

Micah snorted.

"Of course they were aware. It was happening all around them. And Hitler brazenly broadcast his antisemitic leanings in all his propaganda speeches. It's been an open secret since the early stages of war. Did the average German know about mass shootings and the gas chambers?" Micah shrugged. "Undoubtedly, they saw Jews cast out of homes and businesses, spat on in the streets, and placed in squalid ghettos. But did they know of Bergen-Belsen? Or Dachau? Or Auschwitz? It's impossible to know for certain."

"If they understood what was going on, how could they live with themselves – condoning mass murder?" Tillie's eyes were wide.

"Survival, I expect," Micah said. "When you see what your leaders are doing to persecute innocent people, you reckon it might be you next. So, you shut your doors, close your eyes, and look after your own interests."

"Ghastly," Tillie said, with tears in her eyes. "Have you heard they have given it a name? They're calling it the Holocaust."

"Total destruction, slaughter on a mass scale," Micah translated dully.

"Micah, we can only say again how very sorry we are that your parents were killed in such a dreadful way. It must be difficult to bear."

All eyes turned to the serious young man who had lost so much in this war.

"It is, Tillie, and thank you. I can't help but think how pleased they would have been with their two granddaughters. Mama would already try to fatten them up, and Papa would tell stories of their bright futures."

There was no answer to this.

"How is our Hannah reacting to these awful reports? She was so young to lose her parents and endured so much herself." Tillie considered Hannah a sister and would do anything to ease the pain of this little family.

"As best as can be expected. It brings everything back, you see. The photographs and stories in the papers. But our parents would want us to carry on, and we have so much to be grateful for, don't we, little one?" Micah turned to Maggie.

"We do, darling, and we will always keep Bubbe and Zayde alive for Ruth and Rachel."

"More tea?" asked Tillie inadequately. It was the British answer to any circumstance.

It broke the tension.

"I'll get it," Micah jumped up, glad for the distraction. He picked up the brown teapot and hurried to the kitchen. Trevor followed him.

"Is he alright, luv?" Tillie asked her twin.

"He will be. But I don't know how long it will take. Our two little moppets are helping immeasurably."

The sisters lapsed into safer talk about baby schedules, how to get more sleep, and what to do about diaper rash.

In the kitchen, Trevor inquired after Micah's work, trying to understand what needed to be done for the Jewish refugees arriving in England with nothing but the shabby clothes on their backs, and haunted looks in their eyes.

***

With Berlin surrounded, and after Adolf Hitler's suicide at the end of April, his named successor, Grand Admiral Karl Dönitz, assumed command. During his brief spell as Germany's president, Dönitz negotiated an end to the war with the Allies – whilst seeking to save as many Germans as possible from falling into Soviet hands.

Official news confirmed that der Fuhrer and his bride committed suicide together – Eva Braun by taking a cyanide capsule, and Hitler by a shot to the head. As he had ordered, both bodies were moved upstairs to the garden, doused with petrol and burned. Where the ashes were taken, was anyone's guess.

CHAPTER TWENTY-TWO
May 7, 1945

"This tension is making me jumpy," Ruby fiddled with the tiny lamp, book, and pen on her nightstand.

"Why hasn't there been an announcement yet?" Katie paced the small cabin, peering out of the window as if Churchill himself were striding down the street to personally deliver the news. "Is it time to celebrate or not? Will we have a national holiday?"

These questions were on the lips of every Briton. They'd been waiting for days for the last word.

For all intents and purposes, the war in Europe was over. The last Italian troops had surrendered at the end of April, followed by Hitler's suicide. The Red Army had surrounded Berlin, with two weeks of desperate but futile fighting by German defenders, many of them old men and young boys, as Soviet forces overran the city.

By May 2nd, over 300,000 Berliners and 80,000 Red Army soldiers lay dead amongst the ruins.

But the announcement of the end of the war had not happened. Everyone knew it was imminent, but the waiting made them restless.

Katie was doubly fretful. She'd had no answer to her heartfelt letter to Ciaran, and questioned whether she should have sent it. The post was unreliable at best, so she tried to console herself that perhaps his response had been delayed. Yet he was just a short distance from London – surely the post was trustworthy? She chewed her lip and pushed back her curls. Or had he received it and changed his mind about her? Had she come on too strong? Bollocks, it was driving her near mad.

"Let's go for a walk," Ruby tossed Katie her hat. "I'm going dotty waiting in here. And sitting around the wireless for hours with everyone downstairs doesn't suit me either."

"Righto. You're on."

Slipping on her jacket, and swiftly doing up the double-row of buttons, Katie followed Ruby out of their cabin and down the stairs.

"Any news?" called Katie to the crowd assembled around the wireless. Pints were flowing, but the unsmiling faces told the story. More waiting.

"Not yet. I'm sure you'll hear it on the streets."

The girls nodded and strode out into the May sunshine. It was warm, but partly cloudy, the sun bursting through at intervals.

"How soon do you think we'll be demobbed?" Ruby asked. No point in debating when the news would break.

"I heard that the married Wrens will be released first. Which makes sense. As for us, the work has slowed down considerably, so perhaps not too long?" Katie hoped this was true. She was impatient to start her life with Ciaran, and have her family all together again.

"Maybe I should marry that handsome Yank and get out of the Navy that much quicker," teased Ruby.

"Which one?" kidded Katie. "You have 'em queued up like sausages on the cooker."

"Ouch." Ruby gave Katie a gentle shove. "You know I'm soft on Dan from Oklahoma. We've been seeing each other for a few months now."

"I know, luv. I'm just hoping you don't marry him and move to America. I'm a selfish cow."

"Fancy the two of us. We may end up as farmer's wives. Who would have dreamed that?"

"Suits me to the ground. No pun intended," laughed Katie.

They strolled round the streets and returned to the pub in time for a late dinner. As they entered, they could feel the excitement of the throng of locals.

"It's about time for the seven o'clock news. Gather round, girls. Perhaps this is it."

"You said that at three, then five, Timmy."

"Shhh…there's a news flash," shouted another patron.

"This is the BBC. We interrupt our scheduled programming to announce that tomorrow, May 8, 1945, will be Victory in Europe Day. It is to be a national holiday. Prime Minister Winston Churchill will broadcast a special speech tomorrow."

A tremendous cheer erupted in the pub. Every man and woman turned to hug the person closest to them. Tears of joy wet the faces of many. Shouts of God Save the King, and Bless the Allies rang out. Someone raced to the piano and played There Will Always Be an England, whilst people gathered round and sang along. Beer flowed freely, courtesy of the pub owner. From somewhere, bottles of gin and rum were produced and shared about.

Mayhem erupted in the streets. People couldn't contain themselves and spilled out into the warm May night, dancing and laughing by the moonlight.

"Shouldn't we wait for the official broadcast tomorrow?" Katie asked Ruby as they were pulled into the mass of people crowding Portsmouth.

"We'll celebrate now, and until tomorrow, and onwards. We've done it, darling. We've won the war!"

And they did. Into the wee hours of the night, Katie and Ruby and most of Portsmouth danced, and drank, and congratulated each other. Dizzy and exhausted, the two girls fell into bed at four a.m., still half-dressed.

At 7:00 a.m., someone knocked loudly on the door.

"P.O. Kingston, you have a visitor. I wouldn't normally let 'im in, but seeing as how it's V-E Day, I thought you wouldn't mind."

Katie rubbed her bleary eyes, remembered why she had chills of excitement still running through her, and rushed to open the door. Was it possible? Could it be…?

"Irish!" She launched herself into his arms.

"Mavourneen, my darling. I got here as soon as I could get leave, and even so, I must be back tomorrow, but I had to see you."

Katie rained kisses all over his face. His beautiful face. *The face I want to look at forever.*

"You're here. You're here. And we won. A complete and utter German surrender. It's over, darling. The war is finally done."

"Can't a girl get some sleep?" Ruby leaned up on an elbow and grinned at the couple embracing in the doorway.

"Not today, Ruby. Not today. Come on, girls. We don't want to miss a minute."

Sending him downstairs for tea, the girls quickly washed and dressed before meeting him.

"It's Victory in Europe Day." Party makers from the night before were still at it. Home and business owners had hung out bunting and Union Jacks, setting up for the biggest street party in history. Long tables and cloths were being sorted by gleeful mums and grannies. The mood was electric. Instruments of all kinds had materialized, and they heard music throughout the streets. Church bells rang out for the first time in close to six years.

Ciaran, Katie and Ruby joined the revelers, and danced through the streets, with no particular destination in mind. Dressed in uniform, they were hugged and thanked by all and sundry for their service in the glorious victory. Processions formed out of nowhere, people waving flags or whirling football rattles – anything that made a noise – all marching in step with linked arms or doing the Lambeth Walk.

Albeit beer and limited spirits were shared round, the supply was not plentiful, so no one got soused or out of hand.

At three o'clock, Prime Minister Churchill broadcast his victory speech:

"My dear friends, this is your hour. This is not the victory of a party or of any class. It's a victory of the great British nation as a whole. We were the first, in this ancient island, to draw the sword against tyranny. After a while, we were left all alone against the most tremendous military power that has been seen. We were all alone for a whole year…

The lights went out, and the bombs came down. But every man, woman and child in the country had no thought of quitting the struggle. London can take it. So, we came back after long months from the jaws of death, out of the mouth of hell…

Now we have emerged from one deadly struggle. A terrible foe has been cast on the ground and awaits our judgment and our mercy.

But there is another foe who occupies large portions of the British Empire, a foe stained with cruelty and greed: the Japanese. I rejoice we can all take a night off today and another day tomorrow…

Tomorrow, we must begin the task of rebuilding our hearth and homes, doing our utmost to make this country a land in which all have a chance…

We will go hand in hand with our allies. Even if it is a hard struggle, we will not be the ones who will fail. God Save the King."

The noise was deafening as people cheered for Winnie and the King. Ciaran kissed Katie hard on the mouth.

"We need to talk," he shouted over the din.

She nodded as they left the crowd and ducked down a side street. Ruby's beau Dan had turned up, and somehow the pair had been separated from Ciaran and Katie. No matter, they would all meet up later.

Breathless, Ciaran pulled Katie into a doorway as a soft rain fell.

"I received your letter," he said without preamble. "I couldn't believe my eyes. Did you mean it?" Green eyes bored into brown. Ciaran almost shook her by the shoulders.

"Yes, yes, a thousand times, yes." She pulled him closer and kissed him deeply.

He pulled back.

"You want to be with me? Move to Ireland? Live on the farm with me and Da and Ma? You'll be me wife?" He looked hopeful and terrified at the same time.

"Yes, my darling Irishman. I'm so sorry it took me so long to see what is right in front of me. The man I love, who has been so patient. The one I want to spend the rest of my life with." Her smile dazzled. "I love you, Ciaran McElroy."

He picked her up and whooped.

"This is the grandest day of me life." He kissed her again. "We will make plans soon, my mavourneen. A promise made on V-E Day is a promise for life, mind. For now, let's make merry with the rest of England." He grabbed her hand, and they joined a group of uniformed men and women heading for the port.

Clubbing together precious rations, massive street parties offered food and drink to all who came near. Rationing might still be on, and it could well mean stretching what was left till the end of the week, but no one cared.

"Katie, is that you?" A familiar voice shouted down the lane.

"Edi." Katie turned and greeted her old chum from Cape Le Ferne. "How on earth are you here?"

"I'm stationed nearby and stole out for a few hours to meet my fiancé, Archie." She presented a solid Scotsman.

They stopped by a street party and ate a tiny slice of sponge cake and gulped tea offered by a beaming shop owner. The gang thronged towards a bonfire. It was getting dark, and the streets were lit up as if it were daytime – for the first time in years.

"Did you hear the King's speech?" asked Edi as the glow from the bonfires illuminated the dancers and revellers.

"Yes, he thanked us all – those who bore arms so valiantly on land and sea, or in the air. Bloody brilliant." Katie had been smiling so much her face hurt.

"Righto. He even mentioned us service women: 'You have fought, striven, and endured to your utmost,'" Edi repeated. "Our King knows what we've done. Smashing."

The festivities continued on into the night and early hours of the next day. Those scheduled for watch knew they'd be reporting with no sleep, yet full hearts.

***

In London and indeed across the United Kingdom, the same celebrations carried on. There was a sea of red, white, and blue clothing, hats, flags, and signs, as Londoners showed their patriotism. Hyde Park, Piccadilly Circus, and Trafalgar Square heaved with a mass of humanity. Congo lines broke out. Any height that could be scaled for a bird's-eye view, was – be it pole, statue, or rooftop.

People flooded Buckingham Palace throughout the day and night, shouting "We Want the King" over and over again.

The royal family obliged – waving and smiling at the crowds from the balcony no fewer than seven times. Princess Elizabeth looked smashing in her ATS uniform, coupling with her father, the King in his naval blue. Even the Prime Minister joined at one point, causing the amassed horde to go into a frenzy.

At #40 Longridge Road, it was no less mayhem. Maggie and Micah had come with the twins, who contributed their own loud offerings for the day. Isla Drummond and Uncle Thomas joined the party. Trevor hoisted young Jamie on his shoulders to shout, Hooray for the King. Tillie waved her flag from her spot on the couch.

Mum and Pops had put out as much of a spread as they could muster. Long-hoarded wine was poured with many toasts to the King, the Prime Minister, the country, and the family not there.

"What a magnificent day, my dear. As the King said, this is a genuine act of thanksgiving. I'm so grateful for you, the children, and all this." Walter nodded towards the sitting room full of loved ones, young and old, in various stages of joy, disbelief, or with the children – exhaustion.

"Somehow, we've done it, luv. We've made it through this wretched storm. It's all calm waters ahead, isn't it?" Alice's eyes pleaded with her husband.

He gave her a rare public kiss on the cheek and took both her hands in his.

"It will be, Alice. And I'm proper proud of how you've handled all the adversity and awfulness of these last years. You've been through so much and have survived. I know it hasn't been easy." The unspoken loss of Shirley wafted between them, but today was all about merriment and elation. And hopes for the future.

"Mum, do you think Faye will be discharged soon and come back to keep house for us?" Tillie asked from across the room. "I miss her teacakes and sticky toffee pudding," she groaned, rubbing her bulging tummy.

"And her roast beef, mashed potatoes with butter dripping everywhere, Yorkshire pudding, and thick, thick gravy," added Maggie, soothing a fretful baby.

"And her home-baked scones, clotted cream, and fresh blackberry jam," Walter said reverently.

"Walter, don't you like my cooking?" Alice asked, feigning offense.

"You've done your best, dear." Walter patted her hand diplomatically.

They all broke into laughter until Maggie shushed them. Rachel had just fallen asleep in her arms.

"I, for one, think this Faye is a mythical creature. I've never set eyes on this magical lady," Trevor put in, pulling Jamie back from climbing the corner cabinet.

"Oh, she's real," confirmed Micah. "I've tasted her heavenly delights many times, and can vouch for her magic first-hand."

"She's written from time to time," Alice said. "I don't know if she fancies coming to work for someone else after the war. I've assured her we would welcome her with open arms, but I can tell she's hesitant. This war has proven women can be independent and forge fresh paths for themselves. If she decides she doesn't want to come back to Number 40, we'll have to accept that and wish her well."

They all nodded, seeing visions of treacle tarts and madeira cakes fly out the window.

"Hey, this is not a time for gloom. Aren't we meant to be celebrating?" Uncle Thomas boomed from near the window. "I've brought a bottle of brandy that I've been saving for today. Shall I uncork it?"

"Yes, please," squealed Isla Drummond. "I'll fetch the glasses."

"I'm going to put this squirmer to bed so we can have a proper knees-up." Trevor hoisted a wailing toddler to his shoulders.

And they did. Maggie put the twins to sleep in Mum and Dad's room. Micah played the piano, and they sang the poignant war songs that had gotten them through the worst of it all.

CHAPTER TWENTY-THREE

June 1945

"Dear Katie,

Isn't it a glorious time to be alive? Our dreams have come true, and our beloved Allies have vanquished the vile Nazis. I hope you let your hair down and reveled in Portsmouth with the same zeal that we did in London. I would have loved to have seen it all firsthand at Buckingham Palace, but I could scarcely leave the couch. What fun the three Kingston girls could have had if we'd been together.

I know Pops sent you a telegram, but I've been remiss in giving you all the news about our new baby girl. It's been rather busy, sis. She didn't quite make it to Maggie and my birthdays on the 14th. She arrived in a flurry on the 12th. I started having pains at midnight, and by 6:00 a.m., she was here. Katie. It was so wonderful that Trev's eyesight came back in time to see his new baby daughter. Watching him cradle our tiny, sweet girl filled my heart with such love, I can't even tell you.

She has dark hair and looks just like her big brother, Jamie. That little rascal isn't quite sure if he likes his little sister – he sniffs around her as if she's a dog. Mum assures me he will grow to love her in time, and this is all perfectly normal.

We've decided to call her Victoria Shirley. She was born so close to VE-Day and we were all so euphoric that it just seemed like the right name. No one will ever forget our little victory girl.

Mum said you might pop by on your way to visit Ciaran's family in Ireland. We'd love to see you and wee Victoria needs to meet her auntie. The house is madness, but I'm sure you won't mind.

I must dash. I just heard a crash, which means Jamie is up to something, and it's close on time for Victoria's feed.

*Loads of love,
Tillie xx"*

Katie smiled, picturing Tillie's turmoil. Isla would surely stop by to lend a hand with Jamie, the laundry, and so on. It seemed it was all babies, babies, babies in the Kingston households these days. Mum was probably nearly as knackered as Tillie. She put the letter down.

"What time is your train, Queenie?" Ruby asked sleepily, a lump in the other bed.

"Half-past six. Sorry, I didn't mean to wake you," Katie whispered.

"No bother. I'm due on watch this morning," Ruby yawned, arching her back. "Are you nervy about meeting Ciaran's parents?"

"A little. I hope they like me. I could end up living with them, in the event." She raised an eyebrow, as she folded away her letter, and put her sponge bag into her carryall.

"Four people in a small farmhouse together? That sounds like rather a squash." Ruby was unconvinced.

"I'll see when I get there, I suppose. Besides, wherever Ciaran lives is where I want to be. So, I'll just have to learn to like it."

"If you say so, Katie. I'll be eager for the full brief." She threw her feet over the edge of the bed. "I suppose I might as well get a start on the day."

"Ta ra, then, Ruby. I'll see you in five days. Won't it be marvellous not to have to cram our private lives into twenty-four or forty-eight-hour chunks? Even five days feels like a total luxury. What will we do with all that time?"

"I can't wait to find out. Behave yourself, luv."

Katie winked, spun on her heels, and rushed out of the cabin, saying nothing.

* * *

After a whistle stop in London where Katie met her newest niece, brought gifts for the twins, and kissed babies, Katie met up with Ciaran, who had taken the train from Bletchley Park to Euston Station.

"We've got a journey ahead of us, Katie. A train to Liverpool, ferry to Dublin, then, if we're lucky – the number 31 bus to Howth. I told Da not to meet us. I don't want him making the trip, and waiting for uncertain transport."

They'd greeted each other with a warm embrace and a long kiss. People seemed much more willing to show affection in public as the war had waged on. It was all part and parcel of the live for today mindset of so many Britons. On V-E Day, it seemed as if everyone was kissing anyone in sight, albeit Katie didn't fancy the idea of Ciaran kissing any other girls.

"Well, let's shove off then, Irish." She grinned up at him.

He kissed her nose, picked up her holdall, and they moved with the crowd to the stairs.

After a train, ferry, bus and half a mile on shank's pony, it was near nine o'clock when Ciaran and Katie approached the farm gate. The sun was setting, and the orange sky lit their way down the dirt road to the large white stone farmhouse. Katie could just make out the thatched roof, adjacent barn, and several outbuildings.

Having tidied up at the bus station, Katie still felt woefully unprepared to meet her future husband's family. She halted as the house loomed nearer.

"Will I do?" She turned to Ciaran; her brown eyes filled with questions. For a moment, her old insecurities reared up, and she wished it were one of her older, more confident sisters facing the new family.

Ciaran crushed her fear straightaway.

"Katie Kingston, give yourself a shake. You are the woman I love. That will be enough for Ma and Da – even if you were a snaggle-toothed leprechaun. Which you are not. Your natural warmth and kind heart will melt them as it did me, mavourneen." He kissed her. "Better?" Their eyes locked.

"Better, Irish." She took a deep breath and turned to the front door, which was opening. A small couple appeared.

"Ma, Da." Ciaran pulled her hand, and they approached the smiling pair.

"*Mo mhac*," Ciaran's mum murmured over and over, as she clutched her son tightly.

"Don't crush the boy." Ciaran's da gently pulled his wife away. "Welcome home, me son." He gave him a tentative handshake. "How is your hand mending?"

Ciaran easily flexed it.

"Just grand. It's a little stiff at times, but the docs have given me the all-clear for farm duties." He turned to bring Katie forward.

"Da, Ma – this is Katie, the most beautiful girl in England," he presented her with a flourish.

"Aye, a lovely *cailín*, welcome, Katie. An Irish name and all." She kissed Katie on one cheek.

"It's so nice to meet you, Mrs McElroy. And you too, sir." She shook his hand formally.

"She's a Katherine, not a Kathleen, Ma. She's British, not from the green isle," Ciaran corrected softly.

"Come on in, then. Don't stop here on the doorstep," Mrs McElroy ushered the pair into the kitchen. "Yourselves must be near starving."

Within minutes, the couple had washed and were sitting at a worn oak table with tea in their hands, whilst Mrs McElroy served up some Irish stew.

"It's a bit of a warm night for stew, but it's Ciaran's favorite. He always asks for it."

Ciaran's mum was even tinier than Katie herself. An obvious limp didn't slow down her quick motions. Katie could see where Ciaran had gotten his flashing green eyes. Albeit her hair was mostly grey, Katie saw the faded streaks of auburn that she'd passed on to her son.

"It's delicious, Ma." He broke off a piece of soda bread.

"You must be tired after your long journey, Katie." Mr McElroy turned to the young woman eagerly spooning the stew.

"A bit," she admitted. "I'm that eager to go round the farm, but I suppose that will have to wait until tomorrow. Night has fallen swiftly."

"Aye, that's the Irish sky for you," Mr McElroy pushed back. "One minute you're looking at a grand sunset, the next, darkness has fallen."

Katie tried not to slurp the hearty soup. They'd barely eaten all day, and the soft potatoes, carrots, and bits of meat went down a treat.

"Thank you so much for the stew, Mrs McElroy. I have eaten nothing like it since before the war."

"Thank you, dear. That's one of the few advantages of having a farm. Some food is plentiful, and we share across our neighbors. Tea on the ration is a hardship, though," she sighed.

"I couldn't agree more, Mrs McElroy. You should see the stuff that passes for tea on base." Katie smiled, but was drooping.

"Do you fancy a bit of barmbrack before settling in?" Mrs McElroy held the flowered dinner plate aloft.

"Ma, you know you don't need to ask." Ciaran chuckled, as he swept away the bowls. "Have you ever had it, mavourneen?"

"No, but I never say no to afters." She waited expectantly. And she wasn't disappointed. The bread baked with raisins, sultanas, and glacé cherries, lightly coated with butter melted in her mouth. Maybe life on a farm wasn't without its pluses.

"Sure, and it's not the same without a proper smear of butter, but even though we churn it ourselves, most of our butter goes to market," Mrs McElroy tutted.

"Thank you for a lovely dinner." Katie was tempted to lick her dish.

"Would you like another piece?" Ciaran's mum offered.

Katie was tempted, but she supposed the family had made a great effort to put on such a spread.

"I couldn't eat another thing," she refused. "I must confess I'm not much of a cook, but perhaps you could show me how to make the barmbrack." Her tongue tripped over the unfamiliar name. "And Ciaran's other favorites."

"Aye, it will be a pleasure. Now, let's get yourself sorted for the night. Morning comes early at the farm."

Katie helped to clear, whilst Ciaran's mum explained the sleeping arrangements.

"We've changed the parlor into our bedroom. Easier for me with no stairs. Katie, you'll be in our old room upstairs, and Ciaran – of course, you have your own. You'll find it simple, but clean," Mrs McElroy defended.

"I'm sure it's lovely. Thank you for going to so much trouble for me." Katie was knackered and couldn't wait for her head to hit the pillow.

"No bother at all. Ciaran, show her to her room, say your goodnights, and leave our guest to it, and all." She couldn't have been less tactful.

"I'll show herself the outside facilities, and her room, Ma. And that's it." Ciaran winked at Katie.

After a hasty tour, Katie kissed him goodnight, firmly closing her door with him on the other side.

"Goodnight, Ciaran," she announced, as the door shut. "See you in the morning,"

Katie was that tired that she could hardly give her face a swipe with the flannel, shrug out of her clothes, and slide into cotton pajamas. The night had cooled, and a soft breeze wafted through the open window. She climbed into bed and pulled the light coverlet up to her chin. Rolling over, she inhaled the country air and fell into a deep sleep.

The rooster crowing woke her early. It was still mostly dark, with streaks of sun racing across the sky. She stretched, letting the aroma of toast and frying eggs fill her nostrils. And was that bacon she smelled? It couldn't be. Throwing back the coverlet, she made her bed and dressed in casual civvies; wide-legged trousers, a red cotton blouse, and black plimsolls. Washing up in the basin on a corner table, she ran a comb through her tangled curls, tied a turban atop her head, and glanced at herself in the small mirror above the washbasin.

Could I pass for a land girl? Not a chance. But I'm ready for my first day on the farm.

Running lightly down the stairs, she came into the kitchen to see Ciaran flipping an egg at the aga, and his mum pouring water from a kettle into a well-worn brown teapot.

"Good morning, everyone. I hope I'm not late," she said.

Ciaran turned to face her, spatula in hand.

"Just in time. Breakfast is about ready, and Da is expected any minute after the morning feed. I hope yourself slept well?" he asked.

"Like a log, Irish. Good morning, Mrs McElroy. Everything smells delicious. How can I help? I'm hopeless at cooking, but I'm a dab hand at toast buttering and setting the table."

"Good morning, dear." Ciaran's mum handed her a stack of crockery. "It's plain fare, but what we need to put in a good day's work."

Katie took the dishes from Mrs McElroy's trembling hands and laid out four places on the scarred wooden table.

"Is there a cuppa going?" Mr McElroy came through the back door, letting in the early morning sun. He took off his hat, washed his hands at the sink pump, and sat down at the head of the table. The tea was already steaming at his place as Ciaran served the eggs.

"Good morning, sir. Have I missed all the morning chores?" Oh bollocks, she was off to a poor start.

"The animals have their own internal clock, which can't be ignored, so I have fed them. But sure, and there's plenty of work to be done, Katie. Hay needs stacking in the barn, and I've left the eggs for you to collect. Son, I'd like you to take a look at the tractor – it's smoking again." He spooned in big mouthfuls of egg and dipped the toast into the yolks. "Oh, and I expect you'd not say no to a peep at the new piglets." Beneath his bushy eyebrows, his eyes twinkled.

Katie squealed as she tucked into her own breakfast, including heavenly bacon.

"Oh, that sounds splendid, Mr McElroy. I've never seen real piglets before." She finished her plate, resisted the urge to ask for seconds, and cleared away.

"Away with you, and all," shooed Ciaran's mum. "I know me son is keen to show you the farm. I can manage this lot."

"Ta, ma. We'll bring back the eggs. You rest. Katie and I have loads to get on with." He was already up from the table, and putting on his hat.

Katie scrambled to catch up with him.

"Gosh, life on a farm is rather demanding," she trailed after him. "Thank you for a tasty breakfast, Mrs McElroy." Katie's head was spinning with how quickly breakfast had been cooked, eaten, and cleared away. No time to waste.

It was a busy day. Ciaran burst with pride, showing her around, introducing her to Keegan, the chickens, and the new piglets.

After stopping for a ploughman's lunch, they were hard at it again all afternoon. Many jobs had gone wanting in Ciaran's absence. Mr McElroy had done his best, but the place was slightly run down, and needed the attention of the younger man.

Walking back to the farmhouse for supper, Ciaran held Katie's hand. She was blissfully exhausted.

"I'm that impressed with you, mavourneen. You've gotten stuck in all day. And you didn't seem to mind. I'm proud of you." He squeezed her shoulder.

"Did you see how Keegan fancied me, Irish? He ate that carrot right out of my hand. You said he was feisty. And I only broke one egg collecting them. That's not too rubbish, is it?" Katie realized she was babbling, but her excitement overflowed. She had taken to the animals straightaway, picking up wriggling piglets and nuzzling Keegan.

"And you never told me you had an adorable cat named Chester," she scolded good-naturedly.

"He's a scruffer – a barn cat whose job is to keep the mice and rats away. But I'm glad yourself is not running down the lane, screaming for London, and all."

"I even surprised myself, Irish," she replied. "I wasn't all that fond of forking the hay, but I suppose it's all part of the job. My shoulders are aching, I won't deny it."

Ciaran laughed.

"Just wait till tomorrow. Everything will be aching. And I expect you'll have a blister or two. But it's honest work, Katie. And I'm that pleased that you will consider taking it all on."

Katie stopped and pulled him close.

"I love you. I see your mark all over this land. I want to be a part of it. And your family needs you."

"I love you too, my girl. It's a hard life, but farming is respectable, and brings a grand sense of satisfaction. You'll be part of it, too."

He hugged her close as the sun faded into the distance.

CHAPTER TWENTY-FOUR

The next morning, Katie wasn't so sure. Her back and arms ached, and she didn't dare stand up to test the pain in her calves and feet. She heard the rooster's wake up alarm and groaned. *I thought I was in proper shape, working in the Navy, but this small farm has defeated me. How did I ever think I could be a farmer's wife? Am I daft?* She rolled over, ignoring the steady patter of rain thrumming on the roof.

Picturing Ciaran's mum fussing in the kitchen, with Mr McElroy tending the animals in the rain, she grunted and succumbed to the inevitable.

Stretching slowly, she tentatively got to her feet and tried to move a bit. *Not too bad, Petty Office Kingston. I wonder what Ciaran has in mind for me today.* Examining her hands, she noticed the broken fingernails and blister on her right palm – from all they haying, she expected. *I suppose I'll just have to get used to this.*

Calling on her Navy training, she ran through a few exercises to limber up before washing and donning her clothes.

She came into the kitchen, where the little family was already waiting for her.

"Oh dear, I am late again. So sorry," she apologized. *Way to make a good impression, you silly girl.*

"No bother, dear. We were just sitting down. Fancy some porridge and toast with your tea?"

"Yes, please, Mrs McElroy and good morning to you all."

Ciaran wiggled his eyebrows and patted the chair next to him.

"Good morning, mavourneen. We are delighted yourself could join us, and all."

Katie swore at him under her breath, as she took a bowl of steaming porridge from his ma.

"I suppose we have more chores today?" she asked.

The trio laughed heartily.

"That's one thing there's never a shortage of at the farm, young Katie. There are more chores than hours in the day, if I'm honest," Mr McElroy confirmed. "Today, we are going to muck out and wean the piglets, repair the north fence, and stack more hay. Besides the regular feeding and other jobs."

"Wean the piglets? Young Rosie is to be separated from Penny? No, she's too little," Katie objected through a mouthful of sweet porridge.

"You've named them?" Three pairs of McElroy eyes bored into her.

"That little one is so cute. I just had to give her a name. And she's so rosy pink, she seemed to suit Rosie," she explained. "And her mum seemed to need a name, too. Penny just came to me. I'm still working on names for the other seven."

"Well, you'll have to say goodbye to your little friend today, Katie. We're trading the piglets with Murphy Farms for a sheep and her two lambs. Ma is starting her knitting season. Her jumpers and hats are renowned in the county. We'll keep one lamb, who should be fattened up enough for our Christmas dinner."

"Oh, those poor babies." Katie couldn't help herself. Which was worse? Babies separated from mama pig or watching a lamb plump, only to be slaughtered.

"'Tis the way of farming, Katie," Mr McElroy cautioned. "You mustn't get attached to the animals. They come and go, and put all our food on the table – directly or indirectly."

"I'll do my best, sir. It's all so new to me. Please be patient." Katie had so much to learn.

"You can coddle Keegan," Ciaran relented, clearing away the breakfast things. "The beast is here to stay. Let's get on. The rain won't stop us from a full day. We can scrounge up an anorak and old pair of wellies that should fit yourself."

"Righto," Katie nodded, slurping the last of her tea, as she shoved a piece of toast with jam into her mouth.

Mucking out the pigpen in a warm drizzle wasn't the most pleasant task in the world, but Katie was no stranger to hard work and getting the job done. It broke her heart to see the piglets loaded onto a lorry, squealing for their mama. And she was sure she saw tears in Penny's eyes as she searched in vain for her babies.

"You're daft. They don't think like humans. She'll have forgotten about them before long. Next spring, we'll get Murphy's boar over and she'll have a new brood to fuss over."

"Alright, Irish. I get it. What's next?" She pushed back a lock of damp hair. *Will I get it? Farming seems a bit cold-hearted. How will I ever cope with slaughtering a lamb?*

And so the day went. After a hearty lunch of thick soup and more Irish soda bread, Ciaran announced Katie should stay and help Ma with some cleaning, whilst he and his da repaired the fence.

"I'll come for you in an hour to get on with the hay. And then we have a treat for you, luv. We're all going to the pub tonight. Da and Ma are dead keen to introduce you to the locals and have a proper craic. So, you'll need a spot of time to wash the muck out of your hair." He mussed her out-of-control curls and pressed his lips warmly to hers.

"That sounds brilliant," Katie managed, wondering how she would muster up the oomph to pretty herself up and meet a load of Irish strangers.

She hoovered the floors and helped Mrs McElroy scour the kitchen and sort a proper pile of ironing.

"Let's stop for tea, dear. We've earned a wee sit-down."

"Lovely. I'll stick on the kettle. I'd love a cuppa."

The two women sat in companionable silence, sipping tea and crunching home-made biscuits, glad for a few minutes' respite.

"It's not always this hectic, Katie. We've missed Ciaran dreadfully and have imposed too much on the pair o' you during this visit. We'd been doing our best on our own, but it's not been easy going," she stumbled a little over the words.

"I'm sure it's been wretched without him, and with no help whatever. With both of us here after the war, will you be more comfortable? Can you finally retire – at least a smidgen? That's what I want with all my heart – what we both want. Ciaran and I have spent hours talking about it."

What Katie didn't share was that Ciaran had big plans for the farm. He intended to get help straightaway and wanted to expand certain areas and divest of others. Upgrading the farmhouse was a priority – adding a proper indoor bathroom, and ensuring his parents had a comfortable room, for starters. He'd saved what army pay he hadn't sent to his parents, and had a small nest egg with which to get started.

"Bless you, dear. That's will do nicely for Niall and I."

Katie thought this woman was the master of understatement.

Mrs McElroy leaned in.

"You know, me husband has a dickie heart? He doesn't like a fuss made of it, but he's been told time and again to slow down. He can't do near what he used to, and you've doubtless noticed he's often out of breath. I do what I can, but I can't be the help I used to be – or need to be. Please don't let on I've told you any of this. Sure, and he insists he can manage and hates to be seen as a frail old man."

"I understand, Mrs McElroy. I won't breathe a word. And in no time, we'll have you and your husband putting up your feet and enjoying the rest you deserve."

A grateful smile and a pat on the hand told Katie that her words had hit the mark.

Her heart full, she turned to see Ciaran coming through the door, shaking the wet off his yellow mackintosh.

"Is there a cup left in the pot for me? And then we're off to the barn, Katie. You'll be pleased to hear it's stopped raining." He was so cheerful he practically chirped. Katie could see he was in his element.

"Sit down, love, and have a cup before you go out again."

A quarter of an hour later, the young couple tromped through the mud to the barn. The farm had come back to life after the mizzly day. Katie spotted two butterflies fluttering atop the gorse bushes. The air smelt fresh and new, as droplets fell softly off the rooftops and trees, washing the world anew.

"How long will this take, Irish? My back is that sore already, and it will be an uphill battle to get myself tidy enough to present tonight."

"You look smashing – even with mud on your cheek and under your nails. In fact, you're glowing. Farm life suits you, mavourneen." He stopped and hugged her hard.

She put her arms up around his neck and pulled him down for a lingering kiss.

"You're a liar, but a loveable one. Now, let's get stuck in, so we can finish up."

A long shaft of light poured into the barn, shining on piles of freshly stacked hay.

Katie turned in surprise to Ciaran.

"Why, you've gone and piled it all! How did you get it done?" Phew. Katie's back was more than a little relieved.

"The fence work wasn't as bad as I thought, so I came ahead to finish up here. But damn. I must have forgotten a scarf or something up there."

Looking up, Katie saw a flash of red about halfway up the stack.

"Fancy a climb? I'll race you."

"You're on," Katie laughed and started up the offset bales of hay. She was no match for the nimble farmer. He reached the second level and stood there; arms crossed.

Katie scrambled up, not far behind.

"Not bad for a Londoner, eh?" She huffed as she reached him, and saw a red blanket spread on the hay.

"Crikey. What's this then?"

"A wee picnic for us, luv. Sit down." He held out his hand, and she sat, wordless.

He opened two bottles of Irish stout and pulled a bit of cheese and bread from a small basket.

"You rascal, Ciaran. When did you plan this?"

Wiggling his eyebrows, he said nothing.

"How wonderful." She sat back, took a sip of the welcome beer, and nibbled a bit of cheese. This was luxury indeed.

"I thought yourself deserved a bit of pleasure in a long day. You've been working proper hard, and I'm that proud of you."

Katie beamed and lay back, enjoying this quiet moment.

"I should think there's something else in the basket. A pudding of sorts. Can you fetch it?"

Katie obligingly reached into the basket and rooted around. Her fingers encircled a small box and drew it out.

"What?" She gazed at the small velvet box in confusion.

"Open it," he said, his green eyes twinkling.

Katie's heart thumped. She looked into Ciaran's eyes and saw nothing but deep love reflected there. Was this what she thought it was? Was she ready for this?

Her throat dry, Katie opened the small box. A golden ring shimmered before her. She didn't know what to say.

Ciaran took the box from her, removed the ring, got down on one knee, and held it out to her, trembling slightly.

"Katie Kingston, I've loved you for a long time, and we've waited long enough. I couldn't think of a better place to properly ask you to marry me than the home I love almost as much as you. Say you'll be my wife, please."

He held the ring aloft, holding his breath.

Kneeling, she faced him in the hay.

"I will marry you, my Irishman. And I can't wait to make this my home, too. It will be just grand." She smiled, heart full to bursting.

He took the ring and placed it on her finger.

"Oh Ciaran, it's beautiful. I've never seen anything like it. This beautiful heart in the middle is so unique."

He picked up her hand and traced the heart with his finger.

"It's a claddagh ring – an Irish tradition. The emerald heart represents love. The hands clasping it are for friendship, and the crown on top stands for loyalty. Together, they symbolize me commitment to you. The tradition comes from Claddagh, county Galway, and dates back to the seventeenth century. Or so Ma told me." He traced each part in turn.

Katie examined it more closely.

"I love it," she replied simply.

"How you wear it is most important. The point of the heart facing towards the bottom of your fingers means you are engaged. You can turn it round when we're married, or I'll get you a traditional wedding ring if you fancy that. I'm so pleased you like it. It suits yourself and all." He slid it on her finger, point down.

Katie near pounced on him, raining kisses on his face, neck, and anywhere she could find exposed skin.

He returned the kisses, running his fingers up and down her body. Deepening the embrace, his mouth was hot on hers, insisting on more. Rolling her over, he pinned her down on the hay, laying his body on top of hers for the first time, pressing his length to hers.

Feelings shot through Katie's body. The weight of him, the smell of barn and sweat were intoxicating. She looped her arms around his neck, pulling him closer. Resisting the urge to move, she longed to grind her body into his. She felt a bit dizzy as sensations washed over her. She wanted nothing more than to throw off her clothes and to feel his skin on hers.

Rolling her over again, she was now on top of him. He lifted her coat and cupped her bottom, all the while kissing her and murmuring love words in her ear. He unbuttoned her shirt and stroked her breasts. Dipping his head, he pulled one nipple into his mouth, gently kissing and tugging it. Sensations flooded her body like shots of pure heat. *Oh Ciaran, what are you doing to me?*

Moving back to kiss her once more, he resolutely took her arms from around his neck, pulled her off, and sat up – raking a hand through his tussled hair. Trying to break free of a desire-induced haze, Katie struggled to find equilibrium.

"We'd best get back, my girl. A roll in the hay – as enticing as it sounds – is not the way I want to remember this day."

Kissing her once more, she nodded, suddenly embarrassed. Her heart was still racing, and she wanted so much more from him. Blushing, she fastened the loose buttons of her shirt.

"I must look a fright." She pulled straw from her hair and brushed it from her coat.

"Sure, and we both look like we've taken a tumble," he laughed ruefully, pulling straw from his own hair and shirt pocket. "Ma will kill me. I was only to keep you a short while. She has a hot bath waiting for you, so you can get proper ready for tonight."

"I expect we have a good excuse." Katie held up her left hand, admiring the sun sparkling on the emerald. "Do they know about this?"

"They know it's been burning a hole in my pocket since I brought you here, but they don't know when I was going to ask yourself and all. I'm sure they'll be able to tell by the looks on our faces."

The young couple tidied up the picnic, climbed down the pile of haystacks, and hurried to the main house.

"Ciaran, where have you been, me boy? You were meant to be back by half-past."

"We're so sorry, Mrs McElroy. We were held up….by this." Katie extended her hand, eyes shining.

"How grand! Well done, son. And the ring looks lovely on you, dear." She kissed Katie on the cheek. "Congratulations to you both."

"Fair play, Ciaran. We're chuffed that you'll be joining our family, young lady. I suppose a spot of whiskey to celebrate the occasion won't go amiss." Ciaran's dad also kissed Katie and shook his son's hand.

"Go on with you, Niall. But a short nip, mind. We're meant to get to the pub by six."

Small glasses were produced, and tots of Irish whiskey briskly poured.

"Slainte," Niall started the toasting.

"Slainte," echoed Orla and Ciaran.

"Slanty," tried Katie.

Good natured chuckles ensued.

"How was that? Was it grand?" Katie asked.

"It's a good start, mavourneen." Ciaran saluted her kindly with his glass.

And that was just the start of the toasts. After a welcome bath in the large tin tub, Katie felt more like herself again. Donning a pretty blue summer dress from before the war, she fluffed her hair, dashed on a smidge of red lipstick, and slipped on summer sandals.

Ciaran gave a low whistle when she appeared downstairs.

"I'm not sure who has the more beautiful date, Da. Our ladies both look wonderful." But Ciaran only had eyes for Katie.

"I expect I have the grandest date, son," Niall disagreed.

"Go on with your malarkey, boys," Orla sniffed. But Katie could tell she was pleased.

At the Abbey Tavern, Katie lost track of the people she met, and toasts drunk to her and Ciaran's health and future. Local musicians played Irish music and the mood was festive.

By the time they left near midnight and started the two-mile walk back to the farm, they were all pleasantly tipsy.

"Jaysus, Mary and Joseph," Katie exclaimed as she tripped over a bump in the road. "I believe I'm proper langered."

"I suppose we have an Irishwoman in the making, son," Niall observed with a laugh. "I hope she doesn't have a head in the morning, and all. You have an early start."

Waking up with the sun again, Katie's head throbbed and her mouth felt full of cotton. That bloody Irish whiskey. Never again, she swore to herself, dreading the long day of travel ahead before reaching Portsmouth tonight.

The goodbyes were hard, but they all vowed to be together again before long. Ciaran had sorted some help from the Murphy's sixteen-year-old son at the pub, so the McElroys would have a little relief before Ciaran and Katie could return for good.

"Slan leat, dear. We've loved having you," the McElroys bade goodbye from the front door.

"Thank you for everything. We'll see you soon."

CHAPTER TWENTY-FIVE

August 1945

"I'm gobsmacked, Queenie. How could he have lost?" Ruby and Katie walked home from a rare day shift together.

"After all Winnie did for us in the last six years, he must be crushed to be pushed out." Katie was likewise in shock. "He didn't deserve that."

In a stunning reversal, Prime Minister Churchill had suffered a humiliating defeat in the national election. Even with the delayed inclusion of votes from soldiers and residents overseas, it had been a landslide victory for Labor's Clement Attlee. The second-placed Conservatives only secured 197 seats, whilst triumphant Labour won 393.

Attlee had campaigned persuasively on social reform, committing to full employment, affordable housing, and social security and health care for all. It all sounded like progress, relief, and a future-forward life for the shattered British people.

Churchill had banked on his popular appeal, lowering taxes, maintaining defence spending, and focus on private business. Claiming that social reform belonged solidly in the private sector rather than by governmental office, he miscalculated the worn-down Britons, who wanted to put the war years behind them, clamoring for change.

Ruby shrugged.

"Old Winnie did us proud during wartime – none could say different. But I fancy free health care, and the notion of the government taking care of me after all I've done these last years."

"Ruby, did you vote for Attlee?" Katie stopped in the street.

"And why not?" She pushed back her sweat-dampened fringe. It had been a hot August day. "I'm for progress and moving into the modern times. And proud of it." Sticking out her chin, she dared Katie to defy her.

"Keep your hair on, you eejit. You're entitled to your views. And you may well be right. It just seems, I dunno, disloyal somehow to oust the poor bugger after all he's done."

Slightly mollified, Ruby linked arms with her friend.

"Look at you, turning Irish and all. Mark my words. Once you see butter and proper portions of meat and sugar at the table, you'll see it my way."

"Maybe so." Katie didn't want to argue with her mate. "In the event, did you see the first demob list? I wonder when it will be our turn?" She was dead keen to get on with civilian life. Civilian married life. She'd found it hard going being without Ciaran since their last leave together in Howth.

"It makes sense that married women go first. And the work has slowed to such a pace that I don't see how they need us much longer. Seeing as how neither of us is drawn to signing on with the Navy for a further two years, I expect it's just a matter of time – months, maybe weeks."

"Surely, as soon as the Allies declare victory in the Far East, that will speed things along."

On August 6th, an atomic bomb had been launched on the Japanese city of Hiroshima. It had caused massive devastation, reducing five square miles of the city to dust, and killing something like 120,000 people. Just three days later, another bomb caused similar damage to Nagasaki, killing a further 50,000 Japanese civilians outright. It was now just a matter of waiting for the Japanese to officially surrender unconditionally.

"What wreckage this war has cost – not just to us, but all over the world. As much as I am relieved that the war in Japan is all but over – and my brother Kenny will come home at last – I still feel for all those innocent people."

"Maybe I'm just getting numb to it," Ruby said absently. "It doesn't seem real anymore. Is it ghastly that I'm just thinking of spending time with Dan?"

They reached the pub, and went in for a shandy.

"Of course not. We are all impatient for our lives to resume. Or start, really. All I can think about is my wedding to Ciaran."

"Are you still thinking of a Christmas ceremony?" Ruby ordered for them, sinking back in the chair.

"Yes. It seems so far off. Ciaran would like the ceremony to be in Ireland, but I have so much family in London, it doesn't seem sensible. He's worried that the trip will be too much for his da and ma, but I'm sure they can manage it. With men returning in dribs and drabs, there's more help at the farm. If they rest up before and after, they should be able to bear it." Katie thought of her future father-in-law's heart condition, and fervently hoped she was right. Was she being selfish to want to be married at home?

"If Ciaran goes to collect them, and they take their time, surely it will be alright."

Katie brightened.

"And what of your plans? Still Oklahoma-bound? I don't know what I'll do without you, Rubes. We've become like sisters, haven't we?" Katie and Ruby had formed an unbreakable wartime bond. Across the women's forces, attachments had been made amidst the most trying of circumstances, some that would last a lifetime.

"We have, Queenie. All in all, we've had a pretty good war, haven't we? Even though we didn't have a clue what the messages we took meant – we always knew we did vital war work. And we're still here. Do you reckon we'll ever be able to talk about the work we've done? Or always blustering on about 'administrative duties?'" She laughed.

Katie shrugged.

"I try not to think about it, Rubes. We need to just put it behind us. And, haven't we become clever in changing the subject, and fluffing about the vagaries of our work? No one would understand, anyway. We did our bit and we can never talk about it. Even Ciaran and I steer away from those conversations. Perhaps when we're sitting on our rocking chairs, we'll be allowed to reminisce about our dangerous war work."

She gave her mate a friendly push.

"And America?"

"Yes, I plan to make the big move. Just as soon as we're both demobbed, and it's safe, we're going to book ship's passage. And you must come to see us once you have married your Irishman. It's not that far away, really."

Katie nodded slowly, but they both knew it was unlikely to ever see each other again once they'd gone their separate ways. Howth, Ireland and Oklahoma, America were oceans apart.

The next morning, the girls awoke at an absurdly early hour thanks to cheers and whoops from the pub below. They could even hear people shouting in the streets.

"Is this it?" Instantly awake, Katie rubbed her eyes and rushed to the window, throwing open the sash.

"Is it over?" Katie leaned out, heedless of her nightclothes. "Is it really over?"

"Yes, darlin. President Truman announced it last night! The Japanese have finally surrendered. Atlee broadcast it this morning." A stringy young man with unkempt hair shouted back. "It's V-J Day."

Katie shrieked and ran to Ruby's bed to hug her. Her friend was already up and the two danced around the room, screaming.

"It's V-J Day. It's V-J Day. We're going home!"

"Is it a national holiday, I wonder?" Katie paused and asked.

"It is for us, sweetie. Let's get dressed. We're going to celebrate all day."

And they did. Meeting up with the regulars downstairs, they gulped a watery porridge and tea laced with gin. It tasted vile, but they drank it anyway. The party then moved outside, where people danced, music played, and tables were hastily set up for makeshift street parties.

As soon as they discovered it was to be a two-day national holiday, Katie grabbed Ruby's hand and dragged her back to the pub.

"We're going to London. We missed the V-E Day celebrations. I'll be damned if we're going to let this pass. You can stay with me at Earl's Court."

"You're on, Queenie." Ruby's smile ripped her face in half. Her home with Nan was west of London, and a tad too far for this celebratory jaunt.

They threw a few clothes into a bag, and half-ran, half-skipped to the train station. It was jam-packed with travelers cum revellers. Not a seat was to be had on the train, but the girls didn't care. They sang and cheered along with everyone else all the way to London.

Alighting at Waterloo Station, they merged with the moving crowd to Trafalgar Square, where some brave and drunken souls jumped into the fountains. Everyone seemed to wave something: flags, bunting, improvised ticker tape, horns, and newspapers with the screaming headlines WAR OVER! or JAPAN SURRENDERS.

As with V-E Day, it was orderly bedlam. Albeit there was some good-natured drinking, there was little beer or spirits to be had. People moved aimlessly wherever the crowds took them, often breaking into There Will Always Be an England or Rule Britannia. With reckless abandon, scores of Londoners climbed whatever was at hand – buses, cars, billboards, men's shoulders, lampposts, traffic signs – anything to get above the excitement, be cheered, and laugh with the surging throngs.

In uniform, Katie and Ruby were hailed, embraced, and kissed at every turn. Being thanked repeatedly was exhilarating, and filled them both with pride to be part of the Women's Royal Navy.

Joining one of countless congo lines, they kicked and sang along the streets of London.

Word spread later in the afternoon that the King had broadcast a wireless speech. Snatches of *"Our sense of deliverance is overpowering. We have a right to feel that we have done our duty. I send my profound thanks. I thank my peoples for all they have done…for mankind."* could be heard as the masses moved towards Buckingham Palace.

"They must come out on the balcony. We need to see them." Katie struggled to be heard over the din.

Ruby nodded and held fast to Katie's arm so they wouldn't be separated.

Making it to the palace entrance, the girls chanted with the crowd; "We want the King" until they were hoarse. As the doors to the balcony finally opened, an enormous roar rumbled through the thousands of merrymakers.

"Look, it's them!" Katie screamed, and jumped up and down as the King, Queen, and two princesses came out and started waving and smiling.

"Look – Princess Elizabeth is wearing a floral crown. How beautiful," Ruby shrieked.

Indeed, the royal family looked splendid. King George VI was in full military uniform, whilst Queen Elizabeth was festive in a pastel suit and matching hat. Princesses Elizabeth and Margaret shone in flowered dresses with coordinating headpieces. They seemed as joyful as the crowds shouting and howling in front of them.

As night fell, the palace was flooded with light, causing another riot of cheering. As the royal family gave one last wave and left the balcony, the crowd dispersed slowly. Other historic buildings were floodlit, fireworks soared overhead, and bonfires sprung up throughout town. Street parties and vendors fed the crowds with hoarded rations.

Katie and Ruby sat on a bench, contemplating what to do next.

"Are you ready to go home yet? Should we go for a drink?" Ruby asked her chum, still full of elation.

"I'm tired and want to see my folks, but it seems too early to leave the party," Katie replied.

From a distance, she thought she heard someone calling her.

"Katie, wait. Katie!"

An out-of-breath Hannah appeared from nowhere.

"Hannah! Oh, my goodness. I thought you were on base." Katie hugged her youngest sister.

"I saw you from afar, and have been running to catch up," Hannah gasped, catching her breath. "Hold on, I have a stitch in my side."

The girls made room for her on the bench, where Katie and Hannah laughed and cried together.

"Once I heard we had two days of national holiday, I had to come to London."

"Us too," chorused the Portsmouth girls.

"And Ciaran is here too," Hannah puffed. "He came down from Bletchley, hoping against hope you'd come to London."

"Where is he?" shrieked Katie as she seized Hannah's arm. Ciaran – here in London. What joy. But how could she possibly find him in this crush?

"He worked out that you'd likely come to the palace. He's around here somewhere. I lost him just a few minutes ago."

Katie stood and climbed onto the nearest lamppost.

"Irish. Where are you?" It seemed hopeless. The crowds were dissipating, but there were still thousands milling about. She shouted for what seemed like hours, but was just a few minutes.

"Mavourneen, is that yourself up there?"

Katie searched the crush, seeking the face that matched the beloved voice. And then she spotted him. That glorious, familiar, wonderful face. He was about a hundred yards away, striding towards her at an incredible speed.

"Katie, love. Get down from there."

She grinned from ear to ear.

"I can't. I don't know how."

"Jump, you eejit," he urged, holding his arms open and shaking his head in disbelief. Ruby and Hannah encircled the lamppost, creating a hammock of hands.

"I don't think I can." Without warning, Katie grew cold and clammy. She *was* an eejit. What was she thinking – shinnying up the post as if it were a tree in the Kingston backyard?

"Katie, you're going to be fine. It's only a few feet. Just let go of the post and fall. Close your eyes. I'll catch you. I promise," Ciaran encouraged.

"You can do it, Queenie. Come on, there's loads more to see and do tonight," urged Ruby.

"You're so brave, Katie. Just close your eyes and trust your fiancé," Hannah chimed in.

Katie felt foolish and afraid at the same time. Thinking of Ciaran's arms around her, she summoned up the small act of bravery required, and let go. She hoped she was falling in Ciaran's general direction.

A sturdy pair of arms broke her fall. She oomphed as her body seemed to reach the ground before her stomach could catch up. Opening her eyes, she looked into the anxious and oh-so-dear eyes of her beloved. He crushed her with a fierce kiss as she wrapped her arms tightly around his neck.

"I'm sorry, Irish. I just needed to find you is all," she apologized limply.

"I didn't think." He set her on her feet.

"You gave me a fright, but we're alright now." He swept her into his arms once more, bending her backwards into a long, lingering embrace.

"Is there any of that for me?" Ruby interrupted dryly.

Ciaran laughed and released Katie and embraced Ruby and Hannah in turn.

"Come on. The night is young. I'm buying the drinks," he boomed.

The foursome celebrated gaily until the early hours of August 16th. Finally, they gave in to their exhaustion and walked to #40 Longridge Road.

"I hope someone is still up," Katie yawned. "I'd hate to wake up Mum or Pops."

"Someone will be up, no doubt," Ciaran reassured, as they mounted the stairs to the front door. He knocked and was rewarded straightaway. Trevor answered, smiling widely.

"We hoped some of you would find your way to London today. Come in, come in. We're into the brandy, as you can see."

Entering the sitting room, Katie was overjoyed to see Pops in his favorite easy chair. As he rose to his feet, Katie heard Mum from upstairs.

"Is that you, Katie luv? I hoped and hoped." Mum burst into the room and both parents enveloped their youngest daughter in a warm embrace.

"It's over, Mum. The war is over." Tears poured down both their cheeks. Katie's heart swelled. They were so dear to her.

Tillie appeared in the doorway, bleary-eyed in her dressing gown, holding baby Victoria.

"Darling," she cried.

A quarter of an hour passed with congratulations, introductions, and toasts.

"How long can you stay?" Mum asked over a small brandy.

"Just till tomorrow night. We all have to report back for duty on Friday," Ruby declared.

"We have room for everyone," Mum calculated quickly. "Katie, you and Ruby can have your old room. And Ciaran, you can bed down in Kenny's room. Jamie's in there now, but you can take him in with you, can't you, Tillie?" Mum was in her element. "And Hannah, you'll head back to Maggie's?"

"Of course," Tillie yawned. "I'm off for bed. This one doesn't sleep long. She has her days and nights mixed up at the moment, so I need to sleep when I can. Welcome and congratulations to Ciaran and Ruby. Katie, Hannah – we'll have a long chat tomorrow."

The household settled down for the night – what was left of it. It had been a monumental day, with even more to look forward to in the morning. Katie kissed Ciaran at her door, and swiftly undressed, not bothering to wash. Intending to recap the astonishing day they'd just shared, she turned to Ruby, who had already fallen into bed. Opening her mouth, she saw that her mate was fast asleep. Snuggling next to her, Katie closed her eyes and fell into a dead slumber in a matter of seconds.

CHAPTER TWENTY-SIX

The holiday spirit prevailed the next morning, despite little sleep and several sore heads.

"Good morning, Ruby. Isn't it a glorious day?"

Dead silence.

"Come on, then. Haven't we done without sleep loads of times the last five and a half years?" Katie threw the bedcovers off her side. "I don't want to waste a minute today. Tonight will come soon enough."

Katie was bright and breezy. Too cheerful by half for Ruby, who lay motionless on the bed.

"Come on, Ruby. My mum makes a decent breakfast, and you can have a proper bath." She poked the lump next to her.

"A bath?" This created some movement. Ruby peeked out from under the blanket. "A proper bath in a bathtub?"

"The very same." Katie nodded. "Get a move on. I want to see my sisters and their babies, show Ciaran around, and celebrate that we won the war."

"Well, let's start with a bath, and see how we get on," she replied, but Katie knew her mate would bounce back once she'd woken up properly.

"With a full house, I'm not sure when we'll get our turn, mind, but I promise you a bath. Let's get dressed. I'm starving. We hardly ate at all yesterday."

"You just want to see Ciaran, is all," Ruby grumbled as she stretched and climbed out of bed.

"I sure do, you daft cow. I'll meet you downstairs."

The Kingston townhouse was abuzz with activity and excitement when Katie skipped down to the kitchen. Mum had on her familiar, faded, flowered pinny and was serving tea and toast. Trevor was unsuccessfully trying to stuff cereal in Jamie's mouth. Evidence of discarded cornflakes on the high chair table and floor wasn't promising. Ciaran chatted with Pops, and neither Tillie or Victoria were to be seen.

"Good morning, luv," Mum chirped. "I'm still rubbish at porridge, but I've sorted tea and toast. Did you sleep well?"

"For the few hours I slept, like a log, Mum. Good morning, Irish. Where's our Hannah?" She bent for a kiss from her fiancé before pouring herself a cuppa.

"She's at home to help Maggie and Micah with the twins. But I've sent her on messages for Uncle Thomas and Isla first. We're going to have a lovely family dinner before you all have to scatter for trains."

"Alright, Mum, but it will have to be early. Before I get stuck in helping, I'm going to pop upstairs to see Tillie and the baby. Shall I take her a cup of tea?"

"Ta, luv. She would love it. Here, take her some toast as well."

"I'll make a tray, shall I?" Katie busied herself with the tea things.

"Thanks, Katie. This young man is overexcited by all this company, and fussing with his breakfast." Trevor threw her a grateful smile, as Jamie took his bowl of cereal and dumped it on the floor next to his high chair.

"Jamie," Trev exclaimed. "Don't be naughty."

"I'll be back in a tick if they're still asleep. Or it could be half an hour if she's awake and up for a chin wag. Are you alright here, Ciaran?"

"Just fine. Your father and I have a few things to discuss."

Katie wondered what that meant. If Ciaran meant to ask her father for her hand in marriage, it was rather too late. She hoped Pops wouldn't be a stickler on that account. Perhaps he wanted to break the unsettling news that he'd be taking the youngest Kingston daughter away to a foreign country to live. Regardless, she hoped Ciaran could turn on the Irish charm.

"And don't worry about lending a hand, luv," Mum called after her. "Spend the day with your friends. It's only V-J Day once. Isla and I can manage the meal just fine."

"Thanks, Mum," called Katie, as she mounted the stairs.

She was chuffed to find Tillie awake and nursing the baby. Plunking the tea tray on a side table, she sat on the bed.

"How are you getting on, Tils? I hardly remember even seeing you last night."

"Pretty good. Albeit I'd forgotten how exhausting a newborn can be. And chasing after an active two-year-old, to boot. But she's a darling, isn't she?" Tillie gazed with naked adoration at her tiny baby.

"Can I hold her?" Katie asked, sidling up to her sister.

"She needs to be winded. Just pop her over your shoulder and give her a pat. Take this nappy or you may get spit-up on your smashing uniform."

"I don't mind. It's rather wrinkled and fragrant at the moment. A little spit-up from my adorable niece is nothing." Katie took the baby from her sister, bounced her up against her shoulder, and patted furiously.

"A little gentler, sis," Tillie warned, trying not to hover.

"Sorry, luv." She slowed to a rocking pat. What a tender feeling, holding this sweet-smelling infant. *Could I do this? Could I be a mum?*

"So how are you really doing, Tils? You look divine, as always. No one would ever guess you had a baby just a couple of months ago."

"You're joking, right? Look at the bags under my eyes. And I haven't had a bath in a week. And Jamie is acting up like mad. This house is too small to hold our family of four with everyone here. Trev and I talk about it all the time. We desperately need our own place. If I'm honest, I'm a bit wobbly." Tillie fought back tears. Poor Tillie. Katie could see her sister was struggling. Even perfect, sunny Tillie could have her bad days. It made Katie thoughtful.

Victoria chose that moment to let out a large burp, breaking the mood.

"My goodness, that was a good one, Victoria," Katie said with a self-satisfied smirk. "And darling, it's okay not to have everything perfect with a new baby. From my limited knowledge, that's normal, isn't it? You're managing marvellously. Don't be so hard on yourself." Katie laid the baby down gently on the bed and sat next to her sister, putting an arm around her. "None of us knows what we're doing anymore. This war has us at sixes and sevens. And it's over. What the hell do we do now? We are all trying to work it out as we go, luv."

Tillie wiped away her tears.

"I expect it's just the baby blues. It comes over me in waves. I feel so emotional – either happy or weepy – and then it passes. Sorry, darling."

"No need for an apology." Katie was at a loss about how to help her sister. This was beyond her. "How is Maggie getting on? It must be hard for her – twins and all?" Katie poured the tea and passed it to her sister.

"She seems to cope well. She and Micah are both so calm, and it is rubbing off on Ruth and Rachel. They are thriving and even sleeping for longer stretches at night."

"Brilliant. I can't wait to see them at dinner. The first of many family meals again – everyone is here except Kenny. Pretty remarkable, I'd say." Katie skimmed a bit of blackberry jam onto the toast and passed it over. "I can't wait to see him. It's been so long. We'll scarcely recognize him, I expect." She sighed. She missed her younger brother dearly.

The baby wailed.

"It looks like Aunt Katie's magic didn't last long." Katie picked up the red-faced baby and handed her to her mum.

"It's not you. I fear she may have a touch of colic. Can you fetch Trev? He has a way of rocking her that – mostly – soothes her. And then off with you to celebrate. I'll see you at dinner."

"Alright, Tils. And for what it counts, I think you're a smashing mum." She kissed the fussy baby and left. *No one has it all figured out. Even the glamorous Kingston twins had problems. My, maybe I've been putting my sisters on a pedestal for too long. They are just typical wives and mums just getting through the day like everyone else. Bloody hell.* She grinned.

Looking for Trev, she searched the second floor, but the drawing room was empty. Coming into the morning room a level below, Ciaran and Pops were just coming out of the library.

"Hello, you two. Everything alright?" They were smiling, so it couldn't be too bad.

"Your young man and I just had a little talk, poppet. All is well."

"How is your sister getting on?" Ciaran asked.

"Brilliant," Katie replied loyally. She wouldn't give away her sister's secrets for anything. "I need to find Trev, and then shall we go out, Irish? Ruby mentioned something about meeting up with some Wrens at the Old Naval College." They wanted to make the most of their short escape.

Ciaran nodded, and in no time, the trio had popped out for some further V-J Day revelry.

* * *

"He was the best wartime Prime Minister we could have had. We couldn't have won the war without him." Pops shook his head.

"No one will gainsay you, Walter," Thomas replied, helping himself to more cabbage. "But perhaps it is time for a change. The people are heartily sick of war, and don't want to be reminded of it. With so many people homeless from all the bombing and inflow of refugees, social reform is sorely needed."

"Attlee's V-J speech was moving," offered Tillie timidly. "'The last of our enemies laid low.' It inspired me."

"He doesn't have a patch on Churchill. We'll never see the likes of an orator like him again," Pops harrumphed.

"I like the idea of change for the future. What are we going to do with all the men returning from war? And what of us women? We've got a taste of working and serving our King and country. Do you expect us to go back to tending house quietly?"

"There's plenty of work for everyone," Micah put in. "And women have proven more than up to the job. Look what you girls have done. Maggie – firing ack-ack guns against German aircraft under the most perilous of conditions. Ruby and Katie – standing shoulder to shoulder with the men in the Navy. Mum and Isla – keeping the home fires going with impossible rationing and too many nights in the Anderson. And our Hannah – helping our bombers find their targets with intricate weather forecasting. Tillie – driving an ambulance through the Blitz, with bombs crashing all around. We couldn't have won the war without you incredible women."

This was rather a long speech for shy Micah, but one that made the girls glow with pride.

"I'm not sure which is more dangerous – driving an ambulance or having two small children," Tillie observed wryly.

The dining room erupted into laughter.

"You can minimize your efforts, but I think what you have all done for the war effort is nothing short of magnificent," Uncle Thomas beamed.

"And so much hardship, death and tragedy." Maggie looked quietly around the table. "We've all lost so much."

Unspoken was Micah's horrific time in France, the deaths of his and Hannah's parents, Trev's burns and temporary blindness, and losing dear Shirley and her son, Geoffrey.

"So many lives gone and destruction everywhere. No life has been untouched," echoed Isla. Uncle Thomas gave her a warm look.

I wonder what's going on there. Katie turned to Tillie, who gave her a wink. *My, my. More romance round the Kingston household?*

"What are everyone's plans now?" Mum turned expectantly to her growing family.

"We're going to continue our work with Jewish refugees," Micah started them off. "And there's a massive need to help families try to find what's happened to their relatives. We can't ignore them."

"There are so many broken people, desperate to find a mum, child, or brother," Maggie added. They both looked somber indeed. "And so few people to help them."

"It's worthy work." Pops nodded.

"And our Hannah may help us in the future. But for now, she is going to university once she's a civilian again," Micah said proudly.

"That's brilliant," Uncle Thomas smiled. "Too many of our nation's young people have had to forego advanced studies. We need smart minds like yours to help shape the country's future."

"I feel a trifle old to be starting out. But I promised my parents I would get a university education." Hannah straightened. "So, it's important to me."

"Nonsense, you're not too old. You're just eighteen. It's too late for the rest of us Kingston girls, so you'll be carrying the torch for us. Well done, you," encouraged Tillie. She paused. "Is that Victoria I hear?"

They all paused to listen. Maggie half-rose. All three babies had miraculously had good feeds and settled in for afternoon naps. Even young Jamie had gone for a sleep – albeit with loud protests.

"I hear nothing," Trev confirmed. He made a face at Micah. "Phantom baby cry."

Micah chuckled. "Maggie gets them too. These new mothers, I'm telling you."

"Hey, we're right here," Tillie groused.

"Too right, Tils," Maggie echoed, and sat down.

"And what of you two?" Walter returned to the subject at hand.

Trevor and Tillie shared a look.

"You know, we are so grateful for having a room in your home. It's been a godsend to have your help with Jamie, and now Victoria – especially after my injury. But we are bursting out of our room – even with Jamie upstairs in a box room. We need our own place," Trevor plunged in, knowing his mother-in-law would react poorly.

Tillie patted her mum's hand.

"I need my own front door, Mum. Remember those pre-fab homes we toured at the Tate Gallery last year? We put ourselves on a waiting list, and we may get one within a few months."

"Where?" Mum asked faintly. She'd been dreading this day, and now it had come.

"The first ones are in the East End, where the bombing has been the worst. Because Trev served in the RAF, he qualifies to be one of the first several hundred." Tillie pleaded with her eyes, hoping Mum would understand.

"But that's so far away," Alice couldn't keep the emotion out of her voice. She cleared her throat. "And that isn't the best neighborhood, luv."

"Mum, you know the houses have all the latest conveniences – central heating, built-in oven and refrigerator – all so modern."

"I see." Mum struggled for composure.

"May I interject here?" Uncle Thomas spoke softly. He glanced at Isla, who nodded. "I may be able to help with this problem. You may have noticed that Isla and I have gotten close over these past few months. She's brought this lonely widower a great deal of comfort this last year. We've decided that life is too short to go it alone. I am more than pleased that she's agreed to marry me."

Katie gave an involuntary gasp. Had it really been a year since Aunt

Shirley had died? Would Mum be okay with this unexpected development? But Mum was smiling. *Phew*, she must have known.

"We don't need much space for the two of us. Isla's flat is quite lovely, so we're going to live there after the wedding. So, Trevor and Tillie – how do you fancy moving into our house at Number Twelve? You can rent until you decide if you want to buy. I'm sure we can work out an agreeable financial understanding." Thomas sat back, a small smile on his face.

Tillie and Trevor were thunderstruck.

"Ma, how wonderful for you, two!" Trevor jumped to kiss Isla. "We wish you every happiness." He turned to his wife. "What do you reckon, Tils? Would you like your own home just down the street?"

Her shining eyes told him his answer.

"I would love it. Uncle Thomas – how kind and generous of you. Mum, isn't that perfect? We'll be just down the street."

Tears welled up in Alice's eyes. She couldn't help it.

"Absolutely bloody brilliant," Mum swore. "And Thomas, Isla – you know I'm over the moon for you both." She kissed each of them on the cheek. "It will not quite make up for Katie leaving us to move to Ireland."

Katie turned white. Mum knew – and she was fine with this?

"Mum, you are astonishing to me. How did you know we are going to take on the Howth farm?" She stared at Ciaran, wide-eyed.

"I've known for a while, luv. Anyone can see you two are meant to be together, and Ciaran spoke to your father today about your plans. As much as it pains me to let you go – your place is with your future husband, helping your ailing in-laws."

"Mum, you are truly remarkable. I was so afraid to tell you. A heavy weight is lifted off my shoulders. What a day."

Wonderful meal forgotten, everyone hugged, kissed, and exchanged congratulations.

"I should think champagne is in order on all fronts." Pops rose to forage a bottle in the scullery.

"And now we have two weddings to plan." Mum clasped her hands together in bliss. "Christmas for you, isn't it, dear Katie?"

"That would be grand, Mum. Just grand."

CHAPTER TWENTY-SEVEN

October 1945

"Well, this is it. Queenie. Our last day as Wrens." Ruby threw a few last things into her bag. "I didn't think our service numbers would ever come up."

"Well, they have, at last. All we need to do is hand in our uniforms, get our civvy suits, and catch our train to London. Then it's goodbye Portsmouth, hello rest of our lives."

Both girls were jubilant as they said their goodbyes to their billet hosts and tromped through the streets to the naval base.

Katie was unexpectedly emotional saying goodbye to her naval career. Despite the gritty watches that had rendered her numb too many times to count, the inedible grub at the mess, the homesickness, the freezing cold and unbearable heat, and tragedies of war she'd witnessed; she felt slightly weepy.

"Never at sea. Well, that's proved to be true, hasn't it, Katie? Both of us sailors, and never set foot on a ship." The motto of the British Women's Royal Navy had an ironic absurdity to it.

"We never had to find out if we had seasickness or not." Katie sighed. "I'm a bit down about turning in this uniform, Ruby. I've grown attached to it. I've been glad of the warmth of this greatcoat on more than a few frigid nights on watch. I'm proud of what we've done. Dead proud."

It was a blustery October day. Ruby pulled her collar close.

"Me too. We were such green girls when we started. Remember the horrors of basic training? Scrubbing floors till our hands and knees were raw. Some of those blue-blooded debs couldn't cope, and left before the fortnight was up."

"I won't miss that, Ruby. And I suppose that was the Navy's way of sorting who could survive everything the Navy – and the enemy – had to chuck at us."

"What I'll miss most is the camaraderie of other Wrens working alongside us. Battling through the long night watches together, moving from billet to billet, sharing any little treats we had. We really accomplished something, didn't we, Katie?"

Katie stopped.

"Are you going soft on me, Ruby? Are those tears I see?"

"Wrens don't cry, do we? Not going soft, but perhaps a little sentimental. I'm going to miss you something fierce." Ruby hugged her friend hard.

"I know people promise they'll stay in touch and never do. But we will, won't we, Katie? Even though you'll be in America and I'll be in Ireland. We will?" Ruby shook her friend by the arms.

"We must and we will. I promise," Katie assured her. "I intend to show up on your doorstep for some good old American pie. And I have a few pigpens and horse stalls for you to muck out when you come to Ireland. You'll adore it."

Katie knew they were both making light of the day – otherwise it would be tearful, and neither of them wanted that.

At base, they reported to their NCO, turned in their uniforms for utility dresses and shoes, and received their dispatch papers.

"Thank you for your service, Petty Officers. As your King said on V-E Day: *'Armed or unarmed, men and women, you have fought, striven, and endured to your utmost. No one knows that better than I do; and as your King, I thank with a full heart those who bore arms so valiantly on land and sea, or in the air.'*

You have done the British navy proud."

He gave them a salute, which the girls returned.

"Oh my, that was stirring." Katie mingled with the other departing Wrens, saying their goodbyes, writing addresses, and promising to keep in touch with their sisters in blue. Emotions were close to the surface for the lot of them as they held back tears, hugging trusted mates with choked voices.

"Bloody hell, I didn't expect to feel so weepy," Ruby admitted as they ran for the train. "How can you be so fed up with a place, and yet be sad to leave it?"

"It's rather like boarding school, I expect. Glad to be rid of Maths and cold showers, but our shared misery built memories and cozy friendships that mean the world."

Ruby nodded, at a loss for words.

As the train clack-clacked its way to London, thoughts turned to the future.

"Two weddings coming in no time, Ruby. Yours in Reading next month, and then mine on December twenty-seventh. We've got loads to do – dresses, food, flowers to sort. What sort of gown will you be wearing?"

Ruby snorted.

"Not a gown, to be sure. I half-wish Dan and I had married earlier. Wearing a uniform would have been so much easier. And with clothing still on the ration, I'm hoping against hope that Nan can run me up something on her Singer from an old gown in the attic. Otherwise, it will be a dreary day dress for me."

Ruby talked little about her family. She'd lost her parents when she was young and her Nan had brought her up.

"Do you reckon she'll have something suitable?" Katie asked, eyes alight. "Something not too old or moth-eaten?" She had an idea.

"Most probably. She chucks nothing out and is a brilliant seamstress. She made all my clothes growing up. Albeit was more out of necessity than choice. We didn't have much."

"If she really can run you up something from an old dress, do you think I could borrow it for my wedding? We're both having winter ceremonies, so we need long sleeves. You are taller than me – isn't everyone? – so my Aunt Isla could shorten it when you're finished with it. If you don't mind. Would you consider it, dear old pal?" Katie held her breath.

"Consider it? It's a bloody marvellous idea. Why pay for dresses we'll only wear once? You can take a trip out to Reading to see if you like it – whatever we can fashion out of an old evening dress. We are only having a small wedding at the local church. Dan doesn't have any family here, of course. There will only be a few of Nan's friends and chums of mine from childhood. And whoever of the Kingston clan can manage it. Oh, bollocks," she exclaimed.

"What is it?"

"Ciaran will see me in the dress, and then you, just a month later. He's not meant to see you in it so it will spoil your day."

"Don't give it a second thought, Ruby. Ciaran is not due for demobilization until December first, so he won't be able to come to your wedding, more's the pity. I'll accompany Mum and Pops, since you kindly invited them. Problem solved."

"That's alright, then. Aren't we the clever clogs?"

Women all over the United Kingdom had been forced to become resourceful with post-war wedding gowns. Traditional wedding dresses couldn't be had due to the vast number of coupons needed. Some brave souls ripped parachutes apart, and used the silk for frocks, but this was few and far between. Those who hadn't been in the services tended to wear a suit or an outfit with a floral corsage. Many others borrowed wedding frocks from family, neighbors, or friends.

"And you'll still be chief bridesmaid? Well, my only one, if truth be told."

"Of course, you eejit," Katie punched her lightly on the arm. "And you'll be mine, too. Albeit I suppose you'll be a dignified matron of honour, then."

Ruby giggled.

"Sheesh, you make me sound so old."

"Where is Dan stopping until the wedding? In London with mates?"

"He will be demobbed in a fortnight. So yes, he's staying with some soon to be ex-servicemen. And then he'll cram in with us at Nan's just before the wedding."

"Sounds like you have it all planned out."

"Ha. Not even nearly. That's why I need you and your sisters to help. I'm rubbish at these types of things."

"As long as you don't mind bunking in with me again. Tillie and Trevor are in the last throes of packing, so if you help us move them to Number Twelve, I'm sure Tillie will happily exchange some wedding advice."

Ruby flexed a muscle.

"Consider it done. The Wrens have made strongmen out of us lot."

Katie hooted. They spent the rest of the train journey nattering about wedding plans, oblivious to the servicemen and women around them, talking about what they were going to do now that the war was over.

Pops and Mum met their train with a banner, two Union Jacks, and a small bar of chocolate obtained from who-knew-where. Waterloo Station was a riot of activity, with cheers and screaming everywhere as returning soldiers, airmen, and sailors were welcomed by loved ones. Katie even heard music from a small band, but couldn't see where it came from. She was touched to no end to see her parents.

"Mum, Pops. You didn't have to greet us. It's madness here." Katie was thrilled nonetheless, and hugged them tightly. There was something about being met at a train that made one feel loved and special.

"It's your last time in the navy, darling. We couldn't just let you take the underground home. It's cause for enormous celebration. You're home, safe and free." As usual, Mum fought back tears.

"How are you, young lady?" Pops turned to Ruby.

"Couldn't be better, Mr Kingston. Thanks ever so much for meeting us. I didn't dream it would be like this. You'd think it was V-E Day all over again."

"It rather is," Pops replied thoughtfully. "Every man and woman who served us bravely in the last six years deserves a hero's welcome."

On the taxi ride home, Katie pressed her father for all the news.

"Is everyone alright? How is Trev's eyesight? Any word from Kenny? And has Hannah got a demob date yet? How are the twins? And Victoria? How was Uncle Thomas and Aunt Isla's wedding? Was it lovely?" Katie peppered her parents with questions.

"Slow down, luv. Everyone is well. Kenny has written a letter. And it's rather exciting. He's been demobbed and should be home within a fortnight. Isn't that tremendous?" Mum was all smiles now.

Katie clapped her hands.

"Smashing, just smashing. I can't wait to see him. We must have a big party when he returns."

"Alright. Let's do. As for the rest, Trev's eyesight is fine. Still not one-hundred percent, but the doctors say to give it time. All the babies are fine. Maggie is looking a little worn out, but that's to be expected. Hannah should be home by Christmas, but we're not sure exactly when. She joined late during the war, so her demob date is after you lot."

"And the wedding?" Katie prompted.

"It was splendid. Just Pops and I, Maggie and Micah, and Tillie and Trev. Hannah couldn't get leave. It was an elegant ceremony in our drawing room. Isla looked stylish in a pre-war dress that she managed to make look smart. Thomas was serious, but they both seemed quite happy. They didn't want a reception, so we had a lovely dinner at The Ivy restaurant. Everything was tasteful and charming. They are off now on a brief honeymoon in Wales – apparently, they have both always wanted to go there." Mum took a breath. "Is that enough news for you, luv?"

"For now, and ta, Mum. Now the most important question – what's for supper tonight? Ruby and I are fair starving since our spam sandwiches on the train."

"I'm afraid it's just fish pie, darling. But there's loads of it, and custard for afters. Naught too imaginative, but the rationing is unquestionably still on."

"I fear it will be for quite some time, girls," Pops added. "But no moaning. Simple fare, but hearty and filling."

"Pops, you sound like Lord Woolton with one of his speeches on the wireless."

"Oh, Katie. That reminds me of some proper special news. Your father has finally agreed to put in a telephone. They are coming soon to attach it, or wire it, or electrify it, or whatever they need to do to get it working."

Katie starting rumbling, then threw her head back, and, clutching her sides, laughed uncontrollably until the tears splashed down her cheeks.

"What's so funny about that?" Ruby asked, confused. "It seems like an ace idea."

"Grand, just g-g-grand," Katie choked out. "Leave it to Pops to wait until after the war to put in a telephone."

"I wasn't sure I trusted the damn things, poppet," Pops puffed.

This sent Katie into further gales of laughter.

"Darling, get yourself under control. It's not that comical," Mum scolded.

"Sorry, Mum, Pops. It just caught my funny bone is all. When I think of all the times a telephone would have been useful in the last six years, and now that the war is over, Pops is putting one in... but it is a brilliant idea. Now, I'll be able to ring up Ciaran, and Hannah, and even you in America, Ruby. Tops. Just tops." She wiped her eyes. What a turn-up for the books. Pops relenting and moving ahead with modern times. *What else is about to change, I wonder?*

Trev and Tillie greeted them amongst a sea of cartons, cases, and chests.

"Welcome home, luv. We're that glad to see you." The sisters embraced as Jamie tore into the front hall and barrelled into Katie's legs.

"Auntie Katie, Auntie Katie. Me new woom, me new woom."

Katie picked up him and spun him around.

"You're getting a new room? How lovely for you. Has Daddy painted it for you?"

"Boo. Daddy, boo," he replied, throwing his arms around his aunt's neck.

"Come through," Tillie invited. "If you can pick your way through this lot, that is. I'm so sorry, Ruby, but as you can see – we are in the midst of a big move."

Ruby waved away her concern.

"It's no bother, Tillie. I know my way."

Mum served tea and biscuits to the thirsty travellers.

"Supper will be at half-past, luv. Will this keep you until then?"

"It's lovely, Mum. Thanks."

Young Jamie was crawling all over her.

"Katie, could you possibly mind him for an hour or so? Victoria is asleep, so it's just this young lad. The removal van will be here early tomorrow and I'm not near packed." Both Tillie and Trevor looked frazzled.

"Of course, Tils. Ruby and I can manage one squirmy two-year-old, can't we?"

Ruby was slightly more dubious.

"We'll do our best. Go on then, Tillie. We'll give you a hand after supper. We've packed enough in our time, haven't we, Queenie?"

"Just watch our Ruby," warned Katie. "She'll toss everything into one bag without a care."

"That's all that's needed." Tillie pushed back a lock of blonde hair. "And it's just down the street, so nothing fancy."

"Thanks to you both," Trev called as the couple left the morning room.

"I'll get on with supper, then, shall I? You two are alright?"

"Yes, Mum. After the Germans, Jamie should be easy as pie."

Mum raised a knowing eyebrow and left the girls to it. Pops had somehow likewise vanished.

An hour later, the girls were ready to swear off ever having children.

"He's a handful, isn't he?" Ruby lurched after Jamie as he pulled the cushions off the sofa yet again.

"I suppose he loves this game." Katie wearily put them back on the sofa. "It's exhausting keeping up with him. I think I'll have a word with Ciaran about postponing this particular pleasure for some time."

"Me ball," Jamie shouted as he flung a soft ball at Ruby's head. Ruby caught it deftly and sank to the floor to roll it towards the toddler.

He caught it clumsily and tossed it towards Katie. It nearly hit a lamp, and she only avoided calamity by flinging herself in the air and snatching the ball with the ends of her fingertips.

"Brilliant catch, luv," Ruby sighed as she flopped down on top of the cushions. "No more ball." She shook at her head at the demanding little chap. "Can we break out the drinks tray?" She was only half-joking.

Neither of them heard the doorbell, but Mum and Pops stomped up the stairs and burst through the room.

"It's a telegram from Kenny. He'll be home in three days' time. And he's bringing a surprise." Mum held the thin blue paper aloft and literally jumped for joy. "My boy is finally coming home!"

CHAPTER TWENTY-EIGHT

"Whatever could the surprise be? Some exotic foods from the far east? Or carvings or fancy souvenirs?" Tillie trailed in with the baby in her arms after hearing all the ruckus.

"I expect it's a girl," Katie declared. "Kenny has met a girl, and he's bringing her back to England."

"Do you really think so? I just can't imagine." Mum looked totally bemused. "Where would he get a girl?"

The younger generation laughed.

"There are girls all over the world, Mum," Katie explained. "If I'm right, it's unlikely she'll be a British girl."

Trevor had entered the room behind his wife, giving a low whistle.

"I should think you're spot on, Katie. What else could it be?"

They all fell silent, each conjuring up what type of woman Kenny might bring home with him. None of them could fathom who she could be.

"I suppose we'll just have to wait and see, won't we?" Pops concluded dryly. "How about supper?"

"Oh golly, I totally forgot. I hope I haven't burnt it." Mum jumped up.

"We'll help you," Katie said swiftly. "Come on, Ruby." The girls followed Alice out of the room, eager not only to get the supper meal on the table but also to escape child-minding duties.

The fish pie was salvaged, but barely. Slightly dry, it still went down a treat, along with some autumn veg, and the ever-present custard.

"No more navy chow," sighed Katie, her face a picture of elation. "We've dreamt of this, haven't we, Ruby?"

"It's delicious, Mrs Kingston. Really top-notch."

"You girls are exaggerating, but I'll take it." Mum smiled.

"Sorry, Mum, but we have to get back to our packing. As it is, we'll likely be up till midnight."

"We'll clear away, Tils, and then join you. Will the children be going to b-e-d soon?"

"I expect young Jamie is on the brink." Trev pointed to the lad, who was nodding off in his high chair. "As for our young miss, it's anyone's guess. She's at odds with her schedule. Or should I say our schedule? She doesn't seem to work with one." He scooped up Jamie from the chair. "Let's go, lad. Time for a bath."

"Thanks, darling," Tillie threw him a grateful smile. "I'll give Victoria her feed, and then we're back hard at it."

Somehow, everything got packed by the time the lorry arrived the next morning. No one had gotten much sleep, but the mood was buoyant, nonetheless.

By two p.m., all the cases had been moved down the street and into #12, an identical townhouse to #40. Uncle Thomas had left most of the furniture, and even the linens, kitchen crockery, and pots. He said he had no need of it all, as Isla had a beautifully appointed flat. He took only his clothes, books, and other personal belongings. Katie thought he wanted to leave behind painful memories along with the bits and bobs from Shirley's time. He probably also wanted to give Tillie and Trev a boost so they needn't furnish the entire house at this early stage of their married life. So kind of him.

Mum and Pops had bravely offered to look after Jamie and all three babies so that the sisters, their husbands, and Ruby could blast through all the unpacking and organizing. Tillie wanted to at least have the bedrooms set up and kitchen operational by the end of the day. The men moved all the possessions in, whilst the girls unpacked room by room. Katie and Maggie got the kitchen sorted, whilst Tillie dashed out to the shops for several essentials to keep them going for a few days. Ruby had fun setting up the children's beds and ordering the toys onto shelves. Tillie made up the beds when she returned, and laid out pajamas for the little family, so they could collapse when they'd reached their unpacking limit, or the children wore out – whichever came first.

By eight o'clock, the place was looking lived in. Mum and Pops were bringing the children by any moment with duchess soup and some rock cakes for the hungry crew.

"The place looks wonderful already, Tils." Katie flopped onto the sofa, a glass of water in hand.

"Thanks, sis. It doesn't feel like home yet, but once Jamie's toys and Victoria's baby bits are strewn around, it will look more familiar. Little by little, we can replace some of this furniture with some that suit our style. Aunt Shirley had lovely taste, but it will be thrilling to choose things for my own house."

Katie and Ruby walked back with a rather wilted-looking Mum and Pops after they'd brought the grandchildren over. Maggie and Micah left shortly thereafter with the twins, so Tillie and Trev were finally alone with their little family for the first time.

It had been a long day, and everyone was sweaty and dog-tired. Plans were made for a welcome home supper for Kenny in just two days.

The next morning, Mum was up early and brought a tea tray to the girls, who were enjoying a well-deserved lie-in.

"Good morning, girls. It's a bit windy this morning, and it's meant to rain this afternoon. It's such a relief to hear the weather forecasts again. Feels like things are getting back to normal. Routines are comforting."

Throughout the war, no weather forecasts could be broadcast, in fear that they would give the Germans crucial intelligence to aid in bombing accuracy. It had been just one more frustration for the British people, never knowing what weather might be coming.

Katie yawned.

"Good morning, Mum. What a treat. I can't remember the last time anyone brought me tea and toast in bed."

"I should think not." Mum tsked. "It's in the way of a bribe, in the event."

Ruby groaned from somewhere under the covers.

"Kenny will be here tomorrow. We have no idea what time. His telegram was maddeningly vague, so we need to be ready for his arrival at any time. Since we agreed to give him Tillie and Trevor's room, we need to clean it properly and move his bed and belongings down. You two will stay here. We'll need to shift some beds, lamps and so on from the boxrooms. It shouldn't take too long."

By Katie's reckoning, it would take at least a few hours, but she didn't mind. She knew Mum wanted to make everything special and welcoming for her only son's return. And Katie was that keyed up to see her brother that she was pleased to fill a few hours left empty by Tillie and Trevor's departure. Determined not to mention how quiet the house was without Jamie bouncing around or Victoria squealing when tickled, Katie was more than thankful that Mum was in such a cheerful mood.

"Ruby, wake up. Didn't you hear Mum has brought us breakfast?"

An eye appeared over the covers, then another one. "Did you say breakfast?"

"Good morning, Ruby. I'll leave the tea tray. Please bring it down when you're through. I'll meet you in Kenny's new room in three quarters of an hour."

"Yes, Ma'am," Katie gave her a mock salute. "And ta for the breakfast. It's cracking."

"Thanks, Mrs K. We appreciate the first-class treatment," Ruby mumbled through a mouthful of toast and margarine.

***

After Mum was more or less satisfied with Kenny's new room setup, they decorated the front hall with whatever bits and bobs they could find. They turned their hands to organizing a meal that could be ready when Kenny turned up – whenever that would be.

"Remember, luv. As soon as he arrives, we'll ring Maggie and Micah to come round with the girls. And then you'll run to Tillie's to fetch her and Trev."

"Yes, Mum. For the third time, I'll ring Mags and fetch Tillie. Steady on."

"I'll run to Number Twelve so you can stay here with your brother," Ruby offered.

"Ta, luv. That would be brilliant."

Mum was jittery as a cat. She fussed and fidgeted all afternoon, checking and re-checking Kenny's room, the decorations, and supper preparations.

"Shall we lay the table, Mum? Or is it too early?"

"That's a good idea, Katie. I'm sorry I'm right jumpy today. I don't know why. I birthed that boy, bathed and fed him, dried his tears, and tucked him up at night. Why am I so nervy to see my son?"

"Mum, of course you're on edge. You haven't seen him for an age. He was so changed after his ship went down, and lost his memory for such a long time. You're concerned about how much he's changed since what's he's been through – D-Day and fighting in far east. It's to be expected. Don't be so hard on yourself."

Mum gave her a wan smile.

"I suppose you're right, luv. It will all be alright once I see his face, and know for myself that he's really here and safe."

In the event, it was near eight o'clock when the front door opened and Kenny's familiar voice rang out.

"Mum, Pops. Anyone home?"

The family had all gathered, supper had been delayed and finally eaten, and they were playing a lacklustre game of charades, everyone with half an ear cocked.

Mum stifled a scream, jumped up and ran down the stairs, Pops following closely behind.

"Kenny, my boy! Of course, we're home. We're all waiting for you."

Losing the battle with tears, Mum clutched her son tightly and let them flow.

"Kenny, you've gotten so thin. And you're so late! But you're here." Mum was blubbing and there was no stopping her.

"Dear, calm yourself. Son, welcome home. And who is this lovely lady?" Walter shook his son's hand, and turned to the tall blonde at his side.

"Mum, Dad. Sorry we are so late. The trains were heaving with demobbed servicemen and women. And may I present my wife – Mrs Astrid Kingston."

Dead silence.

"Hello everyone." A foreign accent. *What in the world?*

Mum stumbled and recovered herself, holding out her hand.

"Hello, Astrid. I suppose I'm your mother-in-law, Alice. My goodness, Kenny. You've thrown us for six."

The mass of Kingstons, young and old, crowded the newcomers.

"You won't remember us all, but I'm Tillie, the prettiest twin. This is my husband, Trevor. And this jumpy young lad is our son, Jamie. Welcome to London." Tillie kissed Astrid on the cheek, and waved in the general direction of her son, who was trying to climb up his dad's back.

"Rubbish, I'm the better-looking twin." Maggie came forward. "And this is Micah. My baby girls are asleep upstairs. It's lovely to meet you."

"And I'm Katie, the ugly one," Katie pushed in amidst a chorus of protests. "Actually, I'm Kenny's favourite sister, and it's grand to meet anyone that can put up with him. Come through. You must be gasping for a cuppa."

Astrid looked shell-shocked.

"Don't fret, sweetheart." Kenny ushered his bride up the stairs and into the sitting room. "You'll get to know this lot in no time. And yes, we'd love tea, and whatever else is on offer."

"I'll get the tea, Mrs Kingston. I'm Ruby, by the way, Astrid. A navy chum of Katie's. Just to add to the mayhem." Ruby smiled and headed down to the kitchen.

After settling in, everyone looked expectantly at the new couple.

"How was your travel, dear?" Mum hovered at Kenny's elbow, afraid to let him out of her sight.

"Long. We had a rough crossing, and Astrid was green the whole time. After our ship docked, there was a spot of trouble with her paperwork. Once that was sorted, it was just a train home from Portsmouth. Sorry, I missed you, sis. When were you demobbed?" He turned to Katie.

"Ruby and I were released a few weeks ago." She hesitated a moment and then plunged in. "Kenny, Astrid. You must tell us. How did you meet? When did you get married? Fill us in."

Kenny took his wife's hand and grinned at her.

"I told you Katie would be the one to press us. Well, I met Astrid in Norway when HMS Implacable was built there last year. She was part of the resistance movement during the Nazi occupation. We met at the docks."

"My goodness. That all sounds proper mysterious," Tillie spoke first. "Conditions must have been horrendous under the Germans."

"It was," Astrid replied in clipped English. "I did what I could to help."

"Astrid doesn't like to speak about what happened to her and her family," Kenny interrupted. "They were near starving for most of the war. Astrid was a true Norwegian hero."

"Kenneth, stop." Astrid was tall – almost as tall as Kenny – and dreadfully thin. She had long white-blonde hair and frosty blue eyes. Her eyebrows were so blonde they were virtually white. She seemed nervous.

"I brought her some food from the ship, and we struck up a friendship. She agreed to write to me, and we've exchanged letters ever since. I was demobbed three weeks ago, and I made my way back to Norway. After liberation, things eased up a little. I helped Astrid find her brother, then I asked her to marry me. Incredibly, she agreed to come to London with me. We got married aboard ship, and here we are."

"We're very sorry for all you've been through, Astrid. I'm sure there is much more to the story, but we understand it's difficult to talk about. We are so glad you survived, and Kenny is indeed lucky to have found you. Please treat this as your home. We'll be glad to help you settle in any way we can." Pops gave her an encouraging smile.

"And there's my cue. Here's tea, and what I could scrounge from the larder. Sardines on toast, carrots, and prune custard suit you? It's rather a mixed bag, but I thought speed was more important than elegance. And tea, naturally." Ruby burst in at just the right time.

Kenny threw back his head and laughed.

"I've been dreaming of English food for months, but it wasn't prune custard. I'm not whingeing, mind. It all looks delicious. Astrid, ready to tuck in?"

"I never say no to food. Thank you, k-k-kindly," she said formally. She gobbled every crumb on her plate. Ruby offered seconds, which she gratefully accepted.

"It's too soon to ask for your plans, but know you can stay as long as you like, Kenny," Mum said unnecessarily. "We've done up Tillie and Maggie's old room for you. It's the biggest after ours. It will do nicely for the pair of you." Mum was doing her best to accept this peculiar circumstance.

Katie guffawed, and Tillie joined in.

"Mum, you're as transparent as a pane of glass. Kenny and Astrid, you'd better be staying awhile or Mum will pitch a fit." Katie couldn't fight the giggles.

"We are staying put for the moment. I have to sort some kind of job. I've a bit of money put aside from the navy, but I'll need some work to support Astrid and me. For now, I just want to show her 'round London, and get her accustomed to British life."

"Thank you for having me," Astrid said simply. "I make England home now."

Mum beamed. She couldn't help herself.

"I'll show you through the house, dear. Please make yourself at home. Trev, can you manage the cases? I'm sure Astrid is weary from the long trip and wants to see her new bedroom."

"Sure, Ma," Trev tried to keep the chuckle from his voice. "Then we'd best be off. Jamie here is about to fret himself into a sulk."

"Kenny, Astrid. Please come to ours for tea tomorrow. We're just down the street at Number Twelve."

Kenny looked confused.

"I'll explain later, dear," Mum jumped in.

"I need to meet all your babies properly, but I'm just too knackered. Tomorrow will be brilliant."

"Goodnight, everyone." Astrid gave a tiny smile to the assembled family and followed Kenny out of the room.

"Well, I'm bloody gobsmacked," Katie swore. "Life is getting even more interesting round here."

CHAPTER TWENTY-NINE

Kenny and Astrid settled in slowly over the next week. Astrid still seemed quiet, but ate voraciously, and was grateful for any small kindness. Kenny was back to his pre-war temperament – sunny, carefree, and full of jokes. Despite his gaunt frame, he was truly a man now. The war had forced him to grow up.

He took Astrid all over the city, and she was amazed at the size of it, the astronomical bombing damage that London had sustained, and the historical sites that were hundreds of years old.

Kenny wasn't in a rush to find a job. Pops had talked to him about joining his accounting firm, but Kenny's response was lacklustre. After serving in the navy, he wanted more of a hands-on, physical job. He just didn't know what that was yet.

On a bleak November day, Katie was the first down, and gathered the post. Putting aside the letters for her parents, she found one addressed to her. From Buckingham Palace, of all places.

Sinking down to the hallway stairs, she double-checked that it was her name and address: Petty Officer Katherine Kingston, #40 Longridge Road, London, England. *That's me alright.* She ran her finger over the royal seal on the front and flipped over the cream-coloured envelope. She took Pop's letter opener from the library and slid it under the envelope lip.

Taking out the thick, embossed paper, she sat in Pop's chair to read it. King George's red coat of arms blazed from the top of the page.

"28, October 1945

Dear Petty Officer Kingston,

Congratulations on receiving the George Cross for exceptional bravery in non-combat for your efforts to evacuate injured hospital patients at Portsmouth on March 29, 1945. It is valiant endeavors such as yours that helped us to win the war.

Please present yourself and three guests at Buckingham Palace on November 29th at 2:00 p.m. to receive your award from the Queen and I. Afternoon dress is required."

It was signed George VI with an underline flourish.

Katie read it twice, blinked, and still couldn't believe it. She was going to Buck House to be presented with her award by the King himself. She had nearly forgotten all about it.

A slow smile spread across her face. Her heart lifted with pride. Bloody hell.

She ran to the telephone, mentally thanking Pops for finally putting it in. She needed to ring Ciaran straightaway to plead with him to get leave. How could she experience such an important event without her fiancé? And how could she possibly choose just two other guests from her large family to witness the occasion? Oh, shite. What would she wear? She had barely found a suitable dress for Ruby's wedding next week. But what glorious problems. She was going to meet the King and Queen!

* * *

Ruby was chuffed beyond belief that Katie would be recognized in such a significant way. Meeting her and Mum and Pops at the Reading train, Ruby hugged her chum tightly and lifted her off the ground.

"Look at you, Queenie. Grand enough to meet the King. I told you that you were something special. I hope you believe it now. What do you think of our girl, Mr and Mrs K?"

"We are still stunned, if I'm honest." Mum kissed Ruby on the cheek. "And this little scamp never even told us she won the George Cross."

"I didn't know it would come to this, did I?" Katie replied. "One never does."

"We are proper proud of her," Walter confirmed. "To be honored by His Majesty in this way is quite a distinction. And it's nice to see you, Ruby." He gave her a peck.

The trio took a short bus ride to the tiny house that Ruby shared with her nan. It was a grey, bone-chilling day, and they huddled together on the cold bus.

"Just a wee warning. My nan can be a bit – salty – shall we say. She pretty much says whatever comes into her head, with no mind of how it comes out."

"Hmmm. It's a family trait, I expect," Katie teased, blowing on her fingers.

"Leave off. Not here a quarter of an hour, and already having a go at me."

"I'm sure your nan is a perfectly agreeable lady, Ruby. We'll get on just fine. Is everything in order for the wedding?"

Ruby snorted.

"Not by half. We have a church and vicar, some idea of food, and Nan is working on my dress as we speak. No sign of a bridegroom so far, and no flowers or cake. Help." She turned her most charming smile on her best friend.

"Ruby, you said it was all in hand!" Katie was horrified.

"Never fear, Ruby. I'm sure it's not that dire. I'll sort it once I know what needs to be done. Your guest list is small, right?" Mum was all business.

"A few childhood chums and some of Nan's that are still alive. And you. Maybe twenty or so. I'm not quite certain."

Katie felt sweat trickle down her back. This was going to be a load of work.

But as is the way of most things, by the time of the wedding two days later, Mum had worked miracles. She'd moved the reception to the church basement and organized the church ladies to take charge of the food. Helpfully, they'd also provided some banners and paper decorations from their stockpile, and Mum had wheedled one of them to bake a cake, albeit it would only have one layer, the rest being phony cardboard. And the groom had turned up.

"Darling, you look beautiful," Katie breathed, as Ruby twirled in her floor-length yellow satin dress. It skimmed her body in soft waves, with tight long sleeves, and a lace-trimmed bodice. "Nan has done a brilliant job with it."

"You and your mum have done some kind of magic. Bringing a flower garland from London was genius, and how she got Mrs Pruehaven to bake a cake is a mystery to me. Her baking at church sales is always scrummy, but her arthritis keeps her from baking often."

"I'm sure it will all be lovely. None of that is your concern anymore. It's time to enjoy your groom and your day. Is he all set?"

Dan had arrived the night before, full of Yankee bravado and good cheer. He'd won over Nan with chocolate and cigarettes.

"He's not keen on his demob suit, but it will have to do. I'll be looking at his handsome face, anyroad. I'll deal with the suit later." She giggled.

"Sod off. I don't need to think about your groom in that way. I have my own to consider in just a few weeks' time."

Katie was apprehensive and electrified in equal measure about the notion of time alone with her husband. Their passion had grown, and it was becoming increasingly difficult for both of them to hold back. She simmered with longing for him, but feared the unknown. Mum had made half-hearted attempts to talk about the wedding night, which Katie had firmly rebuffed. She might ask Tillie a pertinent question or two in good time, but that was to think about later. Today was Ruby's day. Even if it was sleeting down icy rain and the wind was ferocious. But Katie was saying nothing about the weather.

"Did he manage to get a wedding ring?"

"I believe so." Ruby preened in front of the ancient mirror.

Dan had asked Ruby to wait until they moved to America for a proper engagement ring. There was a family ring that was rumoured to be exquisite, but he hadn't trusted the post to ship it overseas. Ruby couldn't wait to slip it on her finger when she arrived in Oklahoma. A gold band would do for now.

From the family, only Tillie and Trev had made it. They had left the children with Maggie and Micah for the night. Neither Kenny and Astrid, nor Uncle Thomas and Aunt Isla knew the bridal couple well, and elected to stay in London.

It was a ten-minute walk in the driving rain to the church. Pops and Trev did their best to protect Ruby with overcoats, umbrellas, and their own bodies. By the time they got to the church, everyone was soaking wet, but the bride was slightly less so. She repaired her makeup, and Tillie fussed with her hair to bring it to order. Ruby laughed it all off, a trifle nervously.

"Happy is the bride that rain falls on, isn't that right? It's good luck for Dan and me."

"Luv, you are astonishing. Let's get you fixed up proper. Your Dan will never know you've been slogging in the sleet." Katie smoothed out the dress wrinkles as best as she could.

"I expect he has been, too. Your bridegroom may be a tad soggy," Tillie added.

"Perfect. We were meant to be together."

Despite the cold, blustery day, it was a delightful wedding. The bride and groom were obviously in love, and repeated their vows loudly. Nan smiled broadly from the front row.

After the ardent kiss, the couple walked back up the aisle, beaming from ear to ear. It was still teeming, so the guests threw rice at the newlyweds in the church vestibule.

"You take care of her, or I'll be off to America like a shot," threatened Katie, near tears. She would miss her friend dearly.

"She's my best girl, and now my wife. I'm the luckiest man in the old US of A. I promise I'll look after her. And you must come to Oklahoma as soon as you and Ciaran are able."

After the reception turned into a knees up, Ruby and Dan cut the cake. The bride then changed into her going-away outfit. She carefully wrapped the wedding dress in tissue for Katie to take back to Earl's Court.

"On to you now, Queenie. Hopefully, I've used up all the rain, so this dress will be lucky for you on your special day."

The two ex-Wrens embraced tightly. They'd been through so much together, so much that no one else would ever know.

"I'll see you in London the week before the wedding. It will be our last hoorah, darling. Dan is itching to get back to America, but I can't miss your wedding. He'll just have to cool his heels a while longer."

The newlyweds planned a short honeymoon in nearby Woking, before spending a fortnight or so with Nan before leaving England for good.

Katie nodded, a lump in her throat. Damn, she hated the feeling of trying not to cry.

"Till London, then," she said and gave Ruby one last hug.

* * *

Awards day dawned sunny and cold. Katie puttered around, had tea with Tillie down the road, and had a long bath before dressing for the big event.

Unbeknownst to Katie, all the women in the family had been saving clothes coupons for months, hoping to have enough for a proper wedding gown for her. Since Katie had thwarted this plan by borrowing and altering Ruby's frock, they'd had enough to buy a slightly used tea dress in a dusty rose. Katie loved it and felt like she was floating on a cloud when wearing it. Between Isla and Astrid – who had shown herself to be remarkably good at pretty much anything she turned a hand to – they created a fascinator from a cut-down old hat, some dried flowers, and a dash of whimsy.

"Ready to go, luv? You look so lovely. Do you have the invitation?" Mum fussed around as she looked for her handbag.

"Ta, Mum. I feel like royalty myself in this dress. It was so kind of you all to save up your clothing coupons for me. You look smashing, too. The blue suits you. And yes, I have the invitation, and also the detailed instructions that came from the palace. We're meant to be there ninety minutes in advance, so is Pops almost ready? I want to be early to find Ciaran."

"Did he manage leave, then?" Mum was afraid to ask.

"I won't know for sure until I see him. He's been into his CO's office at Bletchley Park every day for the last week, pleading for even a six-hour pass. As of yesterday, the CO was weakening, but it's touch and go."

A loud knock startled them both.

"Bloody hell, who could that be?" Katie started for the door.

"Language, Katie," admonished Mum. "It's likely the taxi that Pops ordered."

Jeremy kept up a friendly chatter as he expertly steered his way through the clogged London traffic to Buckingham Palace. Forgoing his fee upon hearing of the momentous occasion, the cabbie waved them off with good wishes at the gates.

Katie was out of the car just about before it stopped, scanning the crowd, desperately looking for Ciaran. She saw a motion out of the corner of her eye, and spied her wonderful, amazing, gorgeous, resourceful fiancé sprinting towards her.

"Ciaran," she shouted, and they collided with a thud that became a hug. Given the formality of the occasion, she didn't think it appropriate to kiss him outside of the King's home, so she held back, and just drank him in with her eyes. She hadn't seen him for weeks and had sorely missed him.

"You got leave," she exclaimed.

"Finally. He tortured me, but eventually gave way early this morning, so I spiffed up and got the earliest train I could. I've only now arrived, and just in time, I see." He flashed his biggest smile at her.

He greeted her parents, and they presented their identification to the security men at the famous black and gold gates. After carefully examining her official invitation, they were let through.

"We are at Buckingham Palace. I'm pinching myself," Mum gushed, as they crunched the gravel of the palace perimeter. Smiling uniformed staff greeted them, and pointed the way through the inner quadrangle, Bow Room, and up the elaborate staircase, through the breathtaking Picture Galley to the elegant Ballroom. Here, Katie parted from Ciaran and her parents. They were seated in rows of gold-backed chairs, whilst she was whisked into a side room with other honorees.

The Household Comptroller checked the honorees' invitations again and placed the exceptionally well-dressed guests in rows. Another staff placed a pin on their left shoulders (women) or left suit lapel (men). Each pin had a special hook for the King to hang the award onto. *Very splashy. Am I really in the King's anteroom waiting to meet him?* A string quartet played ethereal music from beyond the doors.

The Comptroller reviewed the order of events. Each person would be handed an engraved card with their name on it. Lining up outside the ballroom, each would enter when their turn was next, place the card on a gold tray held by another staff, and wait for the Master of the Household to call their name. Then the long walk to meet the King on a raised dais. Each honoree was to curtsey or bow to both the sovereigns and wait for the King to place the George Cross on the little hook. Once the King had made small talk and shaken their hand, he or she was to curtsey or bow again, and leave by a different door. They would then receive a velvet case for the Cross, and an embossed certificate of congratulations signed by the King.

The instructions were repeated, and as there were no questions (who would dare?), Katie waited expectantly for the ceremony to begin. Her heart was thumping madly in her chest, and she felt dizzy looking around, trying to take it all in and imprint the images on her muzzy brain.

The doors opened, and the music faded. All that Katie could see was a line of Yeoman Warders in traditional red and gold uniforms, guarding the King and Queen.

In no time, it was Katie's turn. She placed her card on the gold tray without dropping it, heard her name called, and stepped forward. Feeling all eyes on her, she held her head high and walked proudly towards the King, who was smiling softly at her. He was quite tall and looked resplendent in his naval uniform. He had kind blue eyes bordered by worry lines, doubtless caused by six years of sleepless nights. She was surprised to notice that he smelled wonderful. Remembering to curtsey, she stopped immediately in front of him.

"Good afternoon, Petty Officer Kingston. I'm given to understand you demonstrated tremendous bravery in Portsmouth earlier this year. You saved the lives of many injured servicemen in an explosion, at great personal risk to yourself. You are a credit to the Women's Royal Navy and to me personally." He pinned the blue-ribboned George Cross to her shoulder pin and firmly shook her hand.

All she could squeak out was a weak Thank you, Your Majesty, before walking past him, and curtseying again to a serene Queen Elizabeth, who sat on a glittering throne. She exited the Ballroom, and found herself in another anteroom, where she was handed her velvet box, framed certificate, and a small bouquet of fresh flowers. She was told to wait until the ceremony was complete, and then tea would be served. *Blimey, I didn't expect to be fed. I'm not sure I could eat a bite.*

Three quarters of an hour later, the assembly of beaming award recipients was shown through to the Blue Drawing Room for a reception. Katie was inordinately thrilled to see Mum, Pops, and Ciaran, and rushed to be congratulated by them. A scrumptious afternoon tea was served, and the family devoured the delicate cucumber, chicken, and watercress sandwiches, freshly-baked scones with real clotted cream and jam, and intricate tiny pastries; all washed down with gallons of tea – with milk and sugar. It was the most delicious tea Katie had ever had – or probably ever would.

Her guests admired the substantial silver cross mounted on the thick blue ribbon that made up the George Cross. In the centre of the cross was a brave warrior atop a stallion with For Gallantry engraved around it. Her name was also inscribed on the medal. Katie would treasure it forever.

"I'm so proud of you, mavourneen. My brave English Wren." Ciaran kissed her, and she didn't care who saw them.

There were tears in Mum's eyes as she and Pops told her what a marvellous daughter she was, and that they couldn't be prouder. It was the happiest day of Katie's life – so far.

She and Mum nattered the entire way home about the ceremony, what the Queen wore (Katie hadn't even noticed she was impeccable in a gauzy, violet ensemble and matching hat), and going over every detail of the day.

Reaching #40, Katie entered with the family behind her. She turned on the hallway lights, and was dumbfounded when the entire rest of the family jumped up and shouted, *Surprise!* And was that Ruby and Dan in the corner, holding up an enormous banner saying CONGRATULATIONS, KATIE!

Not being able to contain the emotions swirling inside her, she fought the lump in her throat and the tears threatening to bubble up.

"Katie, don't cry. This is meant to be a party," Tillie rushed forward.

"I'm alright. Just give me a minute. You all surprised me, is all." *Bloody hell. Was this all for her?*

"Well, don't just stand there gawking at her. Let's celebrate our award winner. If she will deign to join us after meeting the King and Queen." Leave it to Ruby to break the ice and give her a moment to collect herself.

"I might just fit it in to my royal diary," Katie said, wiping her eyes.

Everyone came to hug her, but she gave Ruby an extra squeeze.

The celebration was lovely. As usual, enough food had been scrounged to make it feel like a proper spread, and Aunt Isla had come up trumps with a condensed milk cake. After the delicious royal tea, Katie could hardly eat a bite.

Kenny played some old gramophone records, and they pushed back the rug in the sitting room and danced the evening away.

Everyone gushed over Katie's award, which she proudly wore all night. It was splendid all round.

CHAPTER THIRTY

December 1945

Christmas was rapidly approaching, and as well as planning for the first holiday in six years when the family would be all together, there was another Kingston wedding to organize. Katie and Mum blissfully re-lived the day of the George Cross ceremony many times over. Tillie and Maggie were a rapt audience, and Astrid showed a proper interest in the British royal family.

"Wasn't that tea divine?" Katie sighed as she and Mum sat at the kitchen table a few days later.

"The best I ever had," Mum declared, pulling the brown teapot towards her. "Those scones with clotted cream and fresh strawberry jam melted in my mouth. The King and Queen know how to put on a proper do. I don't suppose we'll ever see the like."

"I wish the whole day was not such a blur. I feel like I was walking through it like a dream."

"The photograph that the palace sent is a keepsake that will remind you forever, luv," Mum replied.

Katie had been delighted when a parcel was delivered with a silver-framed photograph of her receiving her George Cross whilst shaking the King's hand. A reminder that she was worthy in her own right. *Not that I need it anymore. No more doubting myself, and hiding behind my older sisters.*

"It is indeed," Katie mumbled. "I didn't even realize it was being taken. I was that dazed."

"Well, this tick list will not write itself. Let's start with Christmas. Everyone will be here, including Hannah. Won't that be marvellous?"

"Any word on her demob? She's the last one, poor dear."

"Not yet. She expects it to be within the next three months or so. She's that impatient to get on with her life, but what can she do? I'm chuffed that she'll be here for Christmas, at least."

"And Ciaran's parents. We are both happy and relieved they'll be here for Christmas and the wedding. I was worried about the travel, but they insist on making the journey."

"Well, we need to meet them, don't we? It made sense to have them here for the holiday as well, since they are coming from such a long way. We'll take proper care of them."

Turning to her list, she paused for a moment.

"I have some bad news, though. Well, not bad exactly – but disappointing. I've received a letter from Faye. She won't be returning to us as a housekeeper. She finds she loved nursing during the war, and wants to get more training, and keep at it."

"Oh, Mum. That's hard cheese – but not unexpected, is it? Bags of women want to spread their wings now and do more than domestic service."

"Yes, and if I'm honest, I'm not sure we need her anymore. You've all left, save you and Kenny," she turned to Astrid. "The house is not too much for me to cope with anymore. I'm sure I can get a day girl in to help with the washing and seasonal cleaning."

"I'm happy to help," Astrid put in quickly. "I enjoy cooking, and need something to keep busy."

"Thank you, dear. Astrid is a wonder. She is a dab hand in the kitchen, and never whinges about the dishes or running the hoover."

"Makes me useful," Astrid insisted. She'd put on a bit of weight, and was slowly losing the troubled look in her eyes.

"I've wished Faye well, and told her she has a standing invitation to visit anytime. She's sent one of her famous fruitcakes."

"Smashing." Katie counted the family on her hands. "So that's twenty-one for Christmas dinner. My goodness, Mum. That's a houseful."

"It is. Tillie wants everyone for Christmas Eve at hers, so let's sort what we'll have for Christmas dinner."

"Ciaran's parents are bringing some type of game. I expect it's one of the spring lambs grown plump. Perhaps a leg of lamb? Mrs McElroy has also offered eggs, bacon, and I expect she'll tuck in a few other Irish surprises for us."

"What luxury." Mum smiled. "It will be a proper Christmas at last."

"Maybe we can have a Christmas tree…" Katie was in the spirit.

"May I cook some Finnish dishes? We had rutabaga casserole and plum pastries back home." Astrid's eyes were downcast, and she held her breath.

"Of course, Astrid! We would love that. And any other suggestions you have, please bring them forward. This is your first Christmas being away from home and without your family. I'm sure it will be trying for you. We want you to feel as merry as possible."

Astrid nodded, then knit her brows.

"Please can you explain what is 'merry?'"

"It's how we celebrate Christmas, dear. Being merry means being joyful, singing, eating well, and enjoying being together," Mum replied.

"We shall make much merry then. Shall I put on the kettle for more tea?"

Katie and her mum exchanged a fond look. Astrid was settling in.

* * *

By Christmas Eve, the house was brimming with guests. Ciaran had been in Ireland for a fortnight, helping his Da with some heavy winter tasks, and fetching his parents back to London. They'd arrived two days ago, laden with goodies, including two large legs of lamb, a chicken, a massive ham, mince pies, Irish shortbread, and bags more, including homemade gifts for everyone.

Katie's fears for her future in-laws and the difficulty of the journey had been eased as soon as she saw them at Euston Station. Though tired, they wore broad smiles, and moved easily, if not speedily. Kenny and Astrid had insisted on giving up their room, as it was the biggest, with the fewest stairs. They'd moved up to one of the boxrooms on the top floor. Ciaran had another one.

Katie and Astrid had festooned the house with whatever festive ornaments, ribbons, and garlands they could find in the attic. Pops had brought home a Christmas tree, and they'd trimmed it with all the old ornaments packed away for the duration of the war.

And then it was Christmas Eve.

Loading up for the quick trip to Tillie's, Astrid was delighted to see a light snow falling. More was expected on Christmas morning.

"Reminds me of Finland," she cried, opening her mouth for a few flakes to land on her tongue.

Jamie and Trevor answered the door almost before Pops knocked.

"Were you expecting someone, young lad?" Pops asked in all seriousness.

"I told you, Jamie. Father Christmas will not be knocking at the door. He's coming down the chimney."

Jamie's cheeks were flushed with excitement. Slightly crestfallen, he was still happy to see Granny and Gampa.

"Hello, Mum, Pops, everyone." Tillie deposited four-month-old Victoria into Mum's arms, looking slightly frazzled herself. "Everyone's here save Uncle Thomas and Aunt Isla, who are expected momentarily. Come through,"

Christmas carols blared from the wireless, and the rest of the family gathered in the sitting room, dressed in festive red and green, where a Christmas tree took pride of place in the corner.

Tillie had prepared (with Maggie and Isla's help) a feast of hot and cold hors d'oeuvres set up on a long table. This was enjoyed by all, washed down with mulled wine and beer. Toasts to those here and far away were raised again and again. Several off-key Christmas carols were sung, and Silent Night held a new poignancy. Ruby and Dan were kipping here, and joined in with gusto.

Ciaran cleared his throat loudly.

"May I make a traditional Irish Christmas blessing?"

Amidst cries of "yes please," and "we'd love it," Ciaran stood.

"The light of the Christmas star to you
The warmth of home and hearth to you.
The cheer and good will of friends to you.
The hope of a childlike heart to you.

The joy of a thousand angels to you.
Love and God's peace to you.
Slainte."

"Well done, son." Mrs McElroy took a deep swig of mulled wine, and the others followed suit.

"Happy Christmas, mavourneen." Ciaran kissed his fiancée.

"Happy Christmas, Irish." Katie kissed him back with fervor.

The children were getting fractious, so it was time to call it an evening. It would be a big day tomorrow.

A surprise knock came at the door. They all looked around, wondering who could possibly be missing.

"Ho, ho, ho," came the booming voice from the hall. All the young parents rushed to the vestibule with Jamie and the babies.

"Are there any well-behaved children here?" A makeshift Santa pounced on young Jamie, whose mouth was wide open in wonder.

"I shouldn't think so," Trevor answered cheekily.

"Yes, yes, me, me!" Jamie screamed, albeit he didn't approach the intimidating man with white hair and matching beard.

"I suppose you haven't been too naughty," Trev hesitated.

"I think all the children are well-behaved, Father Christmas," Maggie put poor Jamie out of his misery.

"Then you shall have Christmas presents tomorrow morning," the jolly old man declared. "Mind you go to sleep straightaway, with no fuss."

Jamie nodded solemnly, and Santa departed with cries of Merry Christmas all around.

"That Santa looked remarkably like Dan," Katie whispered to Ciaran.

On the way back to #40, Astrid confessed she'd put Dan up to the ruse.

"It's tradition on Christmas Eve in Finland," she explained. "Father Christmas comes to the door to make sure all the children are well-behaved before receiving their gifts."

"Brilliant," Katie replied. "We should adopt it every year."

The festivities continued the next day at Mum and Pops. Whilst rationing still raged, you'd never know it by the bountiful food, imaginative homemade gifts, and good spirits shared by all. There was plenty to be thankful for, and Mum's face shone all day – her babies were all home, and the future beckoned gaily. Much merry was made.

***

"I'm getting married today. Today is my wedding day," Katie tried it on, and was delighted to find it fit.

"It is, and not a cloud in the sky." Ruby came into her room with a loaded tea tray. "Not like the raging ice storm at my wedding, thank goodness."

"Ruby, darling. Join the party."

Tillie and Maggie had left the children at home, and come to help their youngest sister prepare for her wedding.

"Good morning, girls. What's next to be done?"

"Hullo, are you any good at nail varnish? Katie has picked a pastel pink. I'm about to do her makeup." Tillie plucked a cup of tea from the tray.

"Righto." Ruby perched on the bed, where Maggie brushed out Katie's dark curls.

"I feel like a queen with everyone fussing over me." Katie reached for a biscuit.

"It's your day, luv. Enjoy it." Tillie wanted it to be everything her sister had dreamed about.

"Are you all packed for your honeymoon?" Maggie asked. Ciaran and Katie were taking a brief trip to Dover to keep their promise of returning to Abbot's Cliff sound mirror.

"Just about. It takes a little longer without just a uniform to bother about."

"How is the dress? Will it do?" Ruby asked worriedly.

"Aunt Isla has done miracles with it. As well as shortening it, she's taken it in a bit, and added a satin belt. She's also cut the sleeves to three-quarters length and steamed it. It looks like a new gown – mine. I adore it. And it counts for my something borrowed."

"Phew," Ruby sighed. "Will you wear your George Cross with it?"

Amidst a sea of giggles, Katie shook her head emphatically no.

"I'm ignoring you, Ruby. Righto, my shoes are new and the dress is borrowed. I just need something old and blue. Maybe a blue ribbon in my flowers?" She turned to Maggie.

"I expect I can help with both," Aunt Isla came in, carrying a box.

"Bloody hell, what is that?" Katie had elected against a veil, preferring to leave her hair curled and framing her face. She was growing it out now that the Navy didn't insist on her keeping it above shoulder-length, and loved the longer look. What else could it be?

"I hope you don't mind, darling. I've taken Tillie's veil, and with a little inventiveness and some scraps – I've created you a hat with a small veil over the face. Very modern." She handed it to Katie, who took it carefully from the box. Unwrapping the tissue paper revealed a lovely yellow fascinator with netting and delicate flowers.

"And it has a blue flower mixed in with the white. It's absolutely enchanting." She placed it carefully on her head. "How can I ever thank you?"

"I wanted you to have a look that was all your own, dear. And there was fabric left over from the hemming, so it gave me the idea of a perky little hat. Just like you. No need to thank me. It was my pleasure. And thanks to Tillie for supplying some veiling from her own wedding finery."

"It's just perfect, and suits you like a dream." Tillie adjusted the veil slightly. "Let me finish your makeup, luv. Time is ticking."

Thirty minutes later, a beautiful bride stood before her bridesmaids, who were all dressed in various shades of blue.

"Blimey, you look beautiful," Ruby was the first to comment.

"Ciaran is a lucky man, indeed," agreed Maggie.

"Stunning," Tillie echoed.

"Absolutely gorgeous," breathed Hannah who had snuck in behind Aunt Isla.

"A beautiful Christmas bride," Mum called from the doorway, her voice breaking.

"Ta, Mum, and everyone. This dress and hat make me feel like a proper bride."

"Isla's hat is so fetching on you. I got a sneak peek downstairs. Are you nervous, luv?" Mum fussed with the tiny veil.

"I've got butterflies in my tummy, there's no denying. But I've waited so long for this day to come. I'm just that ready to be Mrs Katie McElroy. I expect I'll be nervy just before I walk down the aisle." She fiddled with the claddagh ring.

"Pops will be there to steady you, luv. And just keep your eyes on your young man waiting for you."

"We'd best be going." Maggie checked her watch. "We are quite a load of family to move about."

"Ciaran and the McElroys left some time ago. The rest are expected to go now, if all goes according to plan. Trevor has ordered three taxis." They'd gotten a babysitter for the children. Katie had considered having Jamie as a pageboy, but he was just too young and unpredictable.

"Let's get on, then," Katie glided out the door. They were surprised to see Mrs McElroy downstairs.

"Forgive me, dear. I just wanted to see you in your gown. You're looking grand."

"Thank you. It doesn't even feel like me."

"You look just like yourself, Katie. Sweet, smart, brave, and lovely. I have something for you, if you've the time."

"Of course," she replied quietly.

"It's a tradition in the McElroy family that new brides get started off with a charm bracelet. My mother-in-law gave me one thirty-eight years ago, and Niall has added to it each year. Ciaran too." She held up a frail wrist with a gold charm bracelet dancing in the light. Loaded with charms, it jangled against her tiny hand.

"What a lovely tradition."

Mrs McElroy handed her a slim, black velvet box.

Katie opened it to see a thin gold bracelet with one charm attached. She picked it up and examined it.

"A shamrock. How perfect. Will you help me put it on?" Katie was touched to her core. She was so fortunate to have such a loving family around her, showing how much they cared on her special day.

"Oh, it's a lucky Irish charm. Thank you, Mrs McElroy. A shamrock on a charm bracelet. That's double good luck." Katie kissed her on the cheek.

Pops hurried them along.

"The taxis are waiting. You all go ahead. It's me and poppet in the last one."

In minutes, they'd reached St. Cuthbert's. Katie shrugged off her overcoat and handed it to Ruby in the church vestibule. Tillie gave her the once over, to ensure there wasn't a hair out of place, and handed her the dried flower posy – all that could be found for a winter wedding.

The music started playing, and slowly the girls walked in front of her down the aisle. Then, it was just her and Pops. She shivered, partly from the cold, and partly with nervous excitement. It was all moving so fast.

"Are you alright, darling Katie? You look a picture." Pops gave a reassuring pat as he wrapped his arm through hers. They heard their music cue. Katie nodded.

"Shall we look lively, poppet? Your Irishman is waiting for you."

"That will be grand, Pops." She thrust her shoulders back, held her head high, and gave him a sunny smile.

As the organ played, Katie saw a sea of happy faces – her dearest loved ones. Looking past them, she spied her handsome groom. Ciaran had made a six-year-old suit from Howth look dashing. His auburn hair shone, and his green eyes bore into hers, willing her to move faster. Like always. He had always been urging her to move faster. *But I wasn't ready until it was my time. I had to find my way as my own woman – apart from my sisters, away from my large family, and as a flourishing Wren, serving my country.*

Fragments in her mind – Ciaran rescuing her from an unwelcome suitor, Ciaran walking with her on the Dover cliffs, Ciaran gently tucking her up on the train when she was recovering from measles, Ciaran making a picnic for her in Ireland and giving her the claddagh ring. Steady, loving Ciaran.

This is the right time. Our time.

"Hello, Irish. You look handsome," she whispered to him at the altar.

"Hello, my beautiful mavourneen," he whispered back.

The service was short. Ciaran and Katie exchanged vows in clear voices. Golden wedding rings were exchanged, and the wedding kiss left no one in doubt that this was a couple in love.

Handfasted, they ran back up the aisle, smiling at everyone in the church. Pausing outside in the icy cold, the assembled group threw rice on the newlyweds before they ducked into the waiting car to take them to the reception.

"Darling, we've done it! We are husband and wife. My heart is full, and I can't wait for tonight," she added wickedly.

"Oh, my bride. The light of my life." He leaned over to kiss her most thoroughly. "May we always walk in sunshine." He blessed them both.

ReadMore Press

DISCOVERING THE NEXT BESTSELLER

Would you like a FREE WWII historical fiction audiobook?

This audiobook is valued at 14.99$ on Amazon and is exclusively free for Readmore Press' readers!

To get your free audiobook, and to sign up for our newsletter where we send you more exclusive bonus content every month,

Scan the QR code

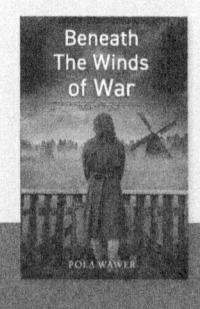

Readmore Press is a publisher that focuses on high-end, quality historical fiction. We love giving the world moving stories, emotional accounts, and tear-filled happy endings.

We hope to see you again in our next book!

Never stop reading, Readmore Press

Glossary

- **Ack-ack guns** – British World War II jargon for anti-aircraft guns.
- **Anderson shelter** – a temporary air raid shelter erected outside UK households during World War II.
- **ATS** – Auxiliary Territorial Service.
- **Billet** – lodgings assigned to soldiers during the war.
- **Biscuit** – unlike an American biscuit, a British biscuit is a hard or crisp cookie.
- **Chuffed** – pleased or proud.
- **Chum** – friend.
- **Civvies** – civilian clothing.
- **CO – commanding officer.**
- **Cuppa** – a cup of tea (shortened).
- **Daft** – silly or stupid.
- **Eejit** – Irish slang for idiot.
- **Fringe** – bangs.
- **Jerry** – an Allied nickname given to Germans and Germany.
- **Kip** – sleep or rest.
- **Lippy** – lipstick (shortened).
- **Lorry** – truck.
- **NAAFI** – Navy, Army, and Air Force Institutes.
- **Natter** – chat, talk conversationally.
- **Pudding** – refers to any kind of dessert.
- **Queue** – line.
- **RAF** – Royal Air Force, the British air force.
- **Supper** – dinner.
- **Ta ra** – goodbye (informal).
- **Trousers** – pants.
- **WAAF** – Women's Auxiliary Air Force.
- **Wren** – member of the Women's Royal Navy Services.
- **WVS** – Women's Voluntary Services.

ACKNOWLEDGEMENTS

Writing about the elder twin sisters Tillie and Maggie in The War Twins of London and A Burning London Sky was riveting for me. Not only the research – where I learned a lot more about World War II than I ever imagined, but also the first-hand accounts of brave women in WWII England. The more stories I read, the more needed to be told. Everywhere I turned in my research, I saw women in all branches of the services, as well as in nursing, munitions factories, and farming the land that showed the heart and soul of how females played a crucial part in winning the war.

A character emerged from the first two books whose story cried out for attention. Katie was in the shadows as the perky younger sister of the glamourous Kingston twins. Smart as a whip, and as courageous as her older sisters, I decided she needed a different role – one of a wireless interceptor – a rare British Wren who signed the Official Secrets Act, and performed undisclosed duties that they never discussed with family or even husbands – many of them for the rest of their lives.

Placing her in the Women's British Navy was a lot of fun. Considered the elite of the armed forces, the smart navy uniform was the envy of ATS and WAAFs across England. I was able to enrich Katie's story by personally visiting Dover Castle and the White Cliffs of Dover which acted as Katie's workplace during the critical D-Day operation. The Imperial War Museum, Bletchley Park, Greenwich Naval Museum, HMS Belfast, and other London landmarks inspired the locations and characters in The Code Girl From London. I even visited the real #40 Longridge Road – the Kingston townhouse in Earl's Court. I was disappointed that no one was home that day. I arrived loaded with signed copies of my books to hand out to any current tenants who might have let me in for a peek. There's nothing like on-the-ground research, and it was a real treat to visit my beloved London again after covid restrictions finally tailed off.

Although (I think) I'm finished with the Kingston girls, my love affair with heroic WWII women is in full swing. More stories are swirling in my brain, and I will definitely explore new characters and settings for the future.

I'd like to thank my two British fact-checkers, Roy Williamson and Jeremy Clinch who always proof my English voice and offer significant background to make London life come alive.

Here are some of the critical sources I mined to make The Code Girl From London as powerfully realistic as possible:

- Barrett, Duncan and Calvi, Nuala. *The Girls Who Went to War.* Harper Element, 2015.
- Brown, Mike and Harris, Carol. *The Wartime House, Home Life in Wartime Britain 1939-1945.* The History Press, 2011.
- Drummond, John D. *Blue for a Girl, The story of the W.R.N.S.* Cax & Wyman Ltd., 1960
- Gray, Andrew & Timereel Studios. *London's War During WWII.* BFS, 2012. (DVD)
- Jeffreys, Alan. *London at War, 1939-1945, A Nation's Capital Survives.* Imperial War Museum, 2018.
- Lamb, Christian. *Beyond the Sea, a Wren at War.* Mardle Books, 2021.
- McKay, Sinclair. *The Secret Listeners.* Aurum Press Ltd., 2012.
- Nicholson, Virginia. *Millions Like Us, Women's Lives During the Second World War.* Penguin Books, 2012.
- Owtram, Patricia and Jean. *Codebreaking Sisters, Our Secret War.* Mirror Books, 2020.
- Storey, Neil R. *WRNS. The Women's Naval Service.* Bloomsbury Shire, 2017.
- Stuart Mason, Ursula. *Britannia's Daughters, The Story of the WRNS.* Leo Cooper, 2011.
- Wynn, Stephen. *City of London at War, 1939-1945.* Pen & Sword Military, 2020.

I'm also thankful for all the online resources, videos, first-hand accounts, podcasts, and so much more at the Imperial War Museum and BBC archives.

Printed in Great Britain
by Amazon